THE HELLHOUNDS' PREY

Coming down the road was a naked man. He stumbled as he walked and he screamed, a senseless, endless screaming that rose and fell, but never broke. Pacing behind him and to either side of him was a pack of Hellhounds, black and evil in the night. Some went on four feet; others shambled erect, their long arms swinging loosely. Their terrible fangs gleamed white against the blackness of their snouts.

The man and the pack of Hellhounds came steadily down the road, the screaming never ending. And now there was another sound, heard as a sort of bass accompaniment to the terrible screaming—the snuffling of the Hellhounds.

The Hellhounds closed in with a rush, not knocking the man down, allowing him to stand, but leaping at him with slashing teeth, then falling back. Half his face was gone, and blood streamed down across his cheek . . .

Also by Clifford D. Simak
Published by Ballantine Books:

Enchanted Pilgrimage

Clifford D. Simak

A Del Rey Book

BALLANTINE BOOKS · NEW YORK

A Del Rey Book
Published by Ballantine Books

Copyright © 1975 by Clifford D. Simak

Library of Congress Catalog Card Number: 74-16617

ISBN 0-345-29869-1

Manufactured in the United States of America

First Ballantine Books Edition: September 1983

Cover art by Darrell K. Sweet

THE rafter goblin spied on the hiding monk, who was spying on the scholar. The goblin hated the monk and had reason for the hate. The monk hated no one and loved no one; he was bigoted and ambitious. The scholar was stealing what appeared to be a manuscript he had found hidden behind the binding of a book.

The hour was late and the library hushed. Somewhere a mouse scrabbled furtively. The candle standing on the desk over which the scholar crouched guttered, burning low.

The scholar lifted the manuscript and tucked it inside his shirt. He closed the book and put it back on the shelf. He snuffed out the candle with a finger and a thumb. Pale moonlight, shining through tall windows that reached almost to the rafters, lit the interior of the library with a ghastly radiance.

The scholar turned from the desk and made his way among the tables of the study room, heading for the foyer. The monk shrank further back into the shadows and let him go. He made no move to stop him. The goblin watched, full of hate for the monk, and scratched his head in perplexity.

• •

MARK Cornwall was eating cheese and bread when the knock came at the door. The room was small and cold; a tiny blaze of twigs burning in the small fireplace did little to warm it.

He rose and brushed crumbs of cheese off his coat before he went to the door. When he opened it a small, wizened creature stood before it—scarcely three feet tall, he was dressed in tattered leathern breeches. His feet were bare and hairy and his shirt was a worn crimson velvet. He wore a peaked cap.

"I am the goblin of the rafters," he said. "Please, may I come in?"

"Certainly," said Cornwall. "I have heard of you. I thought you were a myth."

The goblin came in and scurried to the fire. He squatted in front of it, thrusting his hands out toward the blaze.

"Why did you think of me as a myth?" he asked petulantly. "You know that there are goblins and elves and others of the Brotherhood. Why should you doubt me?"

"I don't know," said Cornwall. "Because I have never seen you, perhaps. Because I have never known anyone who has. I thought it was a student story."

"I keep well hidden," said the goblin. "I stay up in the rafters. There are hiding places there and it is hard to reach me. Some of those monkish characters in the library are unreasonable. They have no sense of humor."

"Would you have some cheese?" asked Cornwall.

"Of course I'd have some cheese. What a foolish question."

He left the fire and hoisted himself onto the rough bench that stood before the table. He looked around the room. "I take it," he said, "that you have no easy life. There is no softness here. It is all hard and sparse."

"I get along," said Cornwall. He took the dagger from the scabbard at his belt and cut a slice of cheese, then sawed a slice off the loaf of bread and handed it to his visitor.

"Rough fare," said the goblin.

"It is all I have. But you didn't come for cheese and bread."

"No," the goblin said. "I saw you tonight. I saw you steal the manuscript."

"Okay," said Cornwall. "What is it that you want?"

"Not a thing," the goblin said. He took a bite of cheese. "I came to tell you that the monk, Oswald, also was watching you."

"If he had been watching, he would have stopped me. He would have turned me in."

"It seems to me," the goblin said, "that there is a peculiar lack of remorse on your part. You do not even make an effort to deny it."

"You saw me," Cornwall said, "and yet you did not turn me in. This business must go deeper than it seems."

"Perhaps," the goblin said. "You have been a student here how long?"

"Almost six years."

"You are no longer a student, then. A scholar."

"There is no great distinction between the two."

"I suppose not," the goblin agreed, "but it means you are no shiny-faced schoolboy. You are beyond simple student pranks."

"I think I am," said Cornwall, "but I don't quite see your point. . . ."

"The point is that Oswald saw you steal it and yet he let you go. Could he have known what you stole?"

"I would rather doubt it. I didn't know what it was myself until I saw it. I wasn't looking for it. I didn't even know that it existed. I noticed when I got the book down that there was something rather strange about the binding on the back cover. It seemed too thick. It gave beneath one's fingers, as if something might be hidden there, between the binding and the board."

"If it was so noticeable," asked the goblin, "how is it that no one else had found it? How about another chunk of cheese?"

Cornwall cut another slice of cheese and gave it to him. "I think there is an easy answer to your question. I imagine I may have been the first one in a century or more who had taken down that book."

"An obscure tome," said the goblin. "There are many such. Would you mind telling me what it was?"

"An old traveler's tale," said Cornwall. "Written many years ago, several hundred years ago. In very ancient script. Some monk of long ago made it a thing of beauty when he copied it, with intricate and colorful initial letters and pretty conceits in the margins. But if you ask me, it was a waste of time. By and large, it is a pack of lies."

"Then why did you go looking for it?"

"Sometimes from many falsehoods one may garner certain truths. I was looking for the mention of one specific thing."

"And you found it?"

"Not in the book," said Cornwall. "In the hidden manuscript. I'm inclined to think the book is the original copy of the tale. Perhaps the only one. It is not the sort of thing that would have been copied extensively. The old monk in the scriptorium probably worked from the traveler's own writings, copying it in style, making it a splendid book that one might be rightly proud of."

"The manuscript?"

"Not really a manuscript. Only a single page of parchment. A page from the traveler's original manuscript. It had something in it that the monk left out."

4

"You think his conscience bothered him and he compromised by binding the page from which he had deleted something under the back cover of the book."

"Something like that," said Cornwall. "Now let us talk about what you came here for."

"The monk," the goblin said. "You do not know this monk, Oswald, as I do. Of all the scruffy crew, he is by far the worst. No man is safe from him, no thing is sacred. Perhaps it has crossed your mind he might have had a purpose in not apprehending you, in not raising an outcry."

"My theft does not seem to perturb you," Cornwall pointed out.

"Not at all," the goblin said. "I am rather on your side. For years this cursed monk has tried his best to make my life a misery. He has tried to trap me; he has tried to hunt me down. I have cracked his shins aplenty and have managed, in one way or another, to pay him back for every shabby trick, but he still persists. I bear him no goodwill. Perhaps you've gathered that."

"You think he intends to inform on me?"

"If I know him," the goblin said, "he intends to sell the information."

"To whom would he sell it? Who would be interested?"

"Consider," said the goblin, "that a hidden manuscript has been filched from its hiding place in an ancient book. The fact that it seemed important enough to be hidden—and important enough to be filched—would be intriguing, would it not?"

"I suppose you're right."

"There are in this town and the university," said the goblin, "any number of unprincipled adventurers who would be interested."

"You think that it will be stolen from me?"

"I think there is no question that it will. In the process your life will not be entirely safe."

Cornwall cut another slice of cheese and handed it to him. "Thank you," said the goblin, "and could you spare me another slice of bread?"

5

Cornwall cut a slice of bread.

"You have been of service to me," he said, "and I am grateful to you. Would you mind telling me what you expect out of this?"

"Why," the goblin said, "I thought it was apparent. I want to see that wretched monk stub his toe and fall flat upon his face."

He laid the bread and cheese on the tabletop, reached inside his shirt and brought out several sheets of parchment. He laid them on the table.

"I imagine, Sir Scholar, that you are handy with the quill."

"I manage," Cornwall said.

"Well, then, here are some old parchments, buffed clean of the writing once upon them. I would suggest you copy the page that you have stolen and leave it where it can be found."

"But I don't . . ."

"Copy it," said the goblin, "but with certain changes you'll know best to make. Little, subtle changes that would throw them off the track."

"That's done quite easily," said Cornwall, "but the ink will be recent ink. I cannot forge the writing. There will be differences and . . ."

"Who is there to know about the different script? No one but you has seen the manuscript. If the style of script is not the same, no one will know or guess. The parchment's old and as far as the erasure is concerned, if that could be detected, it was often done in the olden days when parchment was hard to come by."

"I don't know," said Cornwall.

"It would require a scholar to detect the discrepancies you are so concerned about and the chances are not great the forgery will fall into a scholar's hands. Anyhow, you'll be long gone. . . ."

"Long gone?"

"Certainly," said the goblin. "You can't think you can stay around after what has happened."

"I suppose you're right. I had thought of leaving in any case."

6

"I hope the information in the manuscript is worth all the trouble it will cause you. But even if it isn't . . ."

"I think perhaps it is," said Cornwall.

The goblin slid off the bench and headed for the door.

"Wait a second," said Cornwall. "You've not told me your name. Will I be seeing you again?"

"My name is Oliver—or at least in the world of men that's what I call myself. And it is unlikely we will ever meet again. Although, wait—how long will it take you to make the forgery?"

"Not too long," said Cornwall.

"Then I'll wait. My powers are not extensive, but I can be of certain aid. I have a small enchantment that can fade the ink and give the parchment, once it is correctly folded, a deceptive look of age."

"I'll get at it right away," said Cornwall. "You have not asked me what this is all about. I owe you that much."

"You can tell me," said the goblin, "as you work."

3

LAWRENCE Beckett and his men sat late at drink. They had eaten earlier, and still remaining on the great scarred tavern table were a platter with a ham bone, toward the end of which some meat remained, and half a loaf of bread. The townspeople who had been there earlier were gone, and mine host, having sent the servants off to bed, still kept his post behind the bar. He was sleepy, yawning occasionally, but well content to stay, for it was not often that the Boar's Head had guests so free with their money. The students, who came seldom, were more troublesome than profitable, and the townspeople who dropped in of an evening had long since become extremely expert in the coddling of their drinks. The Boar's Head was not on the direct road into town, but off on one of the many side streets, and it was not often that traders the like of Lawrence Beckett found their way there.

The door opened and a monk came in. He stood for a moment, staring about in the tavern's murky gloom. Behind the bar mine host stiffened to alertness. Some tingling sense in his brain told him that this visit boded little good. From one year's end to the next, men of the saintly persuasion never trod this common room.

After a moment's hesitation the monk pulled his robes about him, in a gesture that seemed to indicate a shrinking from contamination by the place, and made his way down the room to the corner where

Lawrence Beckett and his men sat at their table. He stopped behind one of the chairs, facing Beckett.

Beckett looked at him with a question in his eyes. The monk did not respond.

"Albert," said Beckett, "pour this night bird a drink of wine. It is seldom we can join in cups with a man who wears the cloth."

Albert poured the drink, turning in his chair to hand it to the monk.

"Master Beckett," said the monk, "I heard you were in town. I would have a word with you alone."

"Certainly," said Beckett, heartily. "A word by all means. But not with me alone. These men are one with me. Whatever I may hear is fit for their ears as well. Albert, get Sir Monk a chair, so he may be seated with us."

"It must be alone," said the monk.

"All right, then," said Beckett. "Why don't the rest of you move down to another table. Take one of the candles, if you will."

"You have the air," said the monk, "of humoring me."

"I am humoring you," said Beckett. "I cannot imagine what you have to say is of any great importance."

The monk took the chair next to Beckett, putting the mug of wine carefully on the table in front of him, and waiting until the others left.

"Now what," said Beckett, "is this so secret matter that you have to tell me?"

"First of all," said the monk, "that I know who you really are. No mere trader, as you would have us think."

Beckett said nothing, merely stared at him. But now some of the good humor had gone out of him.

"I know," said the monk, "that you have access to the church. For the favor that I do you, I would expect advancement. No great matter for one such as you. Only a word or two."

9

Beckett rumbled, "And this favor you are about to do me?"

"It has to do with a manuscript stolen from the university library just an hour or so ago."

"That would seem a small thing."

"Perhaps. But the manuscript was hidden in an ancient and almost unknown book."

"You knew of this manuscript? You know what it is?"

"I did not know of it until the thief found it. I do not know what it is."

"And this ancient book?"

"One written long ago by an adventurer named Taylor, who traveled in the Wastelands."

Beckett frowned. "I know of Taylor. Rumors of what he found. I did not know he had written a book."

"Almost no one knew of it. It was copied only once. The copy that we have."

"Have you read it, Sir Monk?"

The monk shrugged. "Until now it had no interest for me. There are many books to read. And travelers' tales are not to be taken entirely at face value."

"You think the manuscript might be?"

"To have been hidden so cleverly as it was, within the binding of the book, it would have to have some value. Why else bother to hide it?"

"Interesting," said Beckett softly. "Very interesting. But no value proved."

"If it has no value, then you owe me nothing. I am wagering that it does have."

"A gentleman's agreement, then?"

"Yes," said the monk, "a gentleman's agreement. The manuscript was found by a scholar, Mark Cornwall. He lodges in the topmost garret of the boardinghouse at the northwest corner of King and Broad."

Beckett frowned. "This Cornwall?"

"An obnoxious man who comes from somewhere in the West. A good student, but a sullen one. He has no friends. He lives from hand to mouth. He stayed on after all his old classmates had left, satisfied with the education they had gotten. Principally he stays on, I think, because he is interested in the Old Ones."

"How interested in the Old Ones?"

"He thinks they still exist. He has studied their language or what purports to be their language. There are some books on it. He has studied them."

"Why has he an interest in the Old Ones?"

The monk shook his head. "I do not know. I do not know the man. I've talked to him only once or twice. Intellectual curiosity, perhaps. Perhaps something else."

"Perhaps he thought Taylor might have written of the Old Ones."

"He could have. Taylor could have. I have not read the book."

"Cornwall has the manuscript. By now he would have hidden it."

"I doubt it has been hidden. Not too securely, anyhow. He has no reason to believe that his theft of it is known. Watching him, I saw him do it. I let him leave. I did not try to stop him. He could not have known I was there."

"Would it seem to you, Sir Monk, that this studious, light-fingered friend of ours may have placed himself in peril of heresy?"

"That, Master Beckett, is for you to judge. All about us are signs of heresy, but it takes a clever man to tread the intricacies of definition."

"You are not saying, are you, that heresy is political?"

"It never crossed my mind."

"That is good," said Beckett, "for under certain, well-defined conditions, the university itself, or more particularly the library, might fall under suspicion because of the material that can be found on its shelves."

"The books, I can assure you, are used with no evil intent. Only for instruction against the perils of heresy."

"With your assurance," said Beckett, "we can let

11

it rest at that. As for this other matter, I would assume that you are not prepared to regain the manuscript and deliver it to us."

The monk shuddered. "I have no stomach," he said, "for such an operation. I have informed you; that should be enough."

"You think that I am better equipped and would have a better stomach."

"That had been my thought. That's why I came to you."

"How come you knew us to be in town?"

"This town has ears. There is little happening that goes unknown."

"And I take it you listen very carefully."

Said the monk, "I've made it a habit."

"Very well," said Beckett. "So it is agreed. If the missing item can be found and proves to have some value, I'll speak a word for you. That was your proposal?"

The monk nodded, saying nothing.

"To speak for you, I must know your name."

"I am Brother Oswald," said the monk.

"I shall mark it well," said Beckett. "Finish off your wine and we shall get to work. King and Broad, you said?"

The monk nodded and reached for the wine. Beckett rose and walked forward to his men, then came back again.

"You will not regret," he said, "that you came to me."

"I had that hope," said Brother Oswald.

He finished off the wine and set the cup back on the table. "Shall I see you again?" he asked.

"Not unless you seek me out."

The monk wrapped his habit close about himself and went out the door. Outside the moon had sunk beneath the rooftrees of the buildings that hemmed in the narrow alley, and the place was dark. He went carefully, feeling his way along the rough, slick cobblestones.

A shadow stepped out of a doorway as he passed.

12

A knife gleamed briefly in the dark. The monk dropped, gurgling, hands clawing at the stones, a sudden rush of blood bubbling in his throat. Then he grew quiet. His body was not found until morning light.

●●●●●●●●●●●●●●●●●●●●●●●●●●●●●●●●●●●

GIB of the Marshes was up before the sun. He was always up before the sun, but on this day there was much to do. This was the day the gnomes had named when the new ax would be ready. He needed the new ax, for the blade of the old one, worn down and blunted, would no longer take a proper edge, no matter how much whetstone might be used.

Ordinarily at this season of the year the marsh would have been wrapped in low-hanging fog early of a morning, but this morning it was clear. A few wisps of layered fog hung above the island where the wood was gotten, but otherwise there was no sign of it. To the east and south, the marsh lay flat and far, brown and silver, with its reeds and grasses. Ducks gabbled in nearby ponds and a muskrat swam through a channel, creating a neat V of an aftermath as he moved along. Somewhere far off a heron croaked. West and north, the forested hills rose against the sky—oaks, maples, hickories, some of them already touched with the first colors of the autumn.

Gib stood and looked toward the hills. Up there, somewhere in that tangled woodland, was the home of his good friend, Hal of the Hollow Tree. Almost every morning, when there was no fog and the hills stood in view, he stood and tried to pick out the home tree, but he never had been able to, for from this distance no one tree could be told from any of the others. He would not, he knew, have time to visit Hal today, for once he had picked up the ax, he must pay his respects to the lonely old hermit who lived in the cave of the limestone capping of one of the distant hills. It had been a month or more since he'd gone calling on the hermit.

He rolled up the goose-down pad and the woolen blanket he had used for sleeping and stored them away in the hut in the center of the raft. Except when the weather was cold or it happened to be raining, he always slept outdoors. On the iron plate on the forward part of the raft he kindled a fire, using dry grass and punk from a rotting log, which he kept in one corner of the woodbox, as kindling, and flint and steel to produce the spark.

When the fire was going, he reached a hand into the live-box sunk beside the raft and brought out a flapping fish. He killed it with a blow of his belt knife and quickly cleaned it, putting the fillets into a pan, which he set on the grill above the fire, squatting to superintend the cooking.

Except for the soft talking of the ducks and the occasional plop of a jumping fish, the marsh was quiet. But, then, he thought, at this time of day it was always quiet. Later in the day there would be blackbirds quarreling in the reeds, the whistling wings of water fowl passing overhead, the harsh cries of shore birds and of gulls.

The east brightened and the marsh, earlier an indistinctness of brown and silver, began to take on new definition. Far off stood the line of willows that edged the narrow height of ground that stood between the distant river and the marsh. The patch of cattails closer to the wooded hill shore could now be seen, waving their full brown clubs in the vagrant wind.

The craft bobbed gently as he ate from the pan, not bothering with a plate. He wondered what life might be like on solid ground, without the bobbing of the raft. He had lived all his years on a bobbing raft, which was only stilled when cold weather froze it in.

Thinking of cold weather, he ran through his mind all that remained to do to get ready for the winter.

He would need to smoke more fish, must gather roots and seeds, try to pick up a few muskrats for a winter robe. And get in wood. But the wood gathering would go faster once he had the new ax from the gnomes.

He washed out the pan in which he'd fried the fish, then put into the boat, tied alongside the raft, the bundles that he had gotten together before he went to sleep. In them were dried fish and packets of wild rice, gifts for the gnomes and the hermit. At the last moment he put his old ax in the craft; the gnomes could make use of the metal to fashion something else.

He paddled quietly down the channel, unwilling to break the morning hush. The sun came up into the east and on the opposite hills, the first autumn colors flamed with brilliance.

He was nearing the shore when he rounded a bend and saw the raft, the forepart of it thrust into the grass, the rest of it projecting out into the channel. An old marshman was sitting at the stern of the raft, mending a net. As soon as Gib came into view, the old man looked up and raised a solemn hand in greeting. It was Old Drood and Gib wondered what he was doing here. The last time he had heard of Drood, he had his raft over near the willow bank close to the river.

Gib pulled his boat against the raft, thrust out a paddle, and held it there.

"Long time since I saw you," he said. "When did you move over here?"

"A few days ago," said Drood. He left his net mending and came over to squat close beside the boat. He was getting old, Gib saw. As long as he could remember, he had been called Old Drood, even when he'd not been old, but now the years were catching up with the name. He was getting gray.

"Figured I'd try for some wood over on the shore," he said. "Not much but willow left over there against the river and willow makes poor burning."

Mrs. Drood came waddling around the hut. She spoke in a high-pitched, squeaky voice. "I thought I heard someone. It's young Gib, isn't it?" She squinted at him with weak eyes.

"Hello, Mrs. Drood," said Gib. "I'm glad you are my neighbors."

"We may not stop here for long," said Drood. "Only long enough to get a load of wood."

"You got any so far?"

"Some," said Drood. "It goes slow. No one to help. The children all are gone. Struck off on their own. I can't work as hard as I once could."

"I don't like it," said Mrs. Drood. "There are all them wolves."

"I got my ax," said Drood. "There ain't no wolf going to bother me long as I have the ax."

"All the children gone," said Gib. "Last time I saw you, there still was Dave and Alice."

"Alice got married three, four months ago," said Drood. "Young fellow down at the south end of the marsh. Dave built himself a raft. Good job he did with it. Wouldn't let me help him much. Said he had to build his own. He built himself a nice raft. Moved over to the east. We see him and Alice every now and then."

"We got some ale," said Mrs. Drood. "Would you like a mug of ale? And I forgot to ask you, have you had your breakfast? It would only take a minute."

"I've had breakfast, Mrs. Drood, and thank you. But I'd like a mug of ale."

"Bring me one, too," said Drood. "Can't let Gib here drink alone."

Mrs. Drood waddled back to the hut.

"Yes, sir," said Drood, "it ain't easy getting in the wood. But if I take my time, I can manage it. Good wood, too. Oak and maple, mostly. All dried out and ready for the fire. Lots of down stuff. No one has touched it for years. Once in a while a pack train camps near here, if they're caught at night, and have to rustle up some camp wood. But they don't make a dent in it. Up the hill a ways there's a down shagbark hickory and it's the best wood that there is.

17

You don't find one of them down too often. It's a far ways to go to reach it, though. . . ."

"I'm busy today," said Gib, "but tomorrow and the next day I can help you with the wood."

"There ain't no need to, Gib. I can manage it."

"I'd like some of that hickory myself."

"Well, now, if that's the way of it, I'd go partners with you. And thanks an awful lot."

"Glad to."

Mrs. Drood came back with three mugs of ale. "I brought one for myself," she said. "Land sakes, it ain't often we get visitors. I'll just sit down while we drink the ale."

"Gib is going to help me with the wood tomorrow," said Drood. "We'll go after that big hickory."

"Hickory is good wood," said Mrs. Drood.

"I am getting me a new ax," said Gib. "The old one is almost worn out. It was one my father gave me."

"Your folks are up near Coon Hollow, so I hear," said Mrs. Drood.

Gib nodded. "Been there for quite a while. Good place to be. Good wood, good fishing, plenty of muskrat, one little slough with a lot of wild rice in it. I think they will stay on."

"You're getting your new ax from the gnomes?" asked Drood.

"That's right," said Gib. "Had to wait awhile. Spoke to them about it way last summer."

"Fine workmen, them gnomes," and Drood judiciously. "Good iron, too. That vein they're working is high-grade ore. Pack trains stop every now and then and take everything they have. Good reputation, no trouble selling it. I sometimes wonder. You hear terrible things of gnomes, and maybe they are sort of scaly things. But these gnomes of ours are all right. I don't know how we'd get along without them. They been here for years, as long as anyone can remember."

"Things can get along together," said Mrs. Drood, "if they have good hearts."

18

"The gnomes ain't people, Mother," Drood reminded her.

"Well, I don't care," said Mrs. Drood. "They're creatures, and they ain't so much different from us. In a lot of ways they are less different from us than we are from humans. The Hill People are a lot like us."

"The main thing," said Drood, "is that all of us manage to get along together. Take us and humans. Humans are twice as big as we are and they have smooth skins where we have fur. Humans can write and we can't. Humans have money and we don't. We trade for what we want. Humans got lots of things we haven't, but we don't begrudge them it and they don't look down on us. Just so long as we get along together, everything's all right."

Gib finished his ale. "I have to go," he said, "I have a long day ahead of me. I have to get my ax, then go calling on the hermit."

"I hear the hermit is right poorly," said Drood. "He is getting on in years. He is half as old as them there hills."

"You're going calling on the hermit?" asked Mrs. Drood.

"That is what he said," Drood told her.

"Well, you just wait a minute. I got something I want to send him. A chunk of that wild honey the Hill People gave me."

"He'd like that," said Gib.

She scurried off.

"I've often wondered," said Drood, "what the hermit has gotten out of life, sitting up there on top of the hill in that cave of his, never going anywhere, never doing nothing."

"Folks come to him," said Gib. "He's got all sorts of cures. Stomach cures, throat cures, teeth cures. But they don't always come for cures. Some just come to talk."

"Yes, I suppose he does see a lot of people."

Mrs. Drood came back with a package that she gave to Gib.

"You stop by for supper," she said. "No matter if you're late, I'll save some supper for you."

"Thanks, Mrs. Drood," said Gib. He pushed away from the raft and paddled down the winding channel. Squawling blackbirds rose in clouds before him, wheeling in dark-winged flight above his head, lighting on distant reeds with volleys of profanity.

He reached the shore, the ground rising abruptly from the margin of the marsh. Giant trees close to the marsh's margin reached great limbs far above the grass and water. A great oak grew so close to the water's edge that some of its roots, once enclosed in earth that had washed away, stuck out like clawing fingers from the bank.

Gib tied the boat to one of the roots, heaved his bundles and the old ax ashore, then scrambled up the bank. He shouldered the bundles and picked his way along a faint path that ran up a hollow between two of the towering hills. He reached and crossed a better-defined path, a trail used by the infrequent pack trains that were either passing through or coming to trade with the gnomes.

The marsh had been noisy with blackbirds, but as Gib walked deeper into the wooded hills a hushed silence closed in about him. Leaves rustled in the wind, and occasionally he could hear the tiny thud of a falling acorn as it hit the ground. Earlier in the morning squirrels would have done some chattering to greet the morning sun, but now they were going quietly about their business of foraging for food, slipping like darting shadows through the woods.

The climb was steep, and Gib stopped for a moment to lean against a lichen-grown boulder. He didn't like the woods, he told himself. Gone from it for only a short time, he already missed the marsh. The woods had a secretive grimness and the marsh was open. In the marsh one knew where he was, but here one could easily become confused and lost.

5

SNIVELEY, the gnome, said, "So you have come for your ax."

"If it is ready," Gib said.

"Oh, it is ready well enough," Sniveley grumbled. "It was ready yesterday, but come on in and sit. It is a tiring climb up here, even for a young one."

The cave opened out from the hillside, and beyond its mouth, half filling the deep ravine that ran below it, was a heap of earth and slag, a huge hog's back, along which ran a wheelbarrow track to reach the dump of mine tailings at its end. So ancient was the earth and slag heap that along its sloping sides trees had sprung up and reached a respectable size, some of them canted out of line so that they hung above the ravine at eccentric angles. Back from the mouth of the cave, extending deep into the hill, forge-flames flared, and there was the sound of heavy hammering.

Sniveley led the way into a small side cave that connected obliquely with the main one that led into the mine. "Here," he said, "we can sit in peace and have some surcease from noise. More than that, we'll be out of the way of the wheelbarrows that come charging from the mine."

Gib laid one of the bundles on the counter that ran against one wall. "Smoked fish," he said, "and some other things. The other bundle's for the hermit."

"I have not seen the hermit for years," said Sniveley. "Here, take this chair. I just recently covered it with a new sheepskin. It is very comfortable."

Gib sat down in the indicated chair, and the gnome took another, hitching it around so he could face his visitor. "Actually," he said, "I only called on the hermit once. A neighborly act, I thought. I took him, as a gift, a fine pair of silver candlesticks. I never went again. I fear that I embarrassed him. I felt an unease in him. He said nothing, of course. . . ."

"He wouldn't," said Gib. "He is a kindly man."

"I shouldn't have done it," said the gnome. "It came from living so long in the land of humans and dealing so much with them that I began to lose the distinction between myself and man. But to the hermit, and I suppose to many other men, I am a reminder of that other world in which I properly belong, against which men still must have a sense of loathing and disgust, and I suppose for a reason. For ages man and the many people of my world fought very hard and viciously against one another, with no mercy, and I suppose, at most times, without a sense of honor. In consequence of this, the hermit, who is, as you say, the kindliest of men, did not quite know how to handle me. He must have known that I was harmless and carried no threat to him or any of his race, and yet he was uneasy. If I had been a devil, say, or any sort of demon, he would have known how to act. Out with the holy water and the sacred spells. But I wasn't a devil, and yet in some obscure way I was somehow connected with the idea of the devil. All these years I have regretted that I called on him."

"And yet he took the candlesticks."

"Yes, he did. Most graciously, and he thanked me kindly for them. He was too much a gentleman to throw them back in my face. He gave me, in return, a length of cloth of gold. Someone, I suppose, perhaps some noble visitor, had given it to him, for the hermit would have had no money to buy so princely a gift. I have often thought, however, that he should have kept it and given me a much more lowly gift. I've wondered all these years what I possibly could do with a length of cloth of gold. I keep it in a chest and I take it out now and then and have a look at it, but that is all I ever do with it. I suppose I could trade it off for something more utilitarian, but I hesitate to do that, for it was the hermit's gift and for that reason seems to me to have a certain sentimental value. One does not sell gifts, particularly a gift from so good a man."

"I think," said Gib, "that you must imagine much of this—the hermit's embarrassment, I mean. I, for example, have no such feeling toward you. Although, in all fairness, I must admit that I am not a human."

"Much closer than I am," said the gnome, "and therein may lie a difference."

He rose. "I'll get your ax," he said, "and there is something else that I want to show you." He patted the bundle Gib had placed on the counter. "I'll give you credit for this. Without it you have credit left, even with the ax."

"There's something I've always wanted to ask you," said Gib, "and never had the courage until now. All the People of the Marshes, all the People of the Hills, even many of the humans who know not how to write, bring you goods and you give them credit. It must be, then, that you know how to write."

"No," said the gnome, "I don't. Few gnomes do. Some goblins, perhaps. Especially those that hang out at the university. But we gnomes, being a trader people, have worked out a system of notation by which we keep accounts. And very honest, too."

"Yes," said Gib, "extremely honest. Most meticulous."

Sniveley went to the back of the room and rummaged around among some shelves. He came back with the ax, mounted on a helve of hickory.

"I think," he said, "the balance is right. If it's not, bring it back and we'll correct it."

Gib hefted it admiringly. "It feels right," he said. "It feels exactly right. If there is need of some slight adjustment, I can manage it."

He took the blade in his hands, rubbing the shiny metal with his thumbs. "Beautiful," he said. "Beautiful. With care it will last me all my life."

23

Sniveley was pleased. "You like it?"

"It is a masterly job," said Gib. "As I knew it would be."

"You will find," said Sniveley, "that it will take a fine edge. It will hold that edge. Be careful of stones. No ax will stand against a stone."

"I am careful," said Gib. "An ax is too fine a tool to mistreat."

"And now," said the gnome, "I have something else to show you."

He sat down and put something that was carefully wrapped in a sheepskin on his knee. He unwrapped it almost reverentially.

As the sheepskin fell away, the object it had covered caught the light and blazed. Gib leaned forward, looking at it, entranced.

"A sword!" he said.

"A man's sword," said Sniveley. "Too large, too long, too heavy for such as you or I. A fighter's sword. No flashy jewels, no fancy glitter. A tool just like your ax. An honest blade. In all the time that I've been here, the swords that we have made you can count upon the fingers of one hand. And this is by far the best of them."

Gib reached out and touched the blade. "It has a personality," he said. "It is the kind of weapon that one could give a name to. Old stories say that olden men often named their swords, as they would name a horse."

"We found one small pocket of richer ore," said Sniveley. "We took it out most carefully and have hoarded it away. Such ore you do not find too often. It shall be used for special things—like this blade and your ax."

"You mean my ax . . ."

"The ax and sword are brothers."

"Let us hope," said Gib, "that the sword passes into worthy hands."

"We shall make certain that it does," said Sniveley.

"I brought you the old ax," Gib said. "The metal

24

still is good, but the bevel has worn so short it cannot be satisfactorily sharpened. There is no rust upon it. I thought perhaps you could reuse the metal. I expect no credit for it."

He lifted it from the floor and handed it to the gnome.

"It was a good ax," Sniveley said. "It was your father's ax?"

Gib nodded. "He gave it to me when I built my raft."

"We made it for him," said Sniveley. "It was a good ax. Not as good as yours."

"My father sends you greetings. And my mother, too. I told them I'd be seeing you."

"It is a good life that you have," said the gnome. "All of you down in the marsh. For many years. You have no history, do you? You don't know how long."

"We cannot write events," said Gib. "We have only the old tales, passed on from father to son. There may be truth in them, but I don't know how much."

"So long as the gnomes have been in the hills," said Sniveley, "your people have been there. There before we came. We have our legends, too. About the one who discovered ore here and the development of the mine. As with you, we cannot judge the truth."

Gib hoisted the hermit's bundle onto his shoulder. "I must get on," he said. "The hermit's cave is a long climb. I want to reach home before the fall of night."

Sniveley wagged his head. "It is good to do so. There are many wolves this year. More than I've ever known. If you are running late, stop here and spend the night. You would be most welcome."

6

● ●

AT first Gib thought the hermit was not at home, although that would have been passing strange. Of late years, since he had grown feeble, the hermit had never left the cave except to sally out on occasions to collect the roots, the herbs, the leaves, and barks that went into his medications.

The fire in the cave was out, and there was no smell of smoke, which meant it had been out for long. Dried egg yolk clung to the lone plate on the rough trestle table.

Gib peered into the darkness. "Hermit," he said softly, half afraid to speak, stricken with a sudden apprehension that he could not understand. "Hermit, are you here?"

A weak sound came from a corner. It could have been a mouse.

"Hermit," Gib said again.

The sound repeated.

Carefully Gib walked toward the corner, crouching to see better.

"Here," said the hermit weakly. The voice was no louder than the fluttering of a leaf.

Then Gib, his eyes becoming accustomed to the darkness, made it out—the low dark mound in the corner, the paleness of the face.

"Hermit, what is wrong?"

Gib crouched above the pallet and saw the wasted form, a blanket pulled up to the chin.

"Bend low," the hermit said. "I can barely speak."

"Are you sick?" Gib asked.

The pale lips barely moved. "I die," they said. "Thank God that you came."

26

"Do you want something? Water? Soup? I could make some soup."

"Listen," said the hermit. "Do not talk, but listen."

"I'll listen."

"The cabinet over against the wall."

"I see it."

"The key is around my neck. Cord around my neck."

Gib reached out his hand.

"No, wait."

"Yes?"

"In the cabinet—in the cabinet . . ."

The hermit struggled to talk.

"A book, leather-bound. A fist ax. Ax made out of stone. Take both to the bishop . . ."

"Which bishop?"

"Bishop of the Tower. Up the river, north and west. Ask. People will tell you."

Gib waited. The hermit did not speak. He did not try to speak.

Gently, Gib reached out a hand, found the cord that lay against the hermit's neck. He lifted the hermit's head to slip it free. A small key dangled at the end.

He let the hermit's head fall back against the pillow.

He waited for a moment, but the hermit did not stir. He rose to his feet and went across the cave to unlock the cabinet. The book was there, a small book bound in leather. Beside it lay the ax. It was like no ax Gib had ever seen before. It was made of stone and was pointed at one end. Even made of stone, it had the smooth look of metal. Only by looking closely could one see where the chips had been flaked off to shape it.

There were other items in the cabinet—a razor, a pair of shears, a comb, a small vial half filled with a blue substance.

He took out the book and ax and went back to the pallet.

27

The hermit opened bleary eyes and looked at him. "You have them? Good."

"I'll take them to the bishop."

"You are Gib. You've been here before."

Gib nodded.

"You'll wait?"

"I'll wait. Is there nothing I can do? No water?"

The hermit rolled his head from side to side. "Nothing," he said.

Gib waited, on his knees beside the pallet. The hermit's breathing was so shallow that his chest scarcely moved and it was a long time between breaths. Occasionally hairs on the upper lip of the hermit's bearded face fluttered slightly when the breath came from his nostrils.

Once the hermit spoke. "I am old," he said. "It is time. Past time." Then he lapsed back into silence. The shallow breathing went on. Twice Gib was almost convinced it had stopped entirely. But it had not stopped. It was only faint.

"Gib?"

"Yes?"

"Leave me here. When it is done, leave me here."

Gib did not answer. The silence hummed. The shallow breathing still went on.

Then: "Wall up the cave. Will you do that?"

"Yes," said Gib, "I will."

"I would not want the wolves . . ."

He did not finish the sentence. Gib continued sitting beside the pallet. Once he went to the cave mouth and looked out. The sun had passed the zenith and was inclining toward the west. From the high point of the cave he could see that part of the marsh from which he had set out that morning. He could see almost to the river.

Gib went back and resumed his vigil. He tried to think and found that he could not think. There were too many things to think, too much to think about. He could not get it sorted out. There was confusion in his mind.

For some time he had not been watching the hermit, but simply sitting there. When he did look at him, he could detect no breathing movement. He waited, remembering there had been times before when he could detect no movement. But time stretched out and there was no flutter of the whiskers on the upper lip, no sign of life at all. He bent his head close against the chest and could detect no heartbeat. He rolled a lid back from an eye and the eye stared back in glassiness.

The hermit, he knew, was dead. But he continued to sit beside him, as if the mere fact of continuing the vigil would beat back the fact of death. He found that now he could think, while he had not been able to before. Had there been, he wondered, anything that he could have done? He remembered in horror that he had not even tried to give the hermit any water. He had asked and the hermit had said that he had no need of water. But even so, should he have tried to give him some? Should he have tried to bring some help? But where could he have gone for help? And who could have been of help? And, he told himself, he could not have brought himself to leave a dying man, to let him die alone.

The hermit, he thought, had been an old man and had not been afraid of death. He wondered if he might not have looked on death as a welcome friend. This very morning Drood had wondered what the hermit had gotten out of life and that, of course, was a question still unanswered. But, Gib told himself, he must have gotten something out of life, perhaps a great deal out of life, to have been able to face death so serenely.

Now there were things to do, he told himself, and the afternoon was waning. He pulled back the blanket and crossed the hands of the hermit decently on his chest, then pulled the blanket up to cover his face. Having done that, he went outside to search for boulders he could use to block the entrance to the cave.

• •

7

HAL of the Hollow Tree climbed over the rail fence and entered the cornfield. He was safe, he knew. The moonshiner and his sons were husking on the other side of the field and the moonshiner's dogs were sleeping off, beneath the stilted corncrib, the effects of last night's hunt.

It had been a long hunt and apparently an unsuccessful one. Hal and Coon had sat for hours outside the hollow tree and listened to its progress. The dogs had barked "treed" once, but the coon must have gotten away, for soon after they struck out on the trail again. Several times the two listeners had seen the lights of the lantern as the moonshiner and his sons had followed the hounds.

The corn crop had been good this year. Not that the moonshiner and his loutish family had contributed to it with outstanding husbandry. They hadn't; the corn had been hoed only two or three times and not at all in the later period of its growth and, as a result, weeds grew thickly between the rows. But the ears hung heavy, and it seemed there were more of them than usual.

Hal went into the corn patch five or six rows. Although there was no great evidence of it, he knew that some of the outer rows had been pilfered by coons and squirrels. That was why, he knew, the moonshiner hunted coons, or at least why he said he hunted them—to cut down their depredations on his corn patch. But it was not entirely that; coonskins had some value and could be sold. Moonshine, coonskins, and hog meat were this farm's stock-in-trade, and with them the family managed to get along.

Hal began husking, moving rapidly, unwilling to stay longer than he had to. Even learning from earlier counting where the family members were, he had no intention of being apprehended. Choosing the best ears, he stripped down the husk, broke the ears free and dropped them in the sack he carried.

Out at the edge of the field bluejays screeched in the autumn sunshine. In a grove of walnut trees, their golden leaves a burst of color against the drabber oaks, squirrels chattered as they went about their harvest. He liked autumn, Hal told himself, best of all the seasons. In these mellow, tawny days, blue-hazed and warm, the land came to fruition and one could sense the satisfactory closing of a long season of growth. It was a respite before the cold closed down again and the long snow came. This year, he knew, he would be well provisioned against the winter. He had bins of nuts and corn, dried berries, a good supply of roots and seeds. One of these days he'd have to go down to the marsh and see if he could trade for some dried fish with his friend, Gib, or perhaps old Drood or some of the other People of the Marsh. Thinking of this, he suddenly realized that it had been a long time since he had seen Gib and now looked forward to a chance to talk with him again.

He hoisted the sack and it was heavier than he had expected; he had picked more ears than he had intended. He wrestled the sack to his shoulder and judged that he could handle it. When he reached the edge of the field, he stopped to look and listen. There seemed no one about. Heaving the heavy sack over the rail fence, he vaulted after it, grabbed the sack and scurried into the woods.

He felt safe now. There was nothing that could catch him in the woods. The woods were home. He knew this forest for miles about, every cranny of it. Angling swiftly down the hill, he headed for the huge hollow oak. As he went, his eyes sought and noted, without too much effort or attention, many different

31

things—the flaming crimson of the ripened berries of the jack-in-the-pulpit, the fact that a small cluster of black haw trees were loaded with fruit that would become edible with the first coming of a killing frost, the heavily laden grapevines, which in many cases masked the very trees in which they grew, the silvery glint of a shed snakeskin left over from the summer, now half concealed in the fallen leaves.

In half an hour or so he reached the oak, a giant that measured at its base a good ten feet in diameter. Twenty feet up its trunk gaped a hole some two feet across. A series of pegs, driven into the wood, formed a ladder by which it could be reached.

There was no sign of Coon. He was probably off somewhere, investigating. It was unlikely, Hal reminded himself, that at this time of day he'd still be inside sleeping.

Hal leaned the sack of corn against the oak, swarmed up the ladder, and crawled through the hold, then climbed down another series of pegs.

The entire interior of the oak was hollowed out. Perhaps not a great deal more than a foot of shell surrounded the cavity. Someday, Hal knew, a wind might snap it off and he'd have to find another home. But here, deep in the forest, the wind was broken up by the many trees, and the oak was further protected by a high, flinty ridge, cutting the course of the prevailing westerlies. The cavity extended up for another twenty feet or so above the opening and here and there the shell was pierced by other smaller holes, admitting some daylight. The floor was made of dry decayed wood, which through the centuries had fallen from the sides of the hole.

A hearth stood to one side of the cavity. There was a table and chairs. Bins and cabinets stood against the walls.

"Hello," a voice said from behind him, and he turned on his heel, his hand going to the knife at his belt. On the edge of the bed sat a wizened creature with big ears. He had on tattered leathern breeches

32

and an old bottle-green jacket over a crimson shirt. He wore a peaked cap.

"Who the hell are you?" asked Hal. "You have your nerve."

"I am the goblin of the rafters from Wyalusing University," said the creature, "and my name is Oliver."

"Well, all right," said Hal, relaxing, "but tell me, what are you doing here?"

"I came to see you," said the goblin, "and you weren't home. I am nervous in the open. You see, a rafter goblin—"

"So you came inside to wait. Lucky for you Coon wasn't around. He'd took you out of here."

"Coon?"

"A big raccoon. He and I are friends. He lives with me."

"Oh, a pet."

"No, not a pet. A friend."

"You going to throw me out?"

"No, you startled me, was all. You hungry?"

"A little," said the goblin. "Have you a bit of cheese?"

"No cheese," said Hal. "How about some cornmeal mush? Or an apple dumpling?"

"The cornmeal mush sounds good."

"All right, then, that will be our supper. I think there still is milk. I get my milk from a woodcutter. Long way to carry it, but he is the nearest with a cow. Maple syrup for sweetening."

The goblin rolled his eyes. "It sounds wonderful."

"I'll stir up the fire. I think there still are coals. You're a long way from home, Master Goblin."

"I have traveled long and far," the goblin said. "My feet are sore and my spirit bruised. There is so much outdoors, and I am unused to space."

Hal went to the hearth and stirred the ash. In its heart was a glow of red. He laid some tinder on it and, bending down, blew on the coals. A tiny flame

33

flickered momentarily, went out, then caught again. Hal fed it tiny twigs.

He squatted back on his heels. "There, now," he said, "we have a fire. There's corn to bring in, but that can be done later. Perhaps you will help me."

"With all my heart," said Oliver.

Hal went to a cupboard, took out a mixing bowl and wooden spoon. From a bin beneath the cupboard he spooned cornmeal into the bowl.

"You say you came to see me."

"Yes, people told me, go see Hal of the Hollow Tree. He'll know, they said, everything that's going on. He knows the woods and all that happens in it. A woodcutter told me how to find the tree. Maybe he was the one who had the cow, although I did not see a cow."

"What do you want to ask me?"

"I am hunting for a man," the goblin said. "A scholar by the name of Cornwall. I had word he was traveling with a pack train that had headed north. It's important that I find him."

"Why important?"

"Because he is in danger. In much greater danger than I had thought."

34

8

• •

THE sun had set, but even here, among the trees, darkness had not fallen. The sky in the west was bright. Dusk was creeping in, but there still was light.

Gib hurried. He still had a mile or more to go, and at this time of year night came swiftly. The path led downhill, but he must go cautiously, on guard against stones or projecting roots that could trip him up. He had stopped briefly at the gnomes' mine to tell Sniveley that the hermit was dead but had passed up the offer to stay overnight since he was anxious to get home. The gnomes, he knew, would swiftly spread the word of the hermit's death and would add a caution against tampering with the boulder wall, which, closing the mouth of the cave, had transformed it to a tomb.

The dusk had deepened as he came down the last stretch of the path before he struck the pack-train trail, and as he began the descent to it, he became aware of snarling. The sound sent a thin chill of terror through him and he halted, straining his ears—now that it was gone, not completely sure he had heard a snarl. But even as he halted, there was another prolonged sound—half snarl, half growl—and other sounds as well, the ghastly sound of teeth tearing at something, a tearing and a slobbering.

Wolves! he thought. Wolves at a kill. Almost instinctively he yelled as loud as he could, a fierce yell, and, lifting his ax, charged down the path. It had been, he knew when he later thought of it, the only thing he could have done. To have tried to retreat, to have tried to go around them, no matter how stealthily, would have been an invitation to attack. But now he did not think at all; he simply yelled and charged.

As he burst out of the heavy undergrowth that grew on either side of the path, onto the trail, he saw what had happened. One look was enough to understand what had happened. There were huddled bodies, the bodies of men and horses, on the trail itself. And on either side of it and crouched over the bodies, fighting over the bodies, was a pack of wolves, great, slavering creatures that swung around to face him or lifted their heads from their feasting to face him.

And something else—a single man, still alive, on his knees, his hands gripping the throat of a wolf, trying to hold it off.

With a scream of fury Gib leaped at the wolf, ax held high. The wolf tried to break away; but the kneeling man's deathlike grip on its throat held the wolf anchored for the moment it took for the ax to crash into its head, to cleave deep into the skull. The wolf fell and lay, its hind legs kicking in reflex reaction, while the man slumped forward and fell on his face.

Gib swung around to face the rest of the pack. They backed away a pace or two but otherwise held their ground. They snarled at him and one, to the side, slunk forward a step or two. Gib took a quick step toward him, flourishing the ax, and the wolf retreated. There were, he saw, eight or ten of them; he did not really count them. They stood as tall as he did, their heads on a level with his head.

The standoff situation, he knew, would not hold for long. Now they were measuring and assessing him, and, in a little time, they would make up their minds and come in with a rush, knocking him off his feet, overwhelming him. It would do no good to turn and run, for they'd simply pull him down.

He did the one thing he could do. With a wild yell, he rushed them, lunging toward the slightly larger, more grizzled one he took to be the leader of the pack. The big wolf, startled, turned, but the ax

36

caught him in the shoulder and sheared through it. Another wolf was coming toward Gib and he spun swiftly to meet it, chopping a short arc with his ax. The blade caught the charging monster in the face and the wolf collapsed in its lunge and went skidding to the ground, flopping loosely as it fell.

Then the pack was gone. They melted into the dark underbrush and there was no sign of them.

Still gripping his ax, Gib turned to the man who had been fighting off the wolf. He gripped him by his shoulders and lifted him, swinging him around so that he was on the path that led down to the marsh. The man was heavy. But the worst was over now. The path sloped sharply, and he could haul him to the water if the wolves did not come back too soon. They would come back, he knew, but there might be time. He backed down the slope, tugging at the man. He reached the sharp pitch that led down to the water and gave a mighty heave. The man's body flopped and rolled, splashing into the water. Backing out into the marsh, Gib hauled the man after him and hoisted him to a sitting position. Here, for the moment, he knew, the two of them were safe. It was unlikely the wolves, with so much feasting left to them on the trail, would follow. Even if they did, they would hesitate to come into the water.

The man lifted an arm and pawed at Gib, as if he might be trying to fight him off.

Gib gripped his shoulder and shook him. "Try to stay sitting up," he said. "Don't fall over. Don't move. I'll get my boat."

The boat, no more than six feet long, he knew, would not carry the man's full weight, but if he could get him to use it as a support, it would keep him from sinking when they moved out into deeper water. They would not have far to go if Drood's raft were still where he'd found it in the morning.

• •

9

THE sky above him was the deepest blue he had ever seen, and there was nothing that obstructed it. All he could see was sky. He was lying on something soft and was being gently rocked and there was a sound like the faint, monotonous slap of water.

He felt an impulse to turn his head, to lift an arm, to try in some manner to discover where he was, but a certain caution, whispering deep inside his mind, told him not to do it, not to make a single motion, to hazard no sign that would draw attention to him.

Thinking back, he remembered a snarling muzzle with slashing teeth. He could still feel the roughness of the grizzled fur his hands had clutched to hold the monster off. It was a memory that was fuzzy and more nightmare than memory and he tried, futilely, to puzzle out whether it was truth or fantasy.

He lay quietly, fighting off the tendency of his nerves to tighten up, and he tried to think. Certainly he was not where he had been when, whether in truth or fantasy, he had contested with the wolf. For there had been trees there; the trail had been edged and roofed over by the trees and here there were no trees.

Something made a harsh sound to one side and above him and he rolled his head slowly and saw the red-winged blackbird swaying on a cattail, its claws clutching desperately to maintain its balance. It spread its wings and flirted its tail and squawked at him, glaring at him out of beady eyes.

Feet came shuffling toward him and he lifted his head a few inches and saw the little woman, short and dumpy, in the checkered dress—like a well-proportioned dwarf and human, but with a furry face.

She came and stood above him. He let his head back on the pillow and stared up at her.

"I have soup for you," she said. "Now that you are awake, I have soup for you."

"Madam," he said, "I do not know . . ."

"I am Mrs. Drood," she said, "and when I bring you soup you must be sure to eat it. You have lost much strength."

"Where am I?"

"You are on a raft in the middle of the marsh. Here you are safe. No one can reach you here. You are with the People of the Marsh. You know the People of the Marsh?"

"I have heard of you," said Cornwall. "I remember there were wolves . . ."

"Gib, he saved you from the wolves. He had this brand new ax, you see. He got it from the gnomes."

"Gib is here?"

"No, Gib has gone to get the clams, to make clam chowder for you. Now I get duck soup. You will eat duck soup? Chunks of meat in it."

She went shuffling off.

Cornwall raised himself on his right elbow and saw that his left arm was in a sling. He struggled to a sitting position and lifted his hand up to his head. His fingers encountered bandages.

It was coming back to him, in bits and pieces, and in a little while, he knew, he would have it all.

He stared out across the marsh. From the position of the sun he gathered that it was midmorning. The marsh stretched far away, with clumps of stunted trees growing here and there—perhaps trees rooted on islands. Far off, a cloud of birds exploded from the grass and reeds, went volleying up into the sky, wheeled with military precision, and floated back to rest again.

A boat came around a bend and cruised down the channel toward the raft. A grizzled marsh-man sat in the stern. With a twist of his paddle he brought the boat alongside the raft.

"I am Drood," he said to Cornwall. "You look perkier than you did last night."

"I am feeling fine," said Cornwall.

"You got a hard crack on the skull," said Drood. "Scalp laid open. And that arm of yours had a gash in it clear down to the bone."

He got out of the boat and tied it to the raft, came lumbering over to where Cornwall sat, and squatted down to face him.

"Guess you were lucky, though," he said. "All the others dead. We went over this morning and searched the woods. Looks like no one got away. Bandits, I suppose. Must have come a far piece, though. One time there were bandits lurking in these hills, but they cleared out. They ain't been here for years. What kind of stuff you carrying?"

Cornwall shook his head. "I'm not sure. Trade goods of all sorts, I think. Mostly cloth, I guess. I wasn't a member of the train. I was just along with them."

Mrs. Drood came shuffling from behind the hut, carrying a bowl.

"Here is Ma," said Drood. "Has some soup for you. Eat all you can. You need it."

She handed him a spoon and held the bowl for him. "You go ahead," she said. "With only one arm, you can't hang onto the bowl."

The soup was hot and tasty and once he had the first spoonful, he found that he was ravenous. He tried to remember when he had had his last meal and his memory failed him.

"It surely does one's heart good," said Drood, "to watch someone spoon in victuals that way."

Cornwall finished up the bowl. "You want another one?" asked Ma. "There is plenty in the kettle."

Cornwall shook his head. "No, thank you. It is kind of you."

"Now you lay back," she said. "You've sat up long enough. You can lay here and talk with Pa."

"I don't want to be a bother. I've put you out

enough. I must be getting on. As soon as I see Gib to thank him."

Pa said, "You ain't going nowhere. You ain't in shape to go. We are proud to have you, and you ain't no bother."

Cornwall lay back, turning on his side so he faced the squatting marsh-man.

"This is a nice place to live," he said. "Have you been here long?"

"All my life," said Drood. "My father before me and his father before him and far back beyond all counting. We marsh people, we don't wander much. But what about yourself? Be you far from home?"

"Far," said Cornwall. "I came from the west."

"Wild country out there," said Drood.

"Yes, it is wild country."

"And you were going back there?"

"I suppose you could say I was."

"You are a tight-lipped creature," Drood told him. "You don't say much of nothing."

"Maybe that's because I haven't much to say."

"That's all right," said Drood. "I didn't mean to pry. You take your rest now. Gib will be coming back almost any time."

He rose and turned to walk away. "A minute, Mr. Drood," said Cornwall. "Before you go—thanks for everything."

Drood nodded at him, his eyes crinkling in a smile. "It's all right, young fellow. Make yourself to home."

The sun, climbing up the sky, was warm upon him and Cornwall closed his eyes. He had no more than closed them when the picture came—the sudden surge of men out of the woods, the chunk of arrows, the shadowed flash of blades. It had been quietly done—there had been no screaming and no bellowing except by the men who had been hit, and not too many of them, for the most of them had died quickly, with arrows through their hearts.

How had it come, he wondered, that he had lived through it? He could remember little—a sword coming down on his head and instinctively throwing up his arms to ward it off, then falling. He could remember falling from the horse he rode, but he had no memory of falling to the ground—just falling, but not striking. Perhaps, he thought, he may have fallen into a heavy patch of undergrowth, for underbrush grew thick and close beside the trail—falling there and being considered dead, not being noticed later.

He heard a grating sound and opened his eyes. Another boat had drifted in against the raft. In it sat a young marsh-man and before him, in the middle of the craft, a basket full of clams.

Cornwall sat up. "You must be Gib," he said.

"That's right," said Gib. "I'm glad to see you looking well."

"My name is Mark Cornwall. They tell me you are the one who saved my life."

"I am glad I could. I got there just in time. You were fighting off a wolf with your bare hands. That took a lot of guts, to do a thing like that. Do you remember any of it?"

"It is all pretty vague," said Cornwall. "Just snatches here and there."

Gib got out of the boat, lifted the basket of clams onto the raft. "A lot of chowder there," he said. "You like chowder?"

"Indeed, I do."

"Mrs. Drood makes it like you never tasted."

He came over and stood beside Cornwall. "Drood and I went out this morning. We found seven bodies. The bodies had been stripped of everything of value. Not a knife, not a purse. All the goods were gone. Even the saddles from the horses. It was the work of bandits."

"I am not so sure," said Cornwall.

"What do you mean, you're not so sure?"

"Look," said Cornwall, "you saved my life. I owe you something. All I can give you is the truth. Drood was asking questions, but I told him nothing."

"You can trust Drood," said Gib. "He's all right.

You can trust any marsh-man. And you don't need to tell me. I don't need to know."

"I somehow feel I should," said Cornwall. "I am not a trader. I am, or rather I was, a student at the University of Wyalusing. I stole a document from the university library, and I was warned by a friendly goblin to flee because others might want the document. So I hunted up a trader and paid him to let me travel with him."

"You think someone attacked the trader's party to get rid of you? Or to get the document? They killed everyone to get rid of you? Did they get the document?"

"I don't think so," said Cornwall. "Pull off my boot, will you? The right boot. With only one hand I can't manage it."

Gib stooped and tugged off the boot.

"Reach into it," said Cornwall.

Gib reached in. "There's something here," he said. He pulled it out.

"That's it," said Cornwall. He awkwardly unfolded the single page and showed it to Gib.

"I can't read," said Gib. "There is no marsh-man who can."

"It's Latin, anyway," said Cornwall.

"What I can't understand," said Gib, "is why it should be there. They would have searched you for it."

"No," said Cornwall. "No, they wouldn't have searched me. They think they have the document. I left a copy, hidden, where it was easy for them to find."

"But if you left a copy . . ."

"I changed the copy. Not much. Just a few rather vital points. If I'd changed too much, they might have been suspicious. Someone might have known, or guessed, something of what it is about. I don't think so, but it is possible. It wasn't the document they were after; it was me. Someone wanted me dead."

43

"You're trusting me," said Gib. "You shouldn't be trusting me. There was no call to tell me."

"But there is," said Cornwall. "If it hadn't been for you, I'd now be dead. There might be danger to you keeping me. If you want to, help me get ashore and I will disappear. If someone asks, say you never saw me. It's only fair to you that you know there might be danger."

"No," said Gib.

"No what?"

"No, we won't put you ashore. No one knows that you are here. No one saw and I have told no one. Anyway, they'll think that you are dead."

"I suppose they will."

"So you stay here until you are well. Then you can go wherever you wish, do what you wish."

"I can't wait for long. I have a long journey I must make."

"So have I," said Gib.

"You as well? I thought you people never left the marsh. Drood was telling me . . ."

"Ordinarily that is so. But there was an old hermit up in the hills. Before he died, he gave me a book and what he called a hand ax. He asked me to deliver them to someone called the Bishop of the Tower . . ."

"North and west from here?"

"That's what the hermit said. Up the river, north and west. You know of this Bishop of the Tower?"

"I have heard of him. On the border of the Wasteland."

"The Wasteland? I did not know. The enchantment world?"

"That's right," said Cornwall. "That's where I am going."

"We could travel together, then?"

Cornwall nodded. "As far as the Tower. I go beyond the Tower."

"You know the way?" asked Gib.

"To the Tower? No, just the general direction. There are maps, but not too reliable."

44

"I have a friend," said Gib. "Hal of the Hollow Tree. He has traveled widely. He might know. He might go with us to point out the way."

"Consider this," said Cornwall, "before you decide we should go together: Already there has been one attempt to kill me; there might be others."

"But whoever is concerned already thinks you dead."

"Yes, of course, at the moment that is true. But there would be many eyes along the way and many tongues. Travelers would be noticed and would be talked about."

"If Hal went with us, we'd travel no roads or trails. We'd travel in the forest. There would be few to see us."

"You sound as if you want to travel with me, even knowing . . ."

"We of the marshes are timid folk," said Gib. "We feel unsafe when we go far from the marsh. I don't mind telling you I shrink from the idea of the journey. But with you and Hal along . . ."

"You are good friends with Hal?"

"The best friend that I have. We visit back and forth. He is young, about as old as I am, and stronger, and he knows the woods. He knows no fear. He steals from cornfields, he raids garden patches . . ."

"He sounds a good man to be with."

"He is all of that," said Gib.

"You think he'd go with us?"

"I think he would. He is not one to turn his back on adventure."

10

SNIVELEY, the gnome, said, "So, you want to buy the sword? What do you want the sword for? It is not for such as you. You could scarcely lift it. It is fashioned for a human. No pretty piece of iron, but a sword for a fighting man."

"I have known you for a long time," said Gib. "You have known my people for a long time. And the People of the Hills. Can I speak in confidence?"

Sniveley twitched his ears and scratched the back of his head. "You should know better than to ask me that. We are not blabbermouths, we gnomes. We are a business people and we are not gossips. We hear many things and we do not pass them on. Loose mouths can be a fertile source of trouble and we want no trouble. You know full well that we of the Brotherhood—the goblins and the elves and all the rest of us—live in the land of humans on their sufferance. It is only by sticking to our business and staying strictly out of matters that are no affair of ours that we can survive at all. The Inquisition forever sniffs around, but it seldom acts against us if we remain somewhat invisible. But let us become ever so faintly obnoxious and some pesty human will go rushing off to inform on us, and then there is hell to pay. Perhaps I should be the one to ask if this confidential matter that you mention might be the cause of trouble to us."

"I don't think so," Gib told him. "If I had thought so, I would not have come. We marsh people need you and through the years you have dealt fairly with us. You have heard, of course, of the massacre of the pack train just two nights ago."

46

Sniveley nodded. "A ghastly business. Your people buried them?"

"We buried what was left of them. We leveled and disguised the graves. We towed the dead animals far out into the marsh. We left no sign of what had happened."

Sniveley nodded. "That is good," he said. "The train will be missed, of course, and the authorities, such as they are, may make some investigation. Not too much of an investigation, I would think, for this is still border country and officialdom does not rest quite easy here. If there had been blatant evidence, they would have had to investigate, and that would have been bad. We, none of us—humans or you or the People of the Hill or the Brotherhood—have any desire for human bloodhounds to be snooping in our yards."

"I feel bad," said Gib, "about one aspect of it. We could not say the proper words above their graves. We do not know the words. Even if we did, we'd not be the proper persons to recite them. We buried them unshrived."

"They died unshrived," said Sniveley, "and it's all foolishness, in any case."

"Foolishness, perhaps," said Gib, "but no more foolishness, perhaps, than many of our ways."

"Which brings us," said Sniveley, "to how all of this is connected with your wanting the sword."

"Not all of them were killed," said Gib. "I stumbled on the massacre and found one who was still alive. It's he who needs the sword."

"He had a sword before and it was looted from him?"

"His sword, his knife, his purse. The killers took the goods the train was carrying and also stripped the bodies. I gather that the sword he had was not a very good one. One his great-grandfather had passed down. And now he needs a good one."

"I have other swords," said Sniveley.

Gib shook his head. "He needs the best. He is going to the Wasteland to hunt out the Old Ones."

47

"That is insanity," said Sniveley. "There may be no Old Ones left. We gnomes have heard ancient tales of them, but that is all they are—old tales. Even if he found them, what would be the use of it?"

"He wants to talk with them. He is a scholar and he wants—"

"No one can talk with them," said Sniveley. "No one knows their language."

"Many years ago—perhaps thousands of years ago—a human lived with them for a time and he wrote down their language, or at least some words of their language."

"Another tale," said Sniveley. "The Old Ones, if they came across a human, would tear him limb from limb."

"I do not know," said Gib. "All of this is what Mark told me."

"Mark? He is your human?"

"Mark Cornwall. He comes from the west. He has spent the last six years at the University of Wyalusing. He stole a manuscript . . ."

"So now he is a thief."

"Not so much thief as finder. The manuscript had been hidden away for centuries. No one knew of it. It would have continued lost if he'd not happened on it."

"One things occurs to me," said Sniveley. "You showed me the book and ax that the dying hermit gave you. To be delivered, I believe, to some bishop. Is it possible you and this Mark will make a common journey?"

"That is our intention," said Gib. "We go together to the Bishop of the Tower. Then he will go into the Wasteland."

"And you have thoughts of going with him?"

"I had thought of it. But Mark will not allow it."

"I should hope not," said Sniveley. "Do you know what the Wasteland is?"

"It's enchanted ground," said Gib.

"It is," said Sniveley, "the last stronghold of the Brotherhood. . . ."

48

"But you—"

"Yes, we are of the Brotherhood. We get along all right because this is the Borderland. There are humans, certainly, but individual humans—millers, woodcutters, charcoal burners, small farmers, moonshiners. The human institutions, government and church, do not impinge on us. You have never seen the lands to the south and east?"

Gib shook his head.

"There," said Sniveley, "you would find few of us. Some in hiding, perhaps, but not living openly as we do. Those who once lived there have been driven out. They have retreated to the Wasteland. As you may suspect, they hold a hatred for all humankind. In the Wasteland are those who have been driven back to it and those who never left, the ones who had stayed there and hung on grimly to the olden ways of life."

"But you left."

"Centuries ago," said Sniveley, "a group of prospecting gnomes found the ore deposit that underlies these hills. For uncounted millennia the gnomes have been smiths and miners. So we moved here, this small group of us. We have no complaint. But if the so-called human civilization ever moved in full force into the Borderland, we would be driven out."

"Humans, however, have traveled in the Wasteland," said Gib. "There was that old traveler who wrote the tale that Mark read."

"He would have to have had a powerful talisman," said Sniveley. "Has this friend of yours a talisman?"

"I do not think he has. He never spoke of it."

"Then he truly is insane. He has not even the excuse of treasure, of finding some great treasure. All he seeks are the Old Ones. And tell me, what will he do if he finds the Old Ones?"

"The ancient traveler did not seek treasure, either," said Gib. "He simply went to see what he could find."

"Then he was insane as well. Are you certain there is no way to dissuade this human friend of yours?"

"I think not. There is no way, I am sure, that one could stop him."

"Then," said Sniveley, "he does have need of a sword."

"You mean you'll sell it to me?"

"Sell it to you? Do you know the price of it?"

"I have some credit with you," said Gib. "Drood has credit. There are others in the marsh who would be willing . . ."

"Take three marshes like the one down there," said Sniveley, "and there would not be credit enough in all of them to buy the sword. Do you know what went into it? Do you know the care and craftsmanship and the magic that was used?"

"Magic?"

"Yes, magic. Do you think that a weapon such as it could be shaped by hands and fire alone, by hammer or by anvil?"

"But my ax—"

"Your ax was made with good workmanship alone. There was no magic in it."

"I am sorry," Gib said, "to have bothered you."

Sniveley snorted and flapped his ears. "You do not bother me. You are an old friend, and I will not sell the sword to you. I will give it to you. Do you understand what I am saying? I will give it to you. I will throw in a belt and scabbard, for I suppose this down-at-heels human has neither one of them. And a shield as well. He will need a shield. I suppose he has no shield."

"He has no shield," said Gib. "I told you he has nothing. But I don't understand. . . ."

"You underestimate my friendship for the People of the Marshes. You underestimate my pride in matching a sword of my fabrication against the howling horrors of the Wasteland, and you underestimate, as well, my admiration for a puny little human who, from his studies, must know what the Wasteland is and yet is willing to face it and its denizens for some farfetched dream."

"I still don't understand you fully," said Gib, "but I thank you just the same."

"I'll get the sword," said Sniveley, rising from his chair. He was scarcely on his feet when another gnome, wearing a heavy leather apron and who, from the soot on his hands and face, had been working at a forge, came bursting unceremoniously into the room.

"We have visitors," he screamed.

"Why must you," asked Sniveley, a little wrathfully, "make so great a hullabaloo about visitors? Visitors are nothing new. . . ."

"But one of them is a goblin," screamed the other gnome.

"So one of them is a goblin."

"There are no goblins nearer than Cat Den Point, and that is more than twenty miles away."

"Hello, everyone," said Hal of the Hollow Tree. "What is all the ruckus?"

"Hello, Hal," said Gib. "I was about to come to see you."

"You can walk back with me," said Hal. "How are you, Sniveley? I brought a traveler—Oliver. He's a rafter goblin."

"Hello, Oliver," said Sniveley. "And would you please tell me just what in hell is a rafter goblin? I've heard of all sorts of goblins . . ."

"My domicile," said Oliver, "is the rafters in the roof atop the library at the University of Wyalusing. I have come here on a quest."

Coon, who had been hidden from view, walking sedately behind Hal, made a beeline for Gib and leaped into his lap. He nuzzled Gib's neck and nibbled carefully at his ears. Gib batted at him. "Cut it out," he said. "Your whiskers tickle and your teeth are sharp." Coon went on nibbling.

"He likes you," said Hal. "He has always liked you."

"We have heard of a pack-train killing," said the goblin, Oliver. "Word of it put much fear in me.

51

We came to inquire if you might have the details."

Sniveley made a thumb at Gib. "He can tell you all about it. He found one human still alive."

Oliver swung on Gib. "There was one still alive? Is he still alive? What might be his name?"

"He is still alive," said Gib. "His name is Mark Cornwall."

Oliver slowly sat down on the floor. "Thank all the powers that be," he murmured. "He is still alive and well?"

"He took a blow on the head," said Gib, "and a slash on his arm, but both head and arm are healing. Are you the goblin that he told me of?"

"Yes, I am. I advised him to seek out a company of traders and to flee with them. But that was before I knew to whom that cursed monk sold his information. Much good that it did him, for he got his throat slit in the bargain."

"What is going on?" squeaked Sniveley. "What is all this talk of throat slitting and of fleeing? I dislike the sound of it."

Quickly Oliver sketched the story for him. "I felt that I was responsible for the lad," he said. "After all, I got myself involved . . ."

"You spoke," said Gib, "of this human to whom the monk sold his information."

"That's the crux of it," said Oliver. "He calls himself Lawrence Beckett and pretends to be a trader. I don't know what his real name is, and I suppose it does not matter, but I know he's not a trader. He is an agent of the Inquisition and the most thorough-going ruffian in the border country. . . ."

"But the Inquisition," said Sniveley. "It is . . ."

"Sure," said Oliver. "You know what it is supposed to be. The militant arm of the Church, with its function to uproot heresy, although heresy, in many instances, is given a definition which far outstrips the meaning of the term. When its agents turn bad, and most of them turn bad, they become a law unto themselves. No one is safe from them, no perfidy too low. . . ."

"You think," said Gib, "that this Beckett and his men massacred the pack train?"

"I would doubt very much they did the actual killing. But I am certain it was arranged by Beckett. He got word to someone."

"In hopes of killing Mark?"

"With the certainty of killing Mark. That was the only purpose of it. All were supposed to be killed. According to what you say, they stripped Mark, took everything he had. They thought that he was dead, although probably they did not know that the purpose of the attack was to kill one certain man."

"They didn't find the page of manuscript. He had it in his boot."

"They weren't looking for the manuscript. Beckett thought he had it. He stole it from Mark's room."

"The fake," said Hal. "The copy."

"That is right," said Oliver.

"And you came all this way," said Gib, "to warn him against Beckett before it was too late."

"I was responsible. And I was late. Small thanks to me that he still lives."

"It seems to me," said Sniveley gravely, "that the key to all of this may lie in what was written in that fake copy Beckett has. Can you enlighten us on that?"

"Willingly," said Oliver. "We worked it out together and, as I remember it, were quite gleeful at the neatness of it. Some things we had to leave as they were, for the monk would tell whoever he sold the information to where the page of parchment had been found, in what book it had been hidden—the book that Taylor had written about his travels in the Wasteland. Most of which, I am convinced, was a tissue of lies. I even have my doubts he was ever in the Wasteland.

"But be that as it may, we had to leave the most of it, only taking out all mention of the Old Ones. In its place we inserted a story based on legend, a very obscure legend that Mark had come upon in his reading of some ancient tome. The legend of a hidden, legendary university, where was housed incredibly ancient, and equally legendary, books, and a great hoard of primeval treasure. Only a hint that it was in the Wasteland, only something that Taylor had heard about. . . ."

"Are you mad?" howled Sniveley. "Do you know what you have done? Of all the nincompoop ideas—"

"What is the matter?" asked Oliver. "What do you mean?"

"You moron!" shouted Sniveley. "You cretin! You should have known. There is such a university!"

He stopped in midsentence and fixed his gaze on Gib, shifted it onto Hal.

"You two," he said, "you're not supposed to know. No one outside the Brotherhood is supposed to know. It is an old secret. It is sacred to us."

He grabbed Oliver by the shoulder and jerked him to his feet. "How come you didn't know?"

Oliver cringed away. "So help me, I never knew. I never heard of it. I am just a lowly rafter goblin. Who was there to tell me? We thought it was a fable."

Sniveley let Oliver loose. Coon crouched in Gib's lap, whimpering.

"Never in my life," said Hal to Sniveley, "have I seen you so upset."

"I have a right to be upset," said Sniveley. "A pack of fools. A set of various fools who have been snared up in something they should have kept their fingers out of. But, worse than that, an agent of the Inquisition has been given knowledge, faked knowledge that happens to be true, and what do you think he'll do with it? I know what he'll do—head straight into the Wasteland. Not for the treasure that was mentioned, but for the ancient books. Can't you see the power and glory that would descend upon a churchly human who found old heathen books and consigned them to the flames?"

"Maybe he won't get them," Gib said hopefully. "He may try for them and fail."

54

"Of course he'll fail," said Sniveley. "He hasn't got a chance. All the hellhounds of the Wasteland will be snapping at his heels, and any human who gets out alive will do so through pure luck. But for centuries now there has been peace—at times unwilling peace—between humans and the Brotherhood. But this will light the fires. The Borderland will become unsafe. There'll be war again."

"There is one thing that puzzles me," said Gib. "You had no great objection to Cornwall going into the Wasteland—foolish certainly, but no great objection. I think you rather admired him for his courage. You were willing to give me a sword for him. . . ."

"Look, my friend," said Sniveley, "there is a vast difference between a lowly scholar going out into the Wasteland on an academic and intellectual search and a minion of the Church charging into it with fire and steel. The scholar, being known as a scholar, might even have a chance of coming out alive. Not that he'd be entirely safe, for there are some ugly customers, with whom I have small sympathy, lurking in the Wasteland. But by and large he might be tolerated, for he would pose no danger to our people. He would not bring on a war. If he were killed, he'd be killed most quietly, and no one would ever know how or when it happened. Indeed, there would be few who would ever mark his going there. And he might even come back. Do you see the difference?"

"I think I do," said Gib.

"So now what do we have?" asked Sniveley of Gib. "There is this journey that you are honor bound to make, carrying the book and ax the hermit gave you for delivery to the Bishop of the Tower. And on this journey your precious scholar will travel with you and then continue on into the Wasteland. Have I got the straight of it?"

"Yes, you have," said Gib.

"You have no intention of going into the Wasteland with him?"

"I suppose I haven't."

"But I have such intentions," said the rafter gob-

55

lin. "I was in at the start of it; I might as well be in at the end of it, whatever that may be. I have come this far and I have no intention whatsoever of turning back."

"You told me," said Hal, "that you had a great fear of open spaces. You had a word for it . . ."

"Agoraphobia," said Oliver. "I still have it. I shiver at the breath of open air. The uncovered sky oppresses me. But I am going on. I started something back there in that Wyalusing garret, and I cannot turn back with it half done."

"You'll be an outlander," said Sniveley. "Half of the Brotherhood, half out of it. Your danger will be real. Almost as much danger to you as there is danger to a human."

"I know that," said Oliver, "but I am still going."

"What about this matter of you carrying something to the Bishop of the Tower?" Hal asked Gib. "I had not heard of it."

"I had meant to ask you if you'd show us the way," said Gib. "We want to travel overland and I fear we might get lost. You must know the way."

"I've never been there," said Hal. "But I know these hills. We'd have to stay clear of paths and trails, especially with this Inquisition agent heading the same way. I suppose he will be coming through the Borderland. So far there has been no word of him."

"If he had passed by," said Sniveley, "I would have had some word of him."

"If I am to go," asked Hal, "when should I be ready?"

"Not for a few days," said Gib. "Mark has to heal a bit, and I promised Drood I'd help him get some wood."

Sniveley shook his head. "I do not like it," he said. "I like no part of it. I smell trouble in the wind. But if the scholar lad's to go, he must have the sword. I promised it for him and it'll be a sorry day when a gnome starts going back on his promises."

56

••••••••••••••••••••••••••••••••••

11

THEY had traveled for five days through sunny autumn weather, with the leaves of the forest slowly turning to burnished gold, to deep blood-red, to lustrous brown, to a pinkness of the sort that made one's breath catch in his throat at the beauty of it.

Tramping along, Mark Cornwall kept reminding himself time and time again that in the past six years he had lost something of his life. Immured in the cold, stone walls of the university, he had lost the color and the smell and the headiness of an autumn forest and, worst of all, had not known he had lost it.

Hal led them, for the most part, along the ridgetops, but there were times when they must cross from one ridge to another or had to leave the high ground to keep out of sight of a ridgetop clearing where a woodcutter or a farmer scratched out a bare existence. While there was no danger in such places, where, indeed, a welcome and a rough sort of hospitality might be accorded them, it was considered best to avoid detection as much as possible. Word would travel fast concerning the movements of such a motley band as theirs and there might be danger in having the fact of their journey noised about.

Plunging down from the ridges into the deep-cut valleys that ran between the hills, they entered a different world—a deep, hushed, and buried world. Here the trees grew closer and larger, rock ledges jutted out of steep hillsides, and massive boulders lay in the beds of brawling creeks. Far overhead one could hear the rushing of the wind that brushed the hilltops, but down below the brows of the rearing bluffs there was no hint of wind. In the quietness of this deeper forest, the startled rush of a frightened squirrel, his foraging disturbed, through the deep layer of autumn leaves, was startling in itself. That, or the sudden explosion of wings as a ruffed grouse went rocketing like a twilight ghost through the tangle of the tree trunks.

At the end of a day's journey they went down into one of the deep hollows between the hills to find a camping place. Hal, scouting ahead, would seek a rock shelter where a fissure in the limestone of a bluff face was overhung either by a ledge of rock or by the bluff itself, offering some protection. The fire was small, but it gave out warmth against the chill of night, holding back the dark, making a small puddle of security and comfort in a woods that seemed to turn hostile with the coming of the night.

Always there was meat, for Hal, wise to the woods and an expert with his bow, brought down squirrels and rabbits, and on the second day, a deer, and on other occasions, grouse. So that, as a result of this, they made lesser inroads on the provisions they carried—wild rice, smoked fish, cornmeal—sparse fare, but sustaining and easy to carry.

Sitting around the fire at night, Cornwall remembered the disappointment of Mrs. Drood when she had been persuaded that she should not have a farewell party for them, inviting in the marsh people, the gnomes and the hill people to speed them on their way. It would have been a good party, but it would have emphasized their going, which all concerned agreed should be kept as quiet as possible.

Five days of sunny weather, but in the middle of the afternoon of the sixth day rain had begun to fall, at first little more than a gentle mist, but increasing as the hours went on, with a wind developing from the west, until, with night about to fall, the rain poured down steadily, driven by the wind that turned it into needles that stung one's face.

Throughout the afternoon Hal hunted for shelter

but had found nothing that would afford more than minimal protection against the driving storm.

Cornwall brought up the rear, following Coon, who humped along disconsolately, his coat of fur plastered down with wetness, his bedraggled tail sweeping the forest floor.

Ahead of Coon, Gib and the rafter goblin walked together, with the marsh-man's wet fur gleaming in the soft light that still remained, the goblin weary and hobbling, walking with an effort. The march, Cornwall realized, had been tougher on the goblin than on any of the others. His days of walking, from Wyalusing to Hal's hollow tree, and now the six days of the march, had played him out. Life in the rafters at the university had not fitted him for this.

Cornwall hurried ahead, passing Coon. He reached down and touched the goblin's shoulder.

"Up, on my back," he said. "You deserve a rest."

The goblin looked up at him. "Kind sir," he said, "there is no need."

"I insist," said Cornwall. He crouched down and the goblin clambered on his shoulder, balancing himself with an arm around the human's neck.

"I am tired," he admitted.

"You have traveled far," said Cornwall, "since that day you came to see me."

The goblin chuckled thinly. "We started a long progression of events," he said, "and not finished yet. You know, of course, that I go into the Wasteland with you."

Cornwall grunted. "I had expected as much. You will be welcome, little one."

"The terror slowly leaves me," said Oliver, the goblin. "The sky no longer frightens me as much as it did when I started out. I am afraid now I might even grow to like the open. That would be a horrible thing to happen to a rafter goblin."

"Yes, wouldn't it?" said Cornwall.

They plodded along, and there was no sign of Hal. Darkness began to sift down into the forest. Would they keep walking all the night, Cornwall wondered.

Was there any end to it? There was no letup in the storm. The slanting rain, coming from the northwest, slashed at his face. The wind seemed to be growing colder and sharper.

Hal materialized in the darkness ahead, moving like a dark ghost out of the darkness of the tree trunks. They stopped, standing in a knot, waiting for him to come up to them.

"I smelled smoke," he said, "and tracked it down. It could have been Beckett and his men, camping for the night; it could have been a charcoal pit or a farmer's homestead. When you smell smoke, you find out what it is."

"Now," said Gib, "that you have sufficiently impressed us, tell us what it was."

"It is an inn," said Hal.

"That does us no good," said Gib. "They'd never let us in, not a marsh-man and a hill-man, a goblin, and a coon."

"They would let Mark in," said Hal. "If he gets too wet and cold, his arm will stiffen up and he'll have no end of trouble."

Cornwall shook his head. "They wouldn't let me in, either. They'd ask to see the color of my coin and I have no coin. In any case, we stick together. I wouldn't enter where they'd not welcome all of you."

"There is a stable," said Hal. "Once it is dark, we can shelter there, be out before the dawn. No one would ever know."

"You found no other shelter?" asked Cornwall. "No cave?"

"Nothing," said Hal. "I think it has to be the stable."

12

THERE was one horse in the stable. It nickered softly at them when they came through the door.

"The innkeeper's horse," said Hal. "A sorry bag of bones."

"Then there are no guests," said Cornwall.

"None," said Hal. "I peered through the window. Mine host is roaring drunk. He is throwing stools and crockery about. He is in a vicious temper. There is no one there, and he must take it out on the furniture and pottery."

"Perhaps, after all," said Gib, "we are better in the stable."

"I think so," said Cornwall. "The loft, perhaps. There appears to be hay up there. We can burrow into it against the cold."

He reached out a hand and shook the pole ladder that ran up into the loft.

"It seems solid enough," he said.

Coon already was clambering up it.

"He knows where to go," said Hal, delighted.

"And I follow him," said Cornwall.

He climbed the ladder until his head came above the opening into the loft. The storage space, he saw, was small, with clumps of hay here and there upon the floor.

Ahead of him Coon was clambering over the piles of hay and, suddenly, just ahead of him, a mound of hay erupted and a shrill scream split the air.

With a surge Cornwall cleared the ladder, felt the rough boards of the hay mow bending and shifting treacherously beneath his feet. Ahead of him the hay-covered figure beat the air with flailing arms and kept on screaming.

He leaped forward swiftly, reaching for the screamer. He sweated, imagining mine host bursting from the inn and racing toward the stable, adding to the hullabaloo that would arouse the countryside, if there were anyone in this howling wilderness of a countryside to rouse.

The screamer tried to duck away, but he reached out and grabbed her, pulled her tight against him, lifted his free hand and clamped it hard against her mouth. The screaming was shut off. Teeth closed on a finger and he jerked it free, slapped her hard, and clamped down the hand across her mouth. She did not bite again.

"Keep quiet," he told her. "I'll take the hand away. I do not mean to hurt you."

She was small and soft.

"Will you be quiet?" he asked.

She bobbed her head against his chest to say she would. Behind him Cornwall heard the others scrabbling up the ladder.

"There are others here," he said. "They will not hurt you, either. Don't scream."

He took the hand away.

"What's the matter, Mark?" asked Oliver.

"A woman. She was hiding up here. Was that what you were doing, miss?"

"Yes," she said. "Hiding."

The loft was not quite dark. Heavy twilight still filtered through the louvered windows set at each end of the gables.

The woman stepped away from Cornwall, then at the sight of Oliver, shrank back against him. A frightened breath caught in her throat.

"It's all right," he said. "Oliver is a very friendly goblin. He is a rafter goblin. You know what a rafter goblin is?"

She shook her head. "There was an animal," she said.

62

"That was Coon. He's all right, too."

"Wouldn't hurt a flea," said Hal. "He is so down-right friendly that it is disgusting."

"We are fugitives," said Cornwall. "Or very close to fugitives. But non-dangerous fugitives. This is Hal, and over there is Gib. Gib is a marsh-man. Hal is hill people."

She was shivering, but she stepped away from him.

"And you?" she asked. "Who are you?"

"You can call me Mark. I am a student."

"A scholar," said Oliver, with fidgety precision. "Not a student, but a scholar. Six years at Wya-lusing."

"We seek shelter from the storm," said Cornwall. "We would have gone to the inn, but they would not have taken us. Besides, we have no money."

"He is drunk," said the girl, "and smashing up the furniture. Madam is hiding in the cellar and I ran out here. I was afraid of him. I've always been afraid of him."

"You work at the inn?"

"I am," she said with some bitterness, "the wench, the scullery maid, the slops girl."

She sat down suddenly in the hay. "I don't care what happens," she said. "I am not going back. I will run away. I don't know what will happen to me, but I'll run away. I will stay no longer at the inn. He is always drunk and madam is handy with a fag-got and no one needs to put up with that."

"You," said Oliver, "can run away with us. What matter if there be one more of us? A brave but a sorry company, and there's always room for anoth-er."

"We go far," said Hal, "and the way is hard."

"No harder than the inn," she said.

"There is no one at the inn?" asked Cornwall.

"Nor likely to be," she said. "Not on a night like this. Not that there is ever any crowd. A few trav-elers now and then. Charcoal burners and woodcut-ters in to get a drink, although not too often, for they seldom have the penny."

63

"Then," said Gib, "we can sleep till morning with no fear of disturbance."

Coon, who had been investigating the crannies of the loft, came back and sat down, wrapping his tail around his feet.

"One of us will have to stand guard for a time," said Cornwall, "then wake another one. We'll have to take turns throughout the night. I will volunteer for the first watch if it's agreeable with the rest of you."

Gib said to the serving wench, "Will you be coming with us?"

"I don't think it wise," said Cornwall.

"Wise or not," she said, "I will leave as soon as it's light enough to travel. With you or by myself. It makes no difference to me. I'm not staying here."

"I think it best," said Hal, "that she travel with us. These woods are no place for a human girl alone."

"If you are to travel with us," said Oliver, "we should know your name."

"My name is Mary," said the girl.

"Does anyone want to eat?" asked Gib. "I have some cold cornbread in my knapsack and a bag of shelled walnuts. Not much, but something we can chew on."

Hal hissed at them.

"What's the matter?"

"I thought I heard something."

They listened. There was only the muffled patter of the rain and the mutter of the wind underneath the eaves.

"I hear nothing," Cornwall said.

"Wait. There it was again."

They listened and it came again, a strange clicking sound.

"That's a horse," said Hal. "A shod horse, the metal of the shoe striking on a stone."

It came again and with it came the faint sound of voices. Then the sound of the stable door creaking open and the shuffle and the thump of feet as a horse was led inside. Voices mumbled.

"This is a foul place," said one whining voice.

"It is better than the open," said another. "Only a little better, but this is a noisome night."

"The innkeeper is drunk," said the other.

"We can find our own food and beds," said his fellow.

More horses were led in. Leather creaked as saddles were taken off. The horses stamped. One of them whinnied.

"Find a fork and get up that ladder," someone said. "Throw down some hay."

Cornwall looked quickly about. There was no place to hide. They could burrow into the hay, of course, but not with someone in the loft, armed with a fork, questing in the darkness for hay to be thrown down the chute.

"All at once," he muttered. "All of us will have to make the break. As soon as he shows above the ladder."

He turned to the girl. "You understand?" he asked. "As fast as you can, then run."

She nodded.

Feet scraped on the ladder and Cornwall reached for the hilt of his sword. A flurry of flying hay went past him and out of the corner of his eye he saw Coon, leaping, spread-eagled, at the head that appeared above the opening into the loft. Coon landed on the head and there was a muffled shriek. Cornwall leaped for the ladder, went swarming down it. Halfway down he caught a glimpse of a fork, its handle lodged in the floor below, its tines spearing up at him, and twisted frantically to one side to miss them. At the bottom of the ladder was a whirling fury of wild motion as the man who had been climbing the ladder fought to dislodge Coon, who was using his claws with terrible execution on his victim's head and face. Even before his feet hit the floor Cornwall snapped out his left hand and, grasping the fork, jerked it free.

65

Three yelling shapes were charging from the front of the barn at him, metal gleaming as one of them drew a sword. Cornwall's left arm came back, carrying the fork backward until the metal of its tines scraped against his jawbone. Then he hurled it, straight at the bellowing shapes that were bearing down on him. Sword held straight before him, he charged to meet them. His shield was still on his back; there had not been the time to transfer it to his arm. And a good thing, too, he thought in a split second of realization. With it on his arm, he never could have grabbed the fork, which, if it had stayed, would have impaled one of the others tumbling down the ladder.

In front of him one of the three shapes was rearing back with a shriek of surprise and pain, clawing at the fork buried in his chest. Cornwall caught the glitter of metal aimed at his head and ducked instinctively, jerking up his sword. He felt his blade bite into flesh, and at the same instant a massive blow on the shoulder that momentarily staggered him. He jerked his sword free and, reeling sidewise, fell against the rump of a horse. The horse lashed out with a foot and caught him a glancing blow in the belly. Doubled up, he went down on his hands and knees and crawled, gasping, the breath knocked out of him.

Someone caught him under the arms and jerked him half erect. He saw, with some surprise, that the sword had not been knocked out of his hand; he still had a grip on it.

"Out of here!" a voice gasped at him. "They'll all be down on us."

Still bent over from the belly kick, he made his legs move under him, wobbling toward the door. He stumbled over a prostrate form, regained his feet and ran again. He felt rain lash into his face and knew he was outdoors. Silhouetted against the lighted windows of the inn, he saw men running toward him, and off a little to his right, the kneeling figure of a bowman who, almost unconcernedly, released arrow after arrow. Screams and curses sounded in the darkness and some of the running men were stumbling, fighting to wrench loose the arrows that bristled in their bodies.

"Come on," said Gib's voice. "We all are here. Hal will hold them off."

Gib grabbed his arm, turning him and giving him a push, and he was running again, straightening up, breathing easier, with just a dull pain in his midriff where the horse had kicked him.

"This is far enough," said Gib. "Let's pull together now. We can't get separated. You here, Mary?"

"Yes, I'm here," said Mary in a frightened voice.

"Oliver?"

"Here," said Oliver.

"Coon? Coon, where the hell are you?"

Another voice said, "Don't worry about Old Coon. He'll hunt us up."

"That you, Hal?"

"It's me. They won't try to follow. They've had enough for one night."

Cornwall suddenly sat down. He felt the wetness of ground soak into his breeches. He struggled to slip the sword back into the scabbard.

"You guys were all right in that barn," said Hal. "Mark got one of them with a pitchfork and another with the sword. The third Gib took care of with his ax. I never had a chance until we got outside."

"You were doing well enough when I saw you," Gib told him.

"And don't forget Coon," said Cornwall. "He led the attack and took his man out of the fighting."

"Will you tell me," Gib asked plaintively, "exactly how it happened. I'm not a fighting man. . . ."

"None of us is a fighting man," said Cornwall. "I never was in a fight before in all my life. A few tavern brawls at the university, but never in a fight. Never where it counted."

"Let's get out of here," said Hal. "We have to build some distance, and once we get started, we might as well stay walking. We won't find a place to stop. Everyone grab hold of hands and don't let loose. I'll lead the way, but we have to take it easy. We can't move too fast. We can't go falling down a cliff or bumping into trees. If one of you loses hold of hands or falls, yell out and everyone will stop."

●●●●●●●●●●●●●●●●●●●●●●●●●●●●●●●●●●●●●

13

HAL crouched in the clump of birches and stared at what the first morning light revealed. The stable and the inn were gone. Where they once had stood lay heaps of embers, smoke tainting the sharp air with an acrid bitterness, rising in thin tendrils.

The rain had stopped and the sky was clear, but water still dripped from the branches of the birches. It would be another splendid autumn day, Hal told himself, but it still was cold. He crossed his arms and put his hands beneath his armpits to warm them.

Not moving, he examined the scene before him, ears tuned for the slightest sound that might spell danger. But the danger now, it seemed, was gone. The men who had done this work had left.

Far off a bluejay screamed and up the hill a squirrel made a skittering sound as it scampered through the fallen leaves. Nothing else made a sound; nothing else was stirring.

His eyes went over the ground inch by inch, looking for the unusual, for something that might be out of place. There seemed to be nothing. The only thing unusual were the ashes where the stable and the inn had stood.

Moving cautiously, he left the birches and scouted up the hill. He stopped behind a huge oak and, shielded by it, peered around its bole. His higher position on the hill now revealed a slope of ground on the opposite side of the inn that had been masked before. On the slope of ground something most unusual was taking place. A huge gray wolf was digging furiously while two others sat leisurely on their haunches, watching as he dug. The wolf was digging in what appeared to be a patch of raw earth and beyond the patch in which he dug were others, slightly mounded.

Hal instinctively lifted his bow and reached over his shoulder for an arrow, then drew back his hand and settled down to watch. There was no point, he mused, in further killing; there had already been killing. And the wolves were engaged in a practice that was quite normal for them. There was meat beneath those mounds and they were digging for it.

He counted the mounds. There were five at least, possibly six; he could not be sure. Three in the stable, he thought, or had there been four? Depending on whether it had been three or four, then his arrows had accounted for one at least, possibly as many as three. He grimaced, thinking of it. The fight had not been that one-sided, he reminded himself; rather, it had been a matter of surprise and simple luck. He wondered, if he and the others had not attacked, would there have been a fight at all? But that was all past and done; no single act could be recalled. The die had been cast when Coon had made his spread-eagled leap at the head of the man who climbed the ladder. Considering the circumstances, they had come out of it far better than could have been expected, with Mark the only one who bore the scars of battle, a sore shoulder, where the flat of a sword had struck him, and a sore belly, where a horse had kicked him.

He squatted beside the tree and watched the wolves. The fact that they were there, he knew, meant that no one else was around.

He rose and stepped around the tree, scuffling in the leaves. The wolves swiveled their heads toward him and leaped to their feet. He scuffled leaves again, and the wolves moved like three gray shadows, disappearing in the woods.

He strode down the hill and circled the two piles of embers. The heat that still radiated from them was welcome in the chilly morning, and he stood for a moment to soak up some of it.

In the muddy earth he found the tracks of men and horses and wondered about the innkeeper and his wife. The serving wench, he recalled, said that the goodwife had been hiding in the cellar from her drunken lord. Could it be that she'd still been there when the inn was fired? If that were so, her charred body must be down among the embers, for the place would have blazed like tinder, and there'd have been no chance to get out.

He followed the trace left by the men and horses down the hill to where it joined the trail and saw that the company had gone on north and west. He went back up the hill, had a look at the raw wetness of the graves, again circled the piles of embers for some clue, wondering what manner of men could have done such a thing, afraid that he might know.

He stood for a moment, nagged by uneasiness. Then he went back down the hill and followed the trail that the company had taken north and west, keeping well up the hillside from it, his ears cocked for the slightest sound, examining each stretch of trail below him before he moved ahead.

A couple of miles away he found the innkeeper, the man he had glimpsed through the window of the inn the night before, smashing crockery and breaking up the furniture. He swung at the end of a short rope tied to the limb of a massive oak tree that leaned out from the hillside to overhang the trail. His hands were tied behind him and his head was twisted strangely by the pressure of the rope. He twirled back and forth at the faint stirring of the breeze. And he dangled; he dangled horribly. A chickadee was perched on one shoulder, a tiny, innocent mite of a gray-white bird, picking at the blood and froth that had run from the corner of the mouth.

Later on, Hal knew, there would be other birds.

He stood in the mud of the trail and looked up at the dangling, twirling man and felt, gathering in his mind, a vague sense of horror and of melancholy.

Leaving the man and the oak, he scouted up the trail and from the tracks he saw that now the mounted company was in something of a hurry. The hoof-marks of the shod horses dug deep into the mud, leaving sharp, incisive tracks. They had been moving at a gallop.

He left the trail and angled back up the hill, studying the conformation of the land, picking up the foggy landmarks he had impressed upon his mind.

So he finally came, slipping through the trees and brush, to the small rock shelter he and his companions had found the night before, after long stumbling through the wet and dark, a few hours before the first hint of dawn.

Oliver, the rafter goblin, and Coon slept far back from the overhang, in the deeper recesses of the shelter, huddled close together for the sake of shared warmth. The other three sat close together toward the front, wrapped in blankets against the chill. He was almost upon them before they saw him.

"So you're back," said Gib. "We wondered what had happened. Can we light a fire?"

Hal shook his head. "We travel fast," he said. "We travel fast and far. We must be out of here."

"But I went out," objected Gib, "and got dry fuel, dug from the heart of a fallen tree. It will give little smoke. We are cold and hungry. . . ."

"No," said Hal. "The country will be up. The inn and stable burned. No sign of the goodwife who was hiding in the cellar, but mine host is hanging from a tree. Someone will find soon what happened, and before they do we must be miles from here."

"I'll shake the goblin and Coon awake," said Gib, "and we'll be on our way."

14

IT had been a punishing day. They had stopped for nothing, pushing ahead as fast as they could manage. There had been only one habitation, the hut of a woodchopper, that they had had to circle. They had not stopped to eat or rest. Cornwall had worried about the girl, but she had managed to keep up with the rest of them with seemingly little effort and made no complaint.

"You may regret throwing in with us," Cornwall said once. But she had shaken her head, saying nothing, conserving her breath for the grim business of clambering up and down the hills, racing down the more open ridges.

Finally, they had come to rest, with early darkness closing in. No rock shelter this time, but the dry bed of a little stream, in a recess where, in spring freshets, a waterfall had carved out a bowl that was protected on three sides by high banks, leaving open only the channel through which the stream ran from the little pool beneath the falls.

Through the centuries, the water, plunging over a ledge of hard limestone, had scoured out all earth and softer shale down to the surface of a harder sandstone stratum. In the center of the bowl stood the small pool of water, but around the pool lay the dry surface of the sandstone.

They had built their fire close against the upstream wall, which was overhung for several feet by the limestone ledge. There had been little talk until, famished, they had wolfed down their food, but now they sat around the blaze and began to talk.

"You feel rather certain," Cornwall asked of Hal, "that the company was that of Beckett?"

"I cannot know, of course," said Hal, "but who else would it be? The horses were shod and a pack train does not shoe its horses and a train would use mostly mules. There were no mules in this bunch, only horses. And who else, I ask you, would visit such terrible, senseless vengeance upon the innocent?"

"They could not have known they were innocent," said Cornwall.

"Of course not," said Hal. "But the point is that they presumed the guilt. They probably tortured the innkeeper and when he could tell them nothing, hanged him. Mine goodwife more than likely died when they burned the inn with her still in the cellar."

He looked at Mary, across the fire from him. "I am sorry, miss," he said.

She put up a hand and ran her fingers through her hair. "There is no need for you to be," she said. "I mourn for them as I would any human being. It is not good to die in such a manner and I feel sorrow at it, but they, the two of them, meant less than nothing to me. Were it not uncharitable, I could even say they deserved what happened to them. I was afraid of him. There was not a moment of the time I spent at the inn I was not afraid of him. And the woman was no better. With but little cause, other than her bad temper, she'd take a stick of firewood to me. I could show you bruises that still are black and blue."

"Why, then, did you stay?" asked Gib.

"Because I had nowhere else to go. But when you found me in the loft, I had decided I would go. By morning light I would have been gone. It was by sheer good luck that I found you to travel with."

"You say that Beckett travels north and west," Cornwall said to Hal. "What happens if we reach the Bishop of the Tower and find him and his men there ahead of us? Even if he has been there and gone, he will have warned the bishop of us and we'll find scant welcome if, in fact, we're not clapped into irons."

"Mark," said Hal, "I think there is little danger of it. A few miles north of where mine host was hanged, the trail branches, the left fork leading to the Tower, the right into the Wasteland. Beckett, I am sure, would have taken the right fork. I should have followed the trail to see, but it seemed to me important we should be on our way as soon as we could manage."

"The Wasteland?" Mary asked. "He is heading for the Wasteland?"

Hal nodded.

She looked around the circle at them. "And you, as well, you go into the Wasteland?"

"Why do you ask?" asked Oliver.

"Because I myself, in my infancy, may have come from the Wasteland."

"You?"

"I do not know," she said. "I do not remember. I was so young I have no memory or almost no memory. There are, of course, certain memories. A great sprawling house sitting on a hilltop. People who must have been my parents. Strange playmates. But whether this was the Wasteland, I do not know. My parents—well, not my parents, but the couple that took me in and cared for me, told me how they found me, toddling down a path that came out of the Wasteland. They lived near the Wasteland, two honest old people who were very poor and had never had a child they could call their own. They took me in and kept me, and I loved them as if they had been my parents."

They sat in silence, staring at her. Finally she spoke again.

"They worked so hard and yet they had so little. There were few neighbors, and those were far away. It was too near the Wasteland. People were not comfortable living so near the Wasteland. Yet it never bothered us. Nothing ever bothered us. We grew some corn and wheat. We raised potatoes and a gar-

75

den. There was wood for chopping. There was a cow, but the cow died one winter of the murrain and there was no way to get another. We had pigs. My father—I always called him father, even if he wasn't—would kill a bear or deer and trap other creatures for their furs. He would trade the furs for little pigs—such cute little pigs. We kept them in the house for fear of wolves until they had grown bigger. I can remember my father coming home with a little pig tucked underneath each arm. He had carried them for miles."

"But you did not stay," said Cornwall. "Happy, you said, and yet you did not stay."

"Last winter," she said, "was cruel. Both snow and cold were deep. And they were old. Old and feeble. They took the coughing sickness and they died. I did what I could, but it was little. She died first and he next day. I built a fire to thaw the ground and chopped out a grave for them, the two of them together. Too shallow, far too shallow, for the ground was hard. After that, I couldn't stay. You understand, don't you, that I couldn't stay?"

Cornwall nodded. "So you went to the inn."

"That is right," she said. "They were glad enough to have me, although you never would have known it from their treatment of me. I was young and strong and willing to work. But they beat me just the same."

"You'll have a chance to rest when we get to the Tower," said Cornwall. "To decide what you want to do. Is there anyone who knows what kind of place the Tower might be?"

"Not much of anything," said Hal. "An old defense post against the Wasteland, now abandoned. Once a military post, but now there is no military there. There is the bishop only, although why he's needed there, or what he does, no one pretends to know. A few servants, perhaps. A farm or two. That would be all."

"You have not answered me," said Mary. "Do you go into the Wasteland?"

"Some of us," said Cornwall. "I go. I suppose

76

Oliver as well. There is no stopping him. If I could, I would."

"I was in at the first of it," said Oliver. "I'll be in at the end of it."

"How far?" asked Gib. "How long before we reach the Tower?"

"Three days," said Hal. "We should be there in three days."

15

●●●●●●●●●●●●●●●●●●●●●●●●●●●●●●●●●●

THE Bishop of the Tower was an old man. Not as old, Gib thought, as the hermit, but an old man. The robes he wore once had been resplendent, with cloth of gold and richest silk, but now they were worn and tattered after many years of use. But, looking at the man, one forgot the time-worn, moth-ravaged robes. A depth of compassion robed him, but there was a sense of power as well, a certain feeling of ruthlessness—a warrior bishop grown old with peace and church. His face was thin, almost skeletal, but fill out those cheeks and broaden out the peaked nose, and one could find the flat, hard lines of a fighting man. His head was covered with wispy white hair so sparse it seemed to rise of itself and float in the bitter breeze that came blowing through the cracks and crevices of the time-ruined tower. The fire that burned in the fireplace did little to drive back the cold. The place was niggardly furnished—a rough hewn table, behind which the bishop sat on a ram-shackle chair, an indifferent bed in one corner, a trestle table for eating, with benches down either side of it. There was no carpeting on the cold stone floor. Improvised shelving held a couple of dozen books and beneath the shelving were piled a few scrolls, some of them mouse-eaten.

The bishop lifted the leather-bound book off the table and, opening it, riffled slowly through the pages. He closed it and placed it to one side. He said to Gib, "My brother in Christ, you say he passed in peace?"

"He knew that he was dying," Gib said. "He had no fear. He was feeble, for he was very old. . . ."

"Yes, old," said the bishop. "I remember him from the time I was a boy. He was grown then. Thirty, perhaps, although I don't remember, if I ever knew. Perhaps I never knew. Even then he walked in the footsteps of the Lord. I, myself, at his age was a man of war, the captain of the garrison that stood on this very spot and watched against the Wasteland hordes. It was not until I was much older and the garrison had been withdrawn, there having been many years of peace, that I became a man of God. You say my old friend lived in the love of the people?"

"There was no one who knew him who did not love him," said Gib. "He was a friend to all. To the People of the Marsh, the People of the Hills, the gnomes . . ."

"And none of you," said the bishop, "of his faith. Perhaps of no faith at all."

"That, your worship, is right. Mostly of no faith at all. If I understand rightly what you mean by faith."

The bishop shook his head. "That would be so like him. So entirely like him. He never asked a man what his faith might be. I distrust that he ever really cared. He may have erred in this way, but, if so, it was erring beautifully. And I am impressed. Such a crowd of you to bring me what he sent. Not that you aren't welcome. Visitors to this lonely place are always welcome. Here we have no commerce with the world."

"Your grace," said Cornwall, "Gib of the Marshes is the only one of us who is here concerned with bringing you the items from the hermit. Hal of the Hollow Tree agreed to guide us here."

"And milady?" asked the bishop.

Cornwall said stiffly, "She is under our protection."

"You, most carefully, it seems to me, say nothing of yourself."

"Myself and the goblin," Cornwall told him, "are

79

on a mission to the Wasteland. And if you wonder about Coon, he is a friend of Hal's."

"I had not wondered about the coon," said the bishop, rather testily, "although I have no objection to him. He seems a cunning creature. A most seemly pet."

"He is no pet, your grace," said Hal. "He is a friend."

The bishop chose to disregard the correction, but spoke to Cornwall, "The Wasteland, did you say? Not many men go these days into the Wasteland. Take my word for it, it is not entirely safe. Your motivation must be strong."

"He is a scholar," said Oliver. "He seeks truth. He goes to make a study."

"That is good," the bishop said. "No chasing after worldly treasure. To seek knowledge is better for the soul, although I fear it holds no charm against the dangers you will meet."

"Your grace," said Cornwall, "you have looked at the book . . ."

"Yes," the bishop said. "A goodly book. And most valuable. A lifetime's work. Hundreds of recipes for medicines that can cure the ills of mankind. Many of them, I have no doubt, known to no one but the hermit. But now that you have brought me the book, in time known to everyone."

"There is another item," Cornwall reminded him, "that the hermit sent you."

The bishop looked flustered. "Yes, yes," he said. "I quite forgot. These days I find it easy to forget. Age does nothing for one's memory."

He reached out and took up the ax, wrapped in cloth. Carefully he unwrapped it, stared at it transfixed once he had revealed it. He said nothing but turned it over and over, examining it, then laid it gently in front of him.

He raised his head and stared at them, one by one, then fixed his gaze on Gib. "Do you know what you have here?" he asked. "Did the hermit tell you?"

"He told me it was a fist ax."

80

"Do you know what a fist ax is?"

"No, your grace, I don't."

"And you?" the bishop asked of Cornwall.

"Yes, your grace. It is an ancient tool. There are those who say . . ."

"Yes, yes, I know. There are always those who say. There are always those who question. I wonder why the hermit had it, why he kept it so carefully and passed it on at death. It is not the sort of thing that a holy man would prize. It belongs to the Old Ones."

"The Old Ones?" Cornwall asked.

"Yes, the Old Ones. You have never heard of them?"

"But I have," said Cornwall. "They are the ones I seek. They are why I am going to the Wasteland. Can you tell if they do exist, or are they only myth?"

"They exist," the bishop said, "and this ax should be returned to them. At sometime someone must have stolen it. . . ."

"I can take it," Cornwall said. "I'll undertake to see that it is returned to them."

"No," said Gib. "The hermit entrusted it to me. If it should be returned, I am the one—"

"But it's not necessary for you to go," said Cornwall.

"Yes, it is," said Gib. "You will let me travel with you?"

"If Gib is going, so am I," said Hal. "We have been friends too long to let him go into danger without my being at his side."

"You are all set, it seems," the bishop said, "to go marching stoutly to your deaths. With the exception of milady . . ."

"I am going, too," she said.

"And so am I," said a voice from the doorway.

At the sound of it Gib swung around. "Sniveley," he yelled, "what are you doing here?"

16

THE bishop, when he was alone, ate frugally—a bowl of cornmeal mush, or perhaps a bit of bacon. By feeding his body poorly, he felt that he fed his soul and at the same time set an example for his tiny flock. But, a trencherman by nature, he was glad of guests, who at once gave him an opportunity to gorge himself and uphold the good name of the Church for its hospitality.

There had been a suckling pig, resting on a platter with an apple in its mouth, a haunch of venison, a ham, a saddle of mutton, a brace of geese, and a peacock pie. There had been sweet cakes and pies, hot breads, a huge dish of fruit and nuts, a plum pudding laced with brandy, and four wines.

Now the bishop pushed back from the table and wiped his mouth with a napkin of fine linen.

"Are you sure," he asked his guests, "that there is nothing else you might require? I am certain that the cooks . . ."

"Your grace," said Sniveley, "you have all but foundered us. There is none of us accustomed to such rich food, nor in such quantities. In all my life I have never sat at so great a feast."

"Ah, well," the bishop said, "we have few visitors. It behooves us, when they do appear, to treat them as royally as our poor resources can afford."

He settled back in his chair and patted his belly. "Someday," he said, "this great and unseemly appetite of mine will be the end of me. I have never been able to settle quite comfortably into the role of

82

churchman, although I do my best. I mortify the flesh and discipline the spirit, but the hungers rage within me. Age does not seem to quench them. Much as I may frown upon the folly of what you intend to do, I find within myself the ache to go along with you. I suppose it may be this place, a place of warriors and brave deeds. Peaceful as it may seem now, for centuries it was the outpost of the empire against the peoples of the Wasteland. The tower now is half tumbled down, but once it was a great watch tower and before it ran a wall, close to the river, that has almost disappeared, its stones being carted off by the country people to construct ignoble fences, hen-houses and stables. Once men manned the tower and wall, standing as a human wall of flesh against the encroachments and the depredations of that unholy horde which dwells within the Wasteland."

"Your grace," said Sniveley, far too gently, "your history, despite the centuries, is too recent. There was a day when the humans of the Brotherhood lived as neighbors and in fellowship. It was not until the humans began chopping down the forest, failing to spare the sacred trees and the enchanted glens, not until they began building roads and cities, that there was animosity. You cannot, with clear conscience, talk of encroachments and depredations, for it was the humans—"

"Man had the right to do what he wished with the land," the bishop said. "He had the holy right to put it to best use. Ungodly creatures such as—"

"Not ungodly," said Sniveley. "We had our sacred groves until you cut them down, the fairies had their dancing greens until you turned them into fields. Even such simple little things as fairies . . ."

"Your grace," said Cornwall, "I fear we are outnumbered. There are but two of us who can make a pretense of being Christian, although I count the rest as true and noble friends. I am glad they have elected to go into the Wasteland with me, although I am somewhat concerned . . ."

"I suppose that you are right," said the bishop,

more good-naturedly than might have been expected. "It ill behooves any one at this jovial board to contend with one another. There are other matters that we should discuss. I understand, Sir Scholar, that you seek the Old Ones out of the curiosity of the intellect. I suppose this comes from the reading you have done."

"Reading most painfully come by," said Oliver. "I watched him many nights, hunched above a table in the library, reading ancient scripts, taking down the books that had not been touched for centuries and blowing off the dust that had accumulated, reading by the feeble light of a too-short candle, since poverty dictated he must use them to their bitter end. Shivering in the winter, since you must know that all the buildings of the university, and perhaps the library most of all, are ill-constructed old stone piles through which the wind has little trouble blowing."

"And, pray," the bishop said to Cornwall, "tell us what you found."

"Not a great deal," said Cornwall. "A sentence here, another sentence there. Enough to convince me that the Old Ones are not, as many think, entirely myth. There is a book, a very thin book, and most unsatisfactory, which purports to instruct one in the language of the Old Ones. I can speak that language, the little that there is of it. I do not know if it is truth or not. I do not know if there is a language or not. No niceties at all, no nuances to the thought that it conveys. I cannot be convinced, however, that such a work could be entirely without basis. Surely the man who wrote it thought the Old Ones had a language."

"There is no clue as to why he might have thought so? He does not explain how he learned the language?"

"He does not," said Cornwall. "I go on faith alone."

"It is not," the bishop said, "when you give it thought, an entirely bad reason for the going."

"Good enough for me," said Cornwall. "Perhaps not good enough for others."

"And it is good enough for me," said Oliver. "It is an excuse for me, if nothing else. I could not spend my life as a rafter goblin. Now that I look back on it, I was getting nowhere."

"Perhaps," said Cornwall, "I can understand you, Oliver. There's something about a university that gets into the blood. It is a place not of the world; it partakes of a certain fantasy. It is, in many ways, not entirely sane. The reaching after knowledge becomes a purpose that bears no relationship to reality. But Gib and Hal I worry over. I could take along the ax."

"You think so," Gib told him, "because you did not know the hermit. He did so much for all of us and we did so little for him. We'd look up at the craggy bluff where he had his cave and knowing he was there made the world seem right. I can't tell you why it was, but that was the way of it. I sat with him the last hour of his life. I pulled up the blanket to shield him from the world once the life was gone. I built the wall of stone to keep away the wolves. There's one thing more I must do for him. No one else, you understand; I'm the one to do it. He put the trust into my hands, and I must see it carried out."

The bishop stirred uncomfortably. "I can see," he said, "that there's nothing I can do to stop the rest of you from going out to get your heads smashed most horribly, and it might be a mercy if the head smashing was all you'd have to suffer. But I cannot understand why the sweet child, Mary, must insist—"

"Your grace," said Mary, "you do not know because I have not told you. When I was no more than a toddler, I came stumbling down a path and an old couple took me in and raised me as their own. I have told the others this, but I did not tell them that I've wondered many times where I might have come from. The path, you see, came out of the Wasteland. . . ."

85

"You cannot think," the bishop said, aghast, "that you came out of the Wasteland. It makes no sense, at all."

"At times," said Mary, "I have a certain memory. An old house high upon a hill and strange playmates that plead to be recognized, but I cannot recognize them. I do not know who or what they were."

"You do not need to know," the bishop said.

"It seems to me, your grace, I do," said Mary. "And if I do not find out now, I will never know."

"Let her go," said Sniveley. "Quit this pestering of her. She goes in goodly company and has every right to go. Perhaps more right than any of the rest of us."

"And you, Sniveley," said Hal, trying to speak lightly. "I imagine it will be old home week for you."

Sniveley snorted. "I could not sleep of nights. Thinking of the hand I had in it, and how destiny had so unerringly guided my hand to take a part in it. I forged the sword that the scholar carries. Fate must have foreordained the shaping of that sword. Otherwise, why would there have been this single pocket of the purest ore? Why the pocket of it in a drift that otherwise was acceptable, but of much poorer grade? It was placed there for a purpose, for there is nothing ever done without a purpose. And I could not put out of my mind the feeling that the purpose was the sword."

"If so," said Cornwall, "it was badly placed. I should be wearing no such sword. I am not a swordsman."

Hal said, "You did all right that night back in the stable."

"What is this?" the bishop asked. "What about a stable? You were brawling in a stable?"

Cornwall said, "We had not told you. I think we felt we should not tell you. We fear we have fallen greatly out of favor with a man named Lawrence Beckett. You may have heard of him."

The bishop made a face. "Indeed, I have," he

86

said. "If you had sat down and thought and planned and really put your mind to it in the picking of an enemy, you could have done no better than Beckett. I never have met the man, but his reputation has preceded him. He is a ruthless monster. If you are at cross-purposes with him, perhaps it is just as well you go into the Wasteland."

"But he is going there as well," said Gib.

The bishop heaved himself straight up in his chair. "You had not told me this. Why did you not tell me this?"

"One reason I can think of," said Cornwall, "is that Beckett is of the Inquisition."

"And you thought, perhaps, because this is so, he stands in the high regard of everyone in Holy Mother Church?"

"I suppose we did think so," said Cornwall.

"The Church is far flung," the bishop said, "and in it is the room for many different kinds of men. There is room for so saintly a personality as our late-lamented hermit and room as well, lamentably, for sundry kinds of rascals. We are too big and too wide-spread to police ourselves as well as might be wished. There are men the Church would be better off with-out, and one of the chief of these is Beckett. He uses the cloak of the Inquisition for his own bloodthirsty purposes; he has made it a political arm rather than ecclesiastical. And you say that now he is heading for the Wasteland?"

"We think he is," Hal said.

"We have had years of peace," the bishop said. "Years ago the military was withdrawn from this outpost because there seemed no need of it. For de-cades there had been no trouble, and there has been no trouble since the soldiers were withdrawn. But now I do not know. Now I fear the worst. A spark is all that's needed to touch the Borderland to flame and Beckett may be that very spark. Let me tell you with all the force at my command that with Beckett loose now is not the time to venture in the Waste-land."

"Nevertheless," said Gib, "we're going."

"I suppose so," said the bishop. "You all are addlepated and it's a waste of honest breath to try to talk with you. A few years younger and I'd join you to protect you from your folly. But since age and occupation bar me from it, I still shall do my part. It is not meet that you should go walking to your deaths. There shall be horses for you and whatever otherwise you need."

17

THE noses of Sniveley and Oliver were greatly out of joint. They had been dealt a grave injustice and had been the victims of heartless discrimination; they had to share a horse.

"Look at me," said Hal. "I am sharing mine with Coon."

"But Coon's your pet," said Oliver.

"No, he's not," said Hal. "He is my friend. The two of us together own a tree back home. We live there together. We share and share alike."

"You only took him up," said Sniveley, "so he wouldn't get wet when we crossed the river. He won't ride with you all the time. He doesn't even like to ride."

"The horse," said Hal, "is his as much as mine."

"I do not think," said Gib, "the horse shares in that opinion. He looks skittish to me. He's never been ridden by a coon."

They had crossed the river ford, the old historic ford once guarded by the tower. But as they wheeled about once the river had been crossed, the tower and wall that flanked it on either side seemed rather puny structures, no longer guarding anything, no longer military, with all the formidability gone out of them, age-encrusted ruins that were no more than an echo of the time when they had stood foursquare against invasion from the Wasteland. Here and there trees grew atop the wall, while the massive stones of the tower were masked and softened by the clinging vines that had gained footholds in the masonry.

Tiny figures, unrecognizable at that distance, grouped together on one section of the ruined wall, raised matchstick arms to them in a gesture of farewell.

"There still is time," Cornwall said to Mary, "to turn back and cross the river. This is no place for you. There may be rough days ahead."

She shook her head stubbornly. "What do you think would happen to me back there? A scullery wench again? I'll not be a scullery wench again."

Cornwall wheeled his horse around, and it plodded slowly along the faint path that angled up the low hill that rose above the river. Once the river had been crossed, the character of the land had changed. South of the river, thick forests crawled up the flanks of massive bluffs, gashed by steep ravines. Here the hills were lower, and the forest, while it still remained, was not so heavy. There were groves of trees covering many acres, but there were open spaces here and there and, looking to the east, Cornwall could see that some of the bluffs on this northern side were bald.

He could have wished, he told himself, that there might have been a map—any sort of map, even a poor one with many errors in it, that might have given some idea of where they might be going. He had talked with the bishop about it, but so far as the bishop knew there was no map and had never been. The soldiery that through the years had guarded the ford had done no more than guard. They had never made so much as a single foray across the river. Any forays that occurred had been made by the people of the Wasteland and these, apparently, had been very few. Duty at the tower had been dreary duty, unbroken, for the most part, by any kind of action. The only people, it seemed, who had ever ventured into the Wasteland had been occasional travelers, like Taylor, who had written the account that now lay in Wyalusing. But whether any of the few accounts written by such travelers had been true was very much a question. Cornwall wrinkled his brow at the

90

thought. There was nothing, he realized, that would argue the Taylor account as any more factual than the rest of them. The man had not actually visited the Old Ones but had only heard of them; and he need not have even traveled to the Wasteland to have heard of them. The ancient fist ax, carried by Gib, was better evidence that they existed than had been Taylor's words. It was strange, he reminded himself, that the bishop had instantly recognized the ax as belonging to the Old Ones. He realized that he should have talked further with the bishop about the matter, but there had been little time and much else to talk about.

It was a matchless autumn day. They had made a late start and the sun already had climbed far into the sky. There were no clouds and the weather was rather warm and as they climbed the hill, the panorama of the river valley spread out below them like a canvas painted by a man mad with the sense of color.

"There is something up there on the ridge," said Mary. "Something watching us."

He raised his head, scanning the horizon.

"I don't see a thing," he said.

"I saw it only for a moment," she said. "Maybe not really seeing it. Maybe just the movement of it. That might have been all. Not really seeing anything, but seeing it move."

"We'll be watched," said Sniveley, who along with Oliver had forced their horse toward the head of the column. "We can count on that. There'll never be a moment we'll be out of their sight. They'll know everything we do."

"They?" asked Cornwall.

Sniveley shrugged. "How is one to know? There are so many different kinds of us. Goblins, gnomes, banshees. Maybe even brownies and fairies, for respectable as such folk may be considered by you humans, they still are a part of all this. And other things as well. Many other things, far less respectable and well intentioned."

"We'll give them no offense," said Cornwall. "We'll not lift a hand against them."

"Be that as it may," said Sniveley, "we are still intruders."

"Even you?" asked Mary.

"Even we," said Sniveley. "Even Oliver and I. We are outlanders, too. Traitors, perhaps deserters. For we or our forefathers deserted the homeland and went to live in the Borderland with their enemies."

"We shall see," said Cornwall.

The horses plodded up the path and finally reached the ridge. Before them spread, not a plateau, as might have been suspected, but a succession of other ridges, each one higher as they spread out horizonward, like regularly spaced and frozen waves.

The path angled down a barren slope covered with browning grass. At the lower edge of the slope, a dense forest covered the span that lay between the hills. There was not a living thing in sight, not even birds. An eerie feeling of loneliness closed in about them, and yet in all that loneliness Cornwall had an uncomfortable feeling between his shoulder blades.

Moving slowly, as if unwilling to go farther, the horse went down the trail, which twisted to one side to bypass a giant white oak tree that stood alone in the sweep of grass. It was a tall, yet squatty tree, with a huge bole and widely spreading branches, the first of which thrust out from the trunk not more than twelve feet above the ground.

Cornwall saw that something apparently had been driven deeply into the hard wood of the trunk. He reined in his horse and stared at it. About two feet of it extended out beyond the wood. It was a couple of inches in diameter, an ivory white and twisted.

Behind him Sniveley involuntarily sucked in his breath.

"What is it?" Mary asked.

"The horn of a unicorn," said Sniveley. "There are not many of the creatures left, and I have never heard of one that left his horn impaled in a tree."

"It is a sign," Oliver said solemnly.

Cornwall nudged his horse closer and reached down to grasp the horn. He pulled and it did not budge. He pulled again and he might as well have tried to pull a branch from the tree.

"We'll have to chop it out," he said.

"Let me try," said Mary.

She reached down and grasped the horn. It came free with a single tug. It measured three feet or so in length, tapering down to a needle point. It was undamaged and unbroken.

They all gazed at it in awe.

"I never saw a thing like this before," said Mary. "Old tales, of course, told in the Borderland, but . . ."

"It is an excellent omen," said Sniveley. "It is a good beginning."

93

18

●●●●●●●●●●●●●●●●●●●●●●●●●●●●●●●●●

THEY camped just before dark in a glade at the head of one of the ravines that ran between the hills. A spring gushed out from the hillside, giving rise to a tiny stream that went gurgling down its bed. Gib chopped firewood from a down pine that lay above the campsite. The day had remained a perfect one and in the west a lemon sky, painted by the setting sun, slowly turned to green. There was grass for the horses, and they were sheltered from the wind by a dense forest growth that closed in on the glade from every side.

Hal said, "They're all around us. We're knee-deep in them. They are out there watching."

"How can you tell?" asked Mary.

"I can tell," said Hal. "Coon can tell. See him over there, huddled by the fire. He doesn't seem to be listening, but he is. Quiet as they may be, he still can hear them. Smell them, likely, too."

"We pay no attention to them," Sniveley said. "We act as if they aren't there. We must get used to it; we can't get our wind up. This is the way that it will be. They'll dog our footsteps every minute, watching, always watching. There's nothing to be afraid of yet. There are nothing but the little ones out there now—the elves, the trolls, the brownies. Nothing dangerous. Nothing really mean. Nothing really big."

Cornwall raked coals out of the fire, pushed them together, set a skillet of cornbread dough on them. "And what happens," he asked, "when something really mean and big shows up?"

Sniveley shrugged. He squatted across the coals

from Cornwall. "I don't know," he said. "We play it by ear—what is it you say, by hunch? It's all that we can do. We have a few things going for us. The unicorn horn, for one. That's powerful medicine. The story of it will spread. In another day or two, all the Wasteland will know about the horn. And there's the magic sword you wear."

"I'm glad you brought that up," said Cornwall. "I had meant to ask you. I've been wondering why you gave it to Gib. Surely, he told you for whom it was intended. You made a slip there, Master Gnome. You should have checked my credentials. If you had, you would have known that, search the world over, you could have found no swordsman more inept than I. I wore a sword, of course, but, then, a lot of men wear swords. Mine was an old blade and dull, a family heirloom, not too valuable, even in a sentimental sense. From one year's end to another, I never drew it forth."

"Yet," said Sniveley, grinning, "I am told you acquitted yourself quite nobly in the stable affair."

Cornwall snorted in disgust. "I fell against the hind end of a horse and the horse promptly kicked me in the gut, and that was the end of it for me. Gib, with his trusty ax, and Hal, with his bow, were the heroes of that fight."

"Still, I am told that you killed your man."

"An accident, I can assure you, no more than an accident. The stupid lout ran on the blade."

"Well," said Sniveley, "I don't suppose it matters too much how it came about. The point is that you managed it."

"Clumsily," said Cornwall, "and with no glory in it."

"It sometimes seems to me," said Sniveley, "that much of the glory attributed to great deeds may derive overmuch from hindsight. A simple job of butchery in aftertimes somehow becomes translated into a chivalrous encounter."

Coon came around the fire, reared up, and put his forefeet on Cornwall's knee. He pointed his nose at

95

the skillet of cornbread and his whiskers twitched.

"In just a little while," Cornwall told him. "It'll take a little longer. I promise there'll be a piece for you."

"I often wonder," Sniveley said, "how much he understands. An intelligent animal. Hal talks to him all the time. Claims he answers back."

"I would have no doubt he does," said Cornwall.

"There is a strong bond between the two of them," said Sniveley. "As if they might be brothers. Coon was chased by dogs one night. He was scarcely more than a pup. Hal rescued him and took him home. They've been together ever since. Now, with the size of him and the smartness of him, no dog in its right mind would want to tangle with him."

Mary said, "The dogs must know him well. Hal says there is a moonshiner out hunting coons almost every night, come fall. The dogs never follow on Coon's track. Even when he's out, the dogs don't bother him. In the excitement of the hunt, they may come upon his track and trail him for a time, but then they break it off."

"Oh, the dogs are smart enough," said Hal. "The only thing that's smarter is Old Coon himself."

Gib said, "They're still out there. You can see one every now and then, moving in the dark."

"They've been with us," said Sniveley, "from the moment that we crossed the river. We didn't see them, of course, but they were there and watching."

Something plucked at Mary's sleeve, and when she turned her head, she saw the little creature with a face that seemed wrinkled up with worry.

"Here is one of them right now," she said. "Come out into the open. Don't make any sudden moves or you will scare him off."

The little creature said, "I am Bromeley, the troll. Don't you remember me?"

"I'm not sure I do," she said, then hesitated. "Are you one of them I used to play with?"

"You were a little girl," said Bromeley. "No bigger than any one of us. There was me and the brown-

96

ie, Fiddlefingers, and at times a stray fairy or an elf that happened to come by. You never thought that we were different. You were not big enough to know. We made mud pies down by the creek, and while neither myself nor Fiddlefingers regarded mud-pie making as a worthwhile enterprise, we humored you. If you wanted to make mud pies, we went and made them with you."

"I remember now," said Mary. "You lived underneath a bridge, and I always thought that under a bridge was the strangest place to live."

"You should know by now," said Bromeley, with a touch of haughtiness, "that all proper trolls must reside beneath a bridge. There is no other place that is acceptable."

"Yes, of course," said Mary, "I know about troll bridges."

"We used to go and pester the ogre," Bromeley said. "We'd toss pebbles and clods and pieces of wood and other things down into his den, and then we'd run as fast as we could manage so he wouldn't catch us. Thinking of it since, I doubt very much the ogre knew about our misbehavior. We were timid characters prone to be scared of shadows. Nothing like the fairies, though. The fairies were really scaredy-cats."

Cornwall started to speak, but Mary shook her head at him. "What are all the other folk doing, watching us?" she asked. "Why don't they come out? We could build up the fire and all of us sit around it talking. We could even dance. There might be something we could eat. We could cook up more cornbread. Enough for all of us."

"They won't come," said Bromeley. "Not even for cornbread. They were against my coming. They even tried to stop me. But I had to come. I remembered you from very long ago. You've been in the Borderland?"

"I was taken there," said Mary.

"I came and hunted for you and I didn't understand. I couldn't understand why you would want to

97

leave. Except for the mud pies, which were boring and terribly messy work, we had good times together."

"Where is Fiddlefingers now?"

"I do not know," said the troll. "He dropped out of sight. Brownies are wanderers. They are always on the move. We trolls stay in one place. We find a bridge we like and settle down and live there all our—"

Suddenly there was a piping, although later, when they thought of it, they realized it had not come so suddenly as it seemed. It had been there for some time while the troll had talked with Mary, but little more than an insect noise, as if some cricket in the grass or underbrush had been doing some quiet chirping. But now the piping welled up into a quavery warbling, then swelled into a wailing that throbbed and beat upon the air, not stopping after a moment, but going on and on, a wild and terrible music, part lament, part war cry, part gibbering of a madman.

Mary, startled, came to her feet, and so did Cornwall, his quick movement upsetting the skillet of cornbread. The horses, lunging at their picket ropes, neighed in terror. Sniveley was trying to scream, but with a voice that was no more than a squeak. "The Dark Piper," he squeaked and kept on saying it over and over again. "The Dark Piper, the Dark Piper, the Dark Piper . . ."

Something round and sodden came rolling down the steep incline that sloped above the camp. It rolled and bounced, and its bouncing made hollow thumps when it struck the ground. It rolled to the edge of the campfire and stopped and lay there, leering back at them with a mouth that was twisted to a leer.

It was a severed human head.

19

ON the afternoon of the next day they found the place the severed head had come from. The head itself lay buried, with scant ceremony and a hastily muttered prayer, at the foot of a great granite boulder at the first night's camp, with a crude cross thrust into the ground to mark its resting place.

Oliver protested the erecting of the cross. "They are leaving us alone," he said. "Why wave an insult at them? Your silly two sticks crossed are anathema to them."

But Cornwall stood firm. "A cross is not an insult," he said. "And how about this business of heaving human heads at us? That's not leaving us alone. This head belonged to a human and presumably a Christian. We owe the owner of the head at least a prayer and cross, and we'll give him both."

"You think," Gib asked, "it could be one of Beckett's men?"

"It could be," Cornwall said. "Since the inn, we've had no word of Beckett. We don't know if he's crossed the border yet, but if there were a human here, it could be one of Beckett's men. He lagged behind the line of march or went wandering and fell afoul of someone who has no love of humans."

"You oversimplify," said Sniveley. "There is no one in the Wasteland who has any love of humans."

"Except for the thrown head," said Cornwall, "they've made no move against us."

"Give them time," said Sniveley.

"You must consider, too," said Oliver, "that

you're the only human here. They may have no great regard for any of us, but you . . ."

"There is Mary," said Hal.

"Mary, sure, but as a child she lived here, and on top of that there is the matter of that horn some addlepated unicorn left sticking in a tree."

"We do not come as an invading army," said Gib. "We are a simple band of innocents—pilgrims, if you will. There is no reason for them to have any fear of us."

"It is not fear with which we are here concerned," said Sniveley. "Rather, it is hate. A hatred that runs through untold centuries, a hatred deeply rooted."

Cornwall got little sleep. Each time that he dropped off he was assailed by a recurring dream that never quite got finished, in which he saw once again the head, or rather a distortion of the head, a weird caricature of the head, twisted out of all reality, but with a screaming horror of its own. Starting up in his blanket, he'd awake in a sweat of fright. Then, when he had fought down the fear and settled back, he'd recall the head once more, not the dream-distortion of it, but as he remembered it, lying by the fire, so close to the fire that little jumping sparks flying from the burning wood set the hair and beard ablaze, and the hair would fry and sizzle, shriveling up, leaving little blobs of expanded, burned material at the end of every strand. The eyes were open and staring, and they had the look of marbles rather than of eyes. The mouth and face were twisted as if someone had taken the head in two strong and hairy hands and bent it to one side. The bared teeth gleamed in the campfire light, and a drool of spittle had run out of one corner of the twisted mouth and lay dried and flaking in the beard.

Finally, toward morning, he fell into a sleep so exhausted that even the dream of the head could not return to taunt him. Breakfast was ready when Oliver finally woke him. He ate, trying very hard, but not succeeding too well, to keep from looking at the

100

cross that stood, canted at an angle, at the foot of the boulder. There was little talk by anyone, and they saddled hurriedly and moved off.

The path they had been following remained a path; it never broadened out to become a road. The terrain grew rougher and wilder, a somehow haunted landscape, deep defiles and gorges, down which the trail wound to reach narrow, rock-rimmed valleys, with the path then climbing tortuously through heavy pines and towering cliffs to reach a hilltop, then plunging down into another gorge. In these places one held his peace, scarcely daring to speak above a whisper, not knowing whether it was the sound of his own voice that he feared or the making of any kind of sound that might alert a lurking something to his presence. There were no habitations, no clearings, no sign that anyone, at any time, had ever lived within these fastnesses.

By common, unspoken consent, they did not halt for a noonday meal.

It was shortly after noon that Hal forced his horse past the others on the trail to come up with Cornwall, who was riding in the lead.

"Look up there," said Hal, pointing upward toward the narrow strip of sky that showed between the massive trees that crowded close on either side.

Cornwall looked. "I don't see anything. A speck or two is all. Birds flying."

"I've been watching them," said Hal. "They've kept coming in. There have been a lot of them. Buzzards. Something's dead."

"A cow, perhaps."

"There aren't any cows. There are no farms."

"A deer, then. A moose, perhaps."

"More than one deer," said Hal. "More than a single moose. That many buzzards, there is a lot of death."

Cornwall reined up. "What are you getting at?" he asked.

"The head," said Hal. "It had to come from some-

101

where. The path goes down into another gorge. A perfect ambush. Trapped in there, no one would get out."

"But we are fairly sure Beckett didn't come this way," said Cornwall. "He didn't cross at the tower. We've seen no sign. No hoofprints. No old campfires. If there had been an ambush . . ."

"I don't know about all that," said Hal. "But I do know about buzzards, and there are too many of them."

Oliver and Sniveley came up behind Hal. "What is going on?" asked Oliver. "Is there something wrong?"

"Buzzards," said Hal.

"I don't see any buzzards."

"The specks up in the sky."

"Never mind," said Cornwall. "They are there, all right. There is something dead. Sniveley, I want to talk with you. Last night, just before someone tossed the head, there was all this piping . . ."

"The Dark Piper," said Sniveley. "I told you who it was."

"I remember now. You told me. But there was so much else happening. Who is the Dark Piper?"

"No one knows," said Sniveley, shivering just a little. "No one has ever seen him. Heard him, is all. Not too often. Sometimes not for many years. He's the harbinger of ill omen. He plays only when there are dark happenings. . . ."

"Cut out the riddles. What kind of dark happenings?"

"The head was a dark happening," said Hal.

"Not the head," protested Sniveley. "Something worse than that."

"Dark happenings to whom?" asked Cornwall.

"I do not know," said Sniveley. "No one ever knows."

"There was something about the piping," said Oliver, "that sounded familiar to me. I thought it at the time, but I couldn't put a finger on it. It was so

102

terrifying that I suppose I was scared out of my wits. But riding along today, I did remember. Just a part of it. A phrase or two of it. It's part of an ancient song. I found the music of it in an ancient scroll at Wyalusing. There was that phrase or two. Passed down, the scroll said, from at least a hundred centuries ago. Perhaps the oldest song on Earth. I don't know how the man who wrote that ancient scroll could know . . ."

Cornwall grunted and urged his horse ahead. Hal fell in behind him. The trail dipped abruptly down, seeming to sink into the very earth, with great walls of jagged rocks rearing up on either side. Little streams of moisture ran down the face of the rocks, where scraggly ferns and mosses clung with precarious rootholds. Out of the rocky crevasses sprang sprawling cedar trees that seemed to have lost their balance and were about to fall at any moment. Cut off from the sun, the gorge grew increasingly darker as they descended it.

A gust of wind came puffing up between the rocky walls, powered by some atmospheric vagary, and with it came a stench, not an overpowering stench, but a whiff of stench, sweet, greenish and sickening—a smell, a presence that settled in the throat and would not go away, that rankled at the guts and turned one slightly sick.

"I was right," said Hal. "There is death down there."

Ahead of them loomed a sharp turn and as they came around it, the gorge came to an end and out in front of them was a rocky amphitheater, a circle closed in by towering cliffs. Ahead of them was the frightening whir of laboring wings as a flock of great black birds launched themselves off the things on which they had been feeding. A few of the ugly birds, too sluggish with their feasting to take off, hopped angrily about in an awkward fashion.

The stench rose up and struck them like a blow across the face.

"Good God!" said Cornwall, gagging at the sight of what lay on the pebbled shore of the little stream that wandered down across the amphitheater.

Out beyond the sodden mass of ragged flesh and protruding bone that bore slight resemblance to a man lay other shapeless lumps—some of them horses, bloated, with their legs extending stiffly; others of the lumps were human or had once been human. There were skulls grinning in the grass; rib cages starkly revealed, with the soft belly ripped away for easy eating; grotesque buttocks thrusting up. Scraps of clothing blew about, fluttering where they had been caught in the thorny branches of low-growing shrubs. A spear, its point buried in the ground, stood stark, a drunken exclamation point. Weak sunlight glittered on fallen shields and swords.

In among the scattered human dead and the bloated horses, other dead things lay—black-furred, grinning with great fangs frozen forever in the grin, short bushy tails, great, heavy shoulders, slender waists, huge hands (hands, not paws) armed with curving claws.

"Over there," said Gib. "There is the way that Beckett came."

At the far end of the amphitheater, a road (not a path such as they had been following, but a rutted road) came snaking out of the wall of rock surrounding the cuplike bowl in which they found themselves. The road continued across the far end of the bowl to plunge into another gorge that rose into the hills.

Cornwall rose in his stirrups and looked back. The others in the band set their horses stiffly, their faces blank with horror.

"There's nothing we can do," said Gib. "We had better ride on through."

"A Christian word," said Cornwall. "Something to speed them on their way, to give them peace and . . ."

"There are no words," Gib said, harshly, "that can do that for them now. There is no peace. Not here, there isn't any peace."

104

Cornwall nodded, kicked his horse into a trot, heading for the road, with the others following. On every side, wings beat as the carrion birds, interrupted at their meat, fought to become airborne. A fox ran frantically across the trail, its tail dragging. Little animals went darting.

When they pulled up on the road, they had left the carnage behind them. There were no bodies by the road. A flock of small gray birds hopped from branch to branch in a tiny thicket, chirping as they hopped. Out on the battlefield the larger, blacker birds were settling down again.

●●●●●●●●●●●●●●●●●●●●●●●●●●●●●●●●●●●

20

THE man was waiting for them when they reached
the top of the ridge that rose above the cuplike amphitheater, where they had found the aftermath of
battle. It was quite apparent that he had been waiting
for them. He was sitting comfortably at the foot of
a great oak tree, leaning back against the trunk, and
watching them with interest as they came clopping
up the wagon road. Just beyond the tree stood a
curious contraption. It was colored red and white,
and it stood on two wheels, as if balancing itself
without any particular difficulty. The wheels were
very strange, for the rims of them were made of
neither wood nor iron, but of some black substance,
and they were not flat, as any proper rim should be,
but somehow rounded. There were far too many
spokes in the wheels and the spokes were not made
of wood, but of many rounded, tiny strips of what
seemed to be gleaming metal, and anyone in his right
mind would have known that spokes so slender and
so fragile would have no strength at all.

As they neared him, the man stood up and dusted
off his seat, brushing away the leaves and dirt his
breeches had picked up from sitting on the ground.
The breeches were white and tight-fitting, and he
wore a shirt of some red material and over that a
vest that was also white. His boots were neatly made.

"So you made it," he said. "I wasn't sure you
would."

Cornwall made a motion backward with his head.
"You mean down there?"

"Exactly," said the man. "The country's all stirred

up. It was just two days ago. You must enjoy running your head into a noose."

"We knew nothing of it," said Cornwall. "We came up from the tower. The men down there took a different route."

"Well," said the man, "you got through safely, and this is the thing that counts. I had been pulling for you."

"You knew that we were coming?"

"I had word of you yesterday. A motley band, they told me. And I see that they were right."

"They?"

"Oh, assorted little friends I have. Skippers-through-the-thickets. Runners-in-the-grass. All eyes and ears. There is not much they miss. I know about the horn and about the head that came rolling to the campfire, and I have been waiting most impatiently to greet you."

"You know, then, who we are?"

"Only your names. And I beg your pardon. I am Alexander Jones. I have a place prepared for you."

Mary said, "Master Jones, I do not like the sound of that. We are entirely capable—"

"I am sorry, Mistress Mary, if I have offended you. All I meant to offer was hospitality. Shelter from the coming night, a good fire, hot food, a place to sleep."

"All of which," said Oliver, "so far as I am concerned, would be most welcome. Perhaps a measure of wine or a mug of beer as well. The stench back there is still clogging up my throat. Something is needed to wash it all away."

"Beer, of course," said Jones. "A full barrel of it is laid in against your coming. Do you agree, Sir Mark?"

"Yes," said Cornwall, "I do agree. I see no harm in it and perhaps some good. But do not call me sir; I am no more than a scholar."

"Then," said Jones, "pray, hold your horses well. For this mount of mine is a noisy beast."

He strode toward the contraption standing on two

107

wheels. He threw one leg over it and settled on what became apparent was the contraption's seat. He reached out and grasped the two handlelike projections extending above and backward of the forward wheel.

"Hold a moment, there," said Gib. "There is one thing you have not told us. With all the dead men lying down there, how come you are still alive? You are human, are you not?"

"I like to think I am," said Jones, "and the answer to your question is an extremely simple one. Folk hereabouts believe I am a wizard, which, of course, I'm not."

He balanced on one foot and kicked with the other. The two-wheeled contraption came alive with an angry roar, breathing out a cloud of smoke. The horses reared in fright. Oliver, who was riding behind Sniveley, fell off and scrambled rapidly on all fours to get out of the way of the lashing hooves.

The two-wheeled monster quit its roaring, settled into a rumbling, throaty purr.

"I am sorry," Jones shouted to Oliver. "I warned you to watch yourselves."

"It's a dragon," said Sniveley. "A two-wheeled dragon, although I did not know that dragons came with wheels. What else but a dragon would make that sort of roar and breathe out fire and brimstone?" He reached down a hand to Oliver and helped him scramble up.

Jones urged the dragon into motion, heading down the road.

"I guess," said Hal, "all we can do is follow him. Hot food, he said. I could do with some."

"I do not like it," Sniveley complained. "I like it not one bit. I am not one to mess around with dragons, even if they be domesticated ones, broken to the saddle."

The dragon speeded up, and they had to force their horses into a rapid trot to keep up with it. The road was not as deeply rutted as it had been coming up the gorge. Now it followed a plateau, running straight between stands of pine and birch, with only an occasional oak tree rearing up above the lesser forest. Then the road dipped down, not sharply, but rather gradually, into a pleasant valley, and there on the valley floor they saw the collection of three tents, all of them gaily striped and with pennons flying from their tops.

The dragon pulled up before the largest tent, and Jones dismounted. To one side was a table made of rough boards and beyond it cooking fires, with spits set above the fires and a huge beer barrel mounted on a pair of sawhorses, with a spigot already driven in the bung. Tending the fires and spits was a ragamuffin crew of brownies, trolls, and goblins, who were going about their work with a tremendous clanging of pans. Some of them dropped their work and ran to take charge of the horses.

"Come," said Jones, "let us sit and talk. I know there must be a deal to talk about."

A half-dozen of the trolls were busy at the beer barrel, filling great mugs from the spigot and bearing them to the table.

"Now, this is fine," said Jones. "We can have a drink or two before the food is ready. For, of course, it is never ready when it is supposed to be. These little friends of mine are willing workers, but most disorganized. Take whatever seat you wish and let's begin our talk."

Oliver scurried to the table and grabbed a mug of beer, dipping his muzzle into it and drinking heartily. Desisting, he wiped the foam from his whiskers. "This is proper brew," he said. "Not like the swill they serve in Wyalusing inns."

"Sniveley calls your mount a dragon," Hal said to Jones, "and while it breathes fire and smoke and bellows most convincingly, I know it is no dragon. I have never seen a dragon, but I've heard stories of them, and the descriptions in the stories are nothing like this creature that you ride. It has no head or wings and a dragon has both head and wings and, I believe, a tail as well."

"You are quite right," said Jones, delighted. "It is not a dragon, although many others than Sniveley have guessed it to be one. It is not a creature at all, but a machine, and it is called a trail bike."

"A trail bike," said Gib. "I've never heard of one."

"Of course you've not heard of one," said Jones. "This is the only one in this entire world."

"You say it is a machine," said Cornwall, "and we have machines, of course, but nothing like this. There are machines of war, the siege machines that are used to hurl great stones or flights of arrows or flaming material against a beleaguered city."

"Or a mill wheel," said Gib. "A mill wheel would be a machine."

"I suppose it is," said Hal.

"But a mill wheel runs by the force of flowing water," Mary said, "and the engines of war by the winding up of ropes. Can you tell us how this machine of yours runs?"

"Not too well," said Jones. "I could not explain it all to you. I could tell you some things, but they would make no sense."

"You don't know, then, how it runs," said Cornwall.

"No, I really don't."

"It must be magic, then."

"I can assure you that it is not magic. There is no magic in my world. You have to come to this world to find magic."

"But that is ridiculous," said Mary. "There has to be magic. Magic is a part of life."

"In my world," said Jones, "magic has been swept away. Men talk of magic, certainly, but they talk of something that is gone. At one time there may have been magic, but it has disappeared."

"And you have to come to this world to find the magic you have lost?"

"That is exactly it," said Jones. "I've come to study it."

"It is strange," said Cornwall. "It is passing strange, all these things you say. You must have some magic in you, even if you do deny it. For here you have all these little people working willingly for you, or at least they appear to be quite willing. Tending the fires and food, carrying the beer, taking care of the horses. They have been following us, but they have not come out to help us. They only hide and watch."

"Give them time," said Jones. "That was the way it was with me when I first arrived. They simply hid and watched, and I went about my business, paying no attention to them. After a time they began coming out to sit and talk with me. From certain things I did and certain things I had, they thought I was a wizard and, therefore, someone who was worthy of them."

"You have advantage of us there," said Cornwall. "There is no wizardry about us."

"I hear otherwise," said Jones. "These little ones of mine tell me otherwise. They heard it from your little ones and came scampering to tell me all about it. There is one of you who can pull the horn of a unicorn from the oak, and there is another who carries a very magic sword, and still another who carries a very special kind of stone."

"How did they know about the stone?" demanded Gib. "The stone is securely wrapped and carried secretly. We've not even talked about it."

"Oh, they know, all right," said Jones. "Don't ask me how they know, but it seems they do. Check me if I'm wrong—the stone is one made by the Old Ones very long ago and now will be returned to them."

Cornwall leaned forward eagerly. "What do you know about the Old Ones? Can you tell me where they might be found?"

"Only what I have been told. You go to the Witch

House and then across the Blasted Plain. You skirt the castle of the Chaos Beast and then you come to the Misty Mountains and there, if you are lucky, you may find the Old Ones. I'm told there are not many of them left, for they are a dying people, and they hide most fearfully, although if you come upon them suddenly, you well may be hard put to defend yourself."

"The Witch House," said Mary anxiously. "You speak about the Witch House. Is it an old, old house? One that appears as if it may be falling down upon itself? Standing on a little knoll above a stream, with an old stone bridge across the stream? An old two-story house, with many, many chimneys and a gallery running all the way across the front?"

"You describe it exactly. Almost as if you might have seen it."

"I have," said Mary. "It is the house where I lived when I was a little girl. There was a troll named Bromeley who lived underneath the bridge. And there was a brownie, Fiddlefingers . . ."

"Bromeley was the one who popped out to see you last night," said Hal.

"Yes, he came to see me. While the others all stayed safely hidden, he came out to greet me. He remembered. If it hadn't been for someone throwing in that horrid head . . ."

"I worried what might have happened," said Jones, "when you reached the battlefield. I was a coward and waited. I should have come out to meet you, but I was afraid that my coming might trigger some reaction, that I might do something that I shouldn't. I started to come down to meet you, then I came back. . . ."

"But there was nothing to harm us," Cornwall said. "It was horrible, of course, but there was no danger. The only ones nearby was this gang of trolls and goblins and other little people. . . ."

"My friend," said Jones, "I am glad you thought so. The belief there were only trolls and goblins may

112

have helped you through it. With no wish to frighten you, I must tell you there were others there."

"What others?" asked Sniveley sharply.

"Hellhounds," said Jones. "A slavering pack of Hellhounds. As well as the little people, they've been with you ever since you crossed the ford."

"Hellhounds?" asked Cornwall. "There were other than human bodies on the battlefield. The ones with tails and fangs."

"You are right," said Jones.

"I knew of them," said Sniveley quietly. "They are a part of our tradition. But I have never seen one, never knew anyone who had." He explained to Cornwall. "They are the enforcers. The executioners. The professional killers."

"But so far," said Cornwall, "they have let us pass."

"They will let you pass," said Jones, "if you continue as you have. They've not made up their minds about you. Make one wrong move and they'll be down on you."

"And what about yourself?" asked Cornwall. "Are they watching you as well?"

"Perhaps," said Jones. "They did at first, of course, and they may still be watching. But, you see, I've built up a marginal reputation as a wizard and, aside from that, they may consider me insane."

"And that would be protection?"

"I have some hope it might be. I've done nothing to disabuse the thought, if indeed they have it."

"There's someone coming up the road," said Sniveley.

They all turned to look.

"It's the Gossiper," said Jones. "He's a goddamn pest. He can scent food from seven miles away and a drink of beer from twice that distance."

The Gossiper came stumping up the road. He was a tall, lean figure, wearing a dirty robe that trailed in the dust behind him. On his shoulder perched a raven, and from a strap slung across one shoulder

113

dangled an oblong package that was encased in sheepskin. He carried a long staff in his left hand and thumped it energetically on the road with every step he took. He was followed by a little white dog with a limp. The dog was all white except for black spots encircling each eye, which made it appear he was wearing spectacles.

The Gossiper came up close beside the table and stopped in front of Cornwall, who swung around to face him. Now that the man was close enough, it could be seen that his robe was very worn and ragged, with gaping rents, through which one could see his hide. Some of the more pronounced rents had been patched, somewhat inexpertly, with cloth of many different colors, but sun and dirt had so reduced the colors that they blended in with the mud color of the robe. The raven was molting, and a couple of loosened feathers hung ragged from its tail; overall the bird looked moth-eaten. The little dog sat down and, with his good hindleg, fell to scratching fleas.

If the Gossiper was human, he was barely human. His ears rose to a point, and his eyes were strangely slanted. His nose was squashed across his face, and his teeth had the look of fangs. His grizzled hair, uncombed, was a writhing rat's nest. The hand that grasped the staff had long, uneven, dirty fingernails.

He said to Cornwall, "You be the scholar, Mark Cornwall? Lately of Wyalusing?"

"That is who I am," said Cornwall.

"You are the leader of this band of pilgrims?"

"Not the leader. We are all together."

"However that may be," said the Gossiper, "I have words of wisdom for you. Perhaps a friendly warning. Go no farther than the Witch House. That is as far as pilgrims are allowed to go."

"Beckett wasn't allowed to go even that far."

"Beckett was no pilgrim."

"And you are sure we are?"

"It's not what I think, Sir Scholar. It is what they think. I only speak their words."

"And who the hell are they?"

"Why, fair sir, must you pretend to so much innocence? If you do not know, there are others of your party who are not so ignorant."

"You are thinking about Oliver and me," said Sniveley. "I would advise you to be careful of your words. I, as a gnome, and Oliver, as a goblin, here stand on home ground. We can go anywhere we please."

"I am not so sure," said the Gossiper, "you can claim that right. You forsook the Brotherhood."

"You still have not answered me," said Cornwall. "Tell me of the 'they' you talk about."

"You have heard of the Hellhounds?"

"I know of them," said Cornwall.

"The Chaos Beast, perhaps. And He Who Broods Upon the Mountain."

"I have heard of them. In old travelers' tales. No more than bare mention of them."

"Then you should pray," said the Gossiper, "that your acquaintanceship becomes no closer."

Cornwall swiveled around to look at Jones. Jones nodded tightly. "He told me the same thing. But, as you know, I am a coward. I did not go beyond the Witch House."

He said to the Gossiper, "How about a beer?"

"I do believe I will," said the Gossiper. "And a slice of meat when it should be done. I have traveled far, and I hunger and I thirst most excessively."

21

A FULL moon had risen above the jagged horizon of the trees, paling the stars, filling the glade with light. The fires burned low, for the meal was over, and out on the grass between the camp and road the little people danced in wild abandon to a violin's shrilling music.

For once the food was eaten, the Gossiper had unshipped the sheepskin bundle he carried and, unwrapping the sheepskin, had taken out a fiddle and a bow.

Now he stood, a ragged figure, with the fiddle tucked beneath his chin, the fingers of his left hand flashing on the frets, while his right arm sent the bow skittering on the strings. The moth-eaten raven still maintained a precarious perch on the Gossiper's right shoulder, hopping and skipping to keep its balance, sometimes climbing out on the upper arm, where it clung desperately, uttering dolorous squawks of protest at the insecurity of its perch. Underneath the table the little lame dog slept, replete with the meat it had been thrown by the festive feasters, its tiny paws quivering and twitching as it chased dream rabbits.

"There are such a lot of them," said Mary, meaning the little dancing people. "When we first arrived, there did not seem so many."

Jones chuckled at her. "There are more," he said. "There are all of mine and most of yours."

"You mean they have come out of hiding?"

"It was the food that did it," he said. "The food and beer. You didn't expect them, did you, to stay lurking in the bushes, watching all the others gorge themselves?"

"Then Bromeley must be out there with them. The sneaky little thing! Why doesn't he come and talk with me?"

"He's having too much fun," said Cornwall.

Coon came lumbering out of the swirl of dancers and rubbed against Hal's legs. Hal picked him up and put him on his lap. Coon settled down, wrapping his tail around his nose.

"He ate too much," said Gib.

"He always does," said Hal.

The violin wailed and whined, sang, reaching for the stars. The Gossiper's arm was busy with the bow, and the hopping raven squalled in protest.

"I don't quite understand you," Cornwall said quietly to Jones. "You said you never went beyond the Witch House. I wonder why you didn't. What are you here for, anyhow?"

Jones grinned. "It is strange that you should ask, for we have much in common. You see, Sir Scholar, I am a student, just the same as you."

"But if you are a student, then why don't you study?"

"But I do," said Jones. "And there's enough to study here. Far more than enough. When you study something, you cover one area thoroughly before you move on to the next. When the time comes, I'll move beyond the Witch House."

"Study, you say?"

"Yes. Notes, recordings, pictures. I have piles of notes, miles of tape . . ."

"Tape? Pictures? You mean paintings, drawings?"

"No," said Jones. "I use a camera."

"You talk in riddles," Cornwall said. "Words I've never heard before."

"Perhaps I do," said Jones. "Would you like to come and see? We need not disturb the others. They can stay here watching."

He rose and led the way to the tent, Cornwall

following. At the entrance to the tent Jones put out a hand to halt him. "You are a man of open mind?" he asked. "As a scholar, you should be."

"I've studied for six years at Wyalusing," said Cornwall. "I try to keep an open mind. How otherwise would one learn anything?"

"Good," said Jones. "What date would you say this is?"

"It's October," said Cornwall. "I've lost track of the day. It's the year of Our Lord 1975."

"Fine," said Jones. "I just wanted to make sure. For your information, it is the seventeenth."

"What has the date got to do with it?" asked Cornwall.

"Not too much, perhaps. It may make understanding easier a little later. And it just happens you're the first one I could ask. Here in the Wasteland, no one keeps a calendar."

He lifted the flap of the tent and motioned Cornwall in. Inside, the tent seemed larger than it had from the outside dimensions of it. It was orderly, but crowded with many furnishings and much paraphernalia. A military cot stood in one corner. Next to it stood a desk and chair, with a stubby candlestick holding a rather massive candle standing in the center of the desk. The flame of the lighted candle flared in the air currents. Piled on one corner of the desk was a stack of black leather books. Open boxes stood beside the books. Strange objects sat upon the desk, leaving little room for writing. There was, Cornwall saw in a rapid glance, no quill or inkhorn, no sanding box, and that seemed passing strange.

In the opposite corner stood a large metallic cabinet and next to it, against the eastern wall, an area hung with heavy black drapes.

"My developing room," said Jones. "Where I process my film."

Cornwall said stiffly, "I do not understand."

"Take a look," said Jones. He strode to the desk and lifted a handful of thin squares from one of the open boxes, spread them on the desk top. "There," he said. "Those are the photos I was telling you about. Not paintings—photographs. Go ahead. Pick them up and look."

Cornwall bent above the desk, not touching the so-called photos. Colored paintings stared back at him—paintings of brownies, goblins, trolls, fairies dancing on a magic green, a grinning, vicious horror that had to be a Hellhound, a two-story house standing on a knoll, with a stone bridge in the foreground. Tentatively Cornwall reached out and picked up the painting of the house, held it close for a better look.

"The Witch House," said Jones.

"But these are paintings," Cornwall exploded in impatience. "Miniatures. At the court many artisans turn out paintings of this sort for hour books and other purposes. Although they put borders around the paintings, filled with flowers and birds and insects and many different conceits, which to my mind makes them more interesting. They work long hours at it and most meticulously, sparing no pains to make a perfect picture."

"Look again," said Jones. "Do you see any brush strokes?"

"It proves nothing," Cornwall said stubbornly. "In the miniatures there are no brush strokes. The artisans work so carefully and so well that you can see no brush strokes. And yet, truth to tell, there is a difference here."

"You're damn right there is a difference. I use this machine," he said, patting with his hand a strange black object that lay on the table, "and others like it to achieve these photos. I point the machine and click a button that opens a shutter so that specially treated film can see what the camera's pointed at, and I have pictures exactly as the camera sees it. Better, more truthfully than the eye can see it."

"Magic," Cornwall said.

"Here we go again," said Jones. "I tell you it's no more magic than the trail bike is. It's science. It's technology. It's a way of doing things."

"Science is philosophy," said Cornwall. "No more

119

than philosophy. Putting the universe into order. Trying to make some sense out of it. You cannot do these things you are doing with philosophy. It must be done with magic."

"Where is that open mind you said you had?" asked Jones.

Cornwall dropped the photo, drew himself up, stiffening in outrage. "You brought me here to mock me," he said, half wrathfully, half sorrowfully. "You would humble me with your greater magic, while trying to make it seem it is not magic. Why do you try to make me small and stupid?"

"Not that," said Jones. "Assuredly not that. I seek your understanding. When I first came here, I tried to explain to the little people. Even to the Gossiper, disreputable and benighted as he may be. I tried to tell them that there is no magic in all of this, that I am not a wizard, but they insisted that I was, they refused to understand. And after their refusal, I found there was some benefit to being thought a wizard, so I tried no longer. But for some reason I do not quite understand I do need to have someone who at least will listen. I thought that, as a scholar, you might be that person. I suppose, basically, that I need to make at least an honest effort to explain myself. I have, underneath it all, a certain contempt for myself parading as something I am not."

"What are you, then?" asked Cornwall. "If you are no wizard, then what are you?"

"I am a man," said Jones, "whit different from you. I happen to live in another world than yours."

"You prate of this world and of your world," said Cornwall, "and there are no more worlds than one. This is the only world we have, you and I. Unless you speak of the Kingdom of Heaven, which is another world, and I find it difficult to believe that you came from there."

"Oh, hell," said Jones, "what is the use of this? I should have known. You are as stubborn and bone-headed as the rest of them."

"Then explain yourself," said Cornwall. "You

keep telling me what you're not. Now tell me what you are."

"Then, listen. Once there was, as you say, only one world. I do not know how long ago that was. Ten thousand years ago, a hundred thousand years ago—there is no way of knowing. Then one day something happened. I don't know what it was; we may never know exactly what it was or how it came about. But on that day one man did a certain thing— it would have to have been one man, for this thing he did was so unique that there was no chance of more than one man doing it. But, anyhow, he did it, or he spoke it, or he thought it, whatever it might be, and from that day forward there were two worlds, not one—or at least the possibility of two worlds, not one. The distinction, to start with, would have been shadowy, the two worlds perhaps not too far apart, shading into one another so that you might have thought they were still one world, but becoming solider and drawing further apart until there could be no doubt that there were two worlds. To start with, they would not have been greatly different, but as time went on, the differences hardened and the worlds diverged. They had to diverge because they were irreconcilable. They, or the people in them, were following different paths. One world to begin with, then splitting into two worlds. Don't ask me how it happened or what physical or metaphysical laws were responsible for the splitting, for I don't know, nor is there anyone who knows. In my world there are no more than a handful of people who know even that it happened. All the rest of them, all the other millions of them, do not admit it happened, will not admit it happened, may never have heard the rumor that it happened."

"Magic," said Cornwall firmly. "That is how it happened."

"Goddamn it. There you go again. Come up against something you can't understand and out pops that word again. You are an educated man. You've spent years at your studies . . ."

121

"Six," said Cornwall. "Six back-breaking, poverty-ridden years."

"Then you should know that magic—"

"I know more of magic, sir, than you do. I have studied magic. At Wyalusing you have to study magic. The subject is required."

"But the Church . . ."

"The Church has no quarrel with magic. Only magic wrongly used."

Jones sat down limply on the bed. "I guess there's no way," he said, "for you and me to talk with one another. I tell you about technology and you say it's magic. The trail bike is a dragon; the camera is an evil eye. Jones, why don't you just give up?"

"I don't know," said Cornwall, "what you're talking about."

"No," said Jones, "I don't suppose you do."

"You say that the world divided," said Cornwall. "That there was one world and it split apart and then there were two worlds."

Jones nodded. "That's the way of it. It has to be that way. Here is your world. It has no technology, no machines. Oh, I know you say machines—your siege engines and your water mills, and I suppose they are machines, but not what my world thinks of as machines. But in the last five hundred years, for more than five hundred years, for almost a thousand, you've not advanced technologically. You don't even know the word. There have been certain common happenings, of course. The rise of Christianity, for example. How this could come about, I have no idea. But the crux of the whole thing is that there has been no Renaissance, no Reformation, no Industrial Revolution . . ."

"You use terms I do not understand."

"I'm sorry," said Jones. "I got carried away. I beg your pardon. None of the events I mentioned have happened here, none of the great turning points of history. And something else as well. Here you have retained your magic and the people of the old folklore—the actual living creatures that in our time

122

are no more than folklore. In my world we have lost the magic, and there are none of these creatures, and it seems to me that we are the poorer for it."

Cornwall sat down on the bed beside him.

"You seek some insight into the splitting of the world," he said. "Not for a moment that I accept this mad tale you tell me, although I must admit I am puzzled by the strange machines you use. . . ."

"Let's not argue about them further," said Jones. "Let us simply agree we are two honest men who differ in certain philosophic matters. And, yes, I would welcome an insight into the divergence of our worlds, although I have not come here to seek it. I doubt it still exists. I think the evidence is gone."

"It might exist," said Cornwall. "There is just a chance it could. Mad as it may sound . . ."

"What are you talking about?" asked Jones.

"You say we are two honest men who differ. We are something else as well. The both of us are scholars . . ."

"That is right. What are you getting at?"

"In this land of mine," said Cornwall, "scholars are members of an unspoken guild, a spectral brotherhood . . ."

Jones shook his head. "With some notable exceptions, I suppose the same is true of my world. Scholars, as a rule, are honorable."

"Then, perhaps," said Cornwall, "I can tell you something that is not really mine to tell. . . ."

"We are from different cultures," said Jones. "Our viewpoints may differ. I would be uncomfortable if you were to tell me secrets that should be kept from me. I have no wish to cause you embarrassment, either now or later."

"Yet," said Cornwall, "we both are scholars. We share a common ethic."

"All right," said Jones, "what is this thing you wish to tell me?"

"There is a university," said Cornwall, "somewhere in this Wasteland. I had heard of it and thought of it as legend, but now I find it is not a legend, but

123

that it actually exists. There are old writings there. . . ."

Outside the music stopped, and the sudden silence was almost like a sound. Jones froze, and Cornwall took a step toward the tent flap, then halted, listening. A new sound came, far off, but there was no mistaking what it was—a screaming, an abandoned, hopeless screaming.

"Oh, my God," Jones whispered, "it's not over yet. They have not let him go."

Cornwall moved quickly through the tent flap, Jones close upon his heels. The band of dancers had drawn back from the road and stood in a huddled mass about the table. They were looking up the road. None of them spoke; they seemed to hold their breaths. The cooking fires still streamed columns of wispy smoke into the moonlit sky.

Coming down the road was a naked man. He stumbled as he walked and it was he who screamed, a senseless, endless screaming that rose and fell, but never broke, his head thrown back as he screamed against the sky. Pacing behind him and to either side of him was a pack of Hellhounds, black and evil in the night, some going on four feet, others shambling erect, with their bodies thrust forward, stooping, not as a man would walk, and their long arms swinging loosely. Their short, bushy tails twitched back and forth in excitement and anticipation, and their terrible fangs gleamed white against the blackness of their snouts.

Oliver broke from the crowd around the table and scurried up to Cornwall. "It's Beckett," he screamed. "It's Beckett that they have."

The man and the pack of Hellhounds came steadily down the road, the screaming never ending. And now they were closer, there was another sound, heard as a sort of bass accompaniment to the terrible screaming—the snuffling of the Hellhounds.

Cornwall strode forward to take his place beside Gib and Hal, who were standing at the edge of the huddled crowd. Cornwall tried to speak, but found

124

he couldn't. A cold trembling had seized him, and he had to clamp his mouth tight shut to keep his teeth from chattering. Oliver was pulling at him. "That's Beckett," he was saying. "That's Beckett. I'd know him anywhere. I have often seen him."

As Beckett came opposite the camp he suddenly ceased his screaming and, stumbling as he turned, shuffled around to face the crowd. He threw out his arms in an attitude of pleading.

"Kill me, please," he babbled. "For the love of Mary, kill me. If there be a man among you, kill me, for the love of God."

Hal, bringing up his bow, reached quickly for an arrow. Sniveley flung himself at the bow and dragged it down. "Are you mad?" he shouted. "Even make a motion and they'll be on us, too. Before you have an arrow nocked, they'll be at your throat."

Cornwall strode forward, his hand reaching for the sword. Jones moved quickly to block him.

"Out of my way," growled Cornwall.

Jones said nothing. His arm, starting back and low, came up. The fist caught Cornwall on the chin, and at the impact he fell like a cut-down tree, crashing to the ground.

Out in the road the Hellhounds closed in on Beckett with a rush, not knocking him down, allowing him to stand, but leaping at him with slashing teeth, then falling back. Half his face was gone and blood streamed down across his cheek. His teeth showed through where the cheek had been sheared away. His tongue moved in agony, and the scream bubbled in his throat. Teeth flashed again and his genitals were torn away. Almost as if by reflex action, he bent forward to clutch at the area where they had been. Snapping fangs tore off half a buttock and he straightened, his arms going up in a flailing motion, and all the time the scream gurgled in his throat. Then he was down, writhing and twisting in the dust, gurgling and whimpering. The Hellhounds drew back and sat in a circle, regarding him with benevolent interest. Slowly the moaning ceased, slowly he drew his knees beneath him and wobbled to his feet. He seemed whole again. His face was whole, the buttock was unmarred, the genitals in place. The Hellhounds rose leisurely. One of them butted him, almost affectionately, with its nose, and Beckett went on down the road, resuming his senseless screaming.

Cornwall rose to a sitting position, shaking his head, his hand groping for the sword.

He gazed up at Jones, saying to him out of the fog that filled his brain, "You hit me. You hit me with your fist. A peasant way of fighting."

"Keep your hand off that toad-stabber of yours," said Jones, "or I'll cream you once again. All I did, my friend, was save your precious life."

22

WHEN Cornwall knocked, the witch opened the door.

"*Ai,*" she said to Mary, "so you came back again. I always knew you would. Since the day I took you down that road, I knew you'd come back to us. I took you down the road into the Borderland, and I patted you on your little fanny and told you to go on. And you went on, without ever looking back, but you didn't fool me none. I knew you would be back once you'd growed a little, for there was something fey about you, and you would not fit into the world of humans. You could never fool Old Granny. . . ."

"I was only three years old," said Mary, "maybe less than that. And you are not my granny. You never were my granny. I never till right now laid my eyes upon you."

"You were too young to know," said the witch, "or knowing, to remember. I would have kept you here, but the times were parlous and unsettled, and it seemed best to take you from enchanted ground. Although it wrenched my heart to do so, for I loved you, child."

"This is all untrue," Mary said to Cornwall. "I have no memory of her. She was not my granny. She was not . . ."

"But," said the witch, "I did take you down the road into the Borderland. I took your trusting little hand in mine and as I hobbled down the road, being much crippled with arthritis at the time, you skipped along beside me and you chattered all the way."

127

"I could not have chattered," Mary said. "I never was a chatterer."

The house was as Mary had described it, an old and rambling house set upon its knoll, and below the knoll, a brook that rambled laughing down the valley, with a stone bridge that spanned its gleaming water. A clump of birch grew at one corner of the house, and down the hill was a lilac hedge, an interrupted hedge that started and ended with no apparent purpose, a hedge that hedged in nothing. Beyond the lilacs a clump of boulders lay and in the land across the creek was a marshy pool.

The rest of the party waited by the stone bridge, looking up the hill toward the porch, where Mary and Cornwall stood before the open door.

"You always were a perverse child," said the witch. "Always in the way of playing nasty tricks, although that was just a childish way that many children have, and no flaw in character. You pestered the poor ogre almost unendurably, popping sticks and stones and clods down into his burrow so that the poor thing got scarcely any sleep. You may be surprised to know that he remembers you rather more kindly than you have the right to deserve. When he heard you were on your way, he expressed the hope of seeing you. Although, being an ogre with great dignity, he cannot bring himself to come calling on you; if you want to see him, you must wait upon him."

"I remember the ogre," said Mary, "and how we threw stuff down into his den. I don't think I ever saw him, although I may have. I've often thought about him and at times have wondered if there really were an ogre. People said there was, but I never saw him, so I couldn't know."

"Indeed, there is an ogre," said the witch, "and most agreeable. But I forget myself. I was so overcome with seeing you again, my dear, that I fear I have been impolite. I have left you standing here when I should have invited you in to tea. And I have not addressed one word of welcome to this handsome gallant who serves as your escort. Although," she said, addressing Cornwall, "I do not know who you are, there have been marvelous tales about you and the members of your company. And you as well," she said to Mary. "I see you no longer have the horn of the unicorn. Don't tell me you lost it."

"No, I have not lost it," said Mary. "But it was an awkward thing to carry. It seemed so much like bragging to carry it all the time. I left it with the others who are waiting at the bridge."

"Ah, well," said the witch, "I'll see it later on. Once I'd heard of it, I had counted so much on the sight of it. You'll show it to me, won't you?"

"Of course I will," said Mary.

The old crone tittered. "I have never seen the horn of a unicorn," she said, "and strange as it may seem, I have never seen a unicorn. The beasts are very rare, even in this land. But let us now go in and sit us down to tea. Just the three of us, I think. It'll be so much cozier with just the three of us. I'll send a basket of cakes down to those waiting at the bridge. The kind of cakes, my dear, that you always liked— the ones with seeds in them."

She opened the door wider and made a motion with her hand, signaling them to come in. The entry hall was dark, and there was a dankness in it.

Mary halted. "It doesn't feel the same," she said. "Not the way I remember it. This house once was bright and full of light and laughter."

"It's your imagination," the witch said sharply. "You always were the one with imagination. You were the one who dreamed up the games you played with that silly troll who lived underneath the bridge and that daffy Fiddlefingers." She cackled with re-membering. "You could talk them into anything. They hated mud-pie making, but they made mud pies for you. And they were scared striped of the ogre, but when you threw stones down into his burrow, they went along and threw their share of stones. You say that I'm a witch, with my humped back and my arthritic hobble and my long and crooked nose, but

129

you are a witch as well, my darling, and a better one than I am."

"Hold there," said Cornwall, his hand going to the sword hilt. "Milady's not a witch."

The old crone reached out a bony hand and laid it gently on his arm. "It's a compliment I pay her, noble sir. There is nothing better said of any woman than that she's a witch."

Grumbling, Cornwall let his arm drop. "Watch your tongue," he said.

She smiled at them with snaggled teeth and led the way down the dark, damp, and musty hall into a small room carpeted with an old and faded rug. Against one wall stood a tiny fireplace blackened by the smoke of many fires. Sunlight poured through wide windows to illuminate the shabbiness of the place. A row of beaten-up houseplants stood on a narrow shelf below the windowsill. In the center of the room stood a magnificently carved table covered by a scarf, and on the scarf was a silver tea service.

She motioned them to chairs, then sat down behind the steaming teapot.

Reaching for a cup, she said, "Now we may talk of many things, of the olden days and how times have changed and what you might be doing here."

"What I want to talk about," said Mary, "are my parents. I know nothing of them. I want to know who they were and why they were here and what happened to them."

"They were good people," said the witch, "but very, very strange. Not like other humans. They did not look down their noses at the people of the Wasteland. They had no evil in them, but a great depth of understanding. They would talk with everyone they met. And the questions they could ask—oh, land sake, the questions they could ask. I often wondered why they might be here, for they seemed to have no business. A vacation, they told me, but it is ridiculous to think that sophisticated people such as they should come to a place like this for their vacation. If it was a vacation, it was a very long one; they were here almost a year. Doing nothing all that time but walking around the countryside and being nice to everyone they met. I can remember the day they came walking down the road and across the bridge, the two of them, my dear, with you between them, toddling along, with each of them holding one of your hands, as if you might need their help, although you never needed any help, then or any other time. Imagine the nerve of them and the innocence of them, two humans walking calmly down a Wasteland road, with their baby toddling between them, walking as if they were out for a stroll of an April afternoon. If there were anyone here in all this land who might have done them any harm, they would have been so shook up by the innocent, trusting arrogance of them that they would have stayed their hand. I can remember them coming up to this house and knocking on the door, asking if they might stay with me and I, of course, good-hearted creature that I am, who finds it hard to say no to anyone . . ."

"You know," said Mary to the witch, "I think that you are lying. I don't believe this is your house. I can't think my parents were ever guests of yours. But I suppose the truth's not in you, and there is no use in trying."

"But, my darling," said the witch, "it all is solemn truth. Why should I lie to you?"

"Let us not fall into argument," said Cornwall. "Truth or not, let's get on with it. What finally happened to them?"

"They went into the Blasted Plain," said the witch. "I don't know why they did this. They never told me anything. They were pleasant enough, of course, but they never told me anything at all. They left this child of theirs with me and went into the Blasted Plain and they've not been heard of since."

"That was when you took Mary, if it was you who took her, into the Borderland?"

"There were ugly rumors. I was afraid to have her stay."

"What kind of rumors?"

"I can't recall them now."

"You see," said Mary, "she is lying."

"Of course she is," said Cornwall, "but we don't know how much. A little or a lot, all of it, or only some of it."

"I take it sadly," said the witch, dabbing at her eyes, "to sit at my own tea table, serving tea to guests who doubt my honest word."

"Did they leave any papers?" Mary asked. "Any letters? Anything at all?"

"Now, that is strange," said the witch, "that you should ask. There was another one who asked, another human. A man who goes by the name of Jones. I told him that I knew of none. Not that I would have looked; I am not a snoop. No matter what else I may be called, I am not a snoop. I told him there might be some on the second floor. That I wouldn't know. Crippled as I am, I cannot climb the stairs. Oh, I know that you think a witch need but use her broomstick to go anywhere she wishes. But you humans do not comprehend. There are certain rules . . ."

"Did Jones look upstairs?"

"Yes, indeed he did. He told me he found nothing, although he has shifty eyes, and one can never know if he told the truth. I remember asking him and . . ."

The front door burst open, and feet came pounding down the hall. Gib skidded to a stop when he burst into the room.

"Mark," he said to Cornwall, "we've got trouble. Beckett has showed up."

Cornwall sprang to his feet. "Beckett! What about the Hellhounds?"

"He escaped from them," said Gib.

"That's impossible," said Cornwall. "How could he escape from them? Where is he now?"

"He's down by the bridge," said Gib. "He came running up to us, naked as a jaybird. Bromeley got a towel for him—"

The door banged, and feet pattered rapidly down

132

the hallway. It was Sniveley, panting with his running.

"It's a trick!" he yelled. "We can't let him stay here. The Hellhounds let him escape. Now they'll say we're sheltering him, and they'll come swarming in here—"

"Pouf," said the witch. "These pitiful little puppy dogs. Let me get my broom. There ain't no Hellhounds getting gay with me. They may act vicious, but give them a whack or two . . ."

"We can't turn him back to them," said Cornwall. "Not after what we saw last night. He has a right to ask protection of us. After all, he's a Christian, although a very shabby one."

Cornwall hastened down the hall, the others trailing after him.

Outside, coming up the hill toward the house, was a motley procession. Beckett, with a towel wrapped about his middle, was in front. He was not proceeding by himself. Hal walked behind him, and Hal's bowstring was looped about his neck. Hal held the bow and, twisting it, drew the cord close about his captive's throat. Behind the two came Oliver and a bunched-up group of trolls, brownies, gnomes, and fairies.

Hal made a thumb over his shoulder. "We got company," he said, speaking to Cornwall, but not taking his eyes off Beckett.

Cornwall looked in the direction of the thumb. On the top of the barren hill across the brook sat a row of Hellhounds, not doing anything, with the look of not being about to do anything—just sitting there and watching, waiting for whatever was about to happen.

Coming down the hillside, heading for the bridge, was a giant, although a very sloppy giant. From where Cornwall stood on the gallery that ran before the house, he seemed to be all of twelve feet tall, but large as his body was, his head was small. It was no larger, Cornwall thought, than the head of an ordinary man, perhaps smaller than that of an

133

ordinary man. And large as the body was, it was not muscular. It was a flabby body, a soft body, with no character to it. The pin-headed giant wore a short kilt and a half shirt that had a strap across one shoulder. He moved slowly, his great splay feet plopping squashily on the ground. His long and flabby arms dangled down, not moving back and forth the way a man's arms usually do when he is walking, but just hanging and joggling with every step he took.

Cornwall came down the steps and started walking down the hill.

"You stay here with Beckett," he told Hal. "I will handle this."

The giant halted short of the bridge. He planted his feet solidly beneath him, and his voice boomed out so that all could hear him.

"I am the messenger of the Hellhounds," he roared. "I speak to all who have no right to be here. I bring you measured warning. Turn back, go back to where you came from. But first you must give up the one who fled."

He stopped and waited for the answer.

Cornwall heard a commotion behind him and swung hastily around. Beckett had broken loose from Hal and was running up the slope to one side of the house, toward a pile of boulders. The bow was still looped around his neck. Hal was racing after him, with others of the crew whooping along behind. Suddenly Beckett swerved and appeared to dive headlong into the earth. He disappeared; the earth appeared to have swallowed him.

The witch, hobbling painfully along, let out a screech. "Now," she screamed, "there'll be sheeted hell to pay. He dived down the ogre's hole."

"Answer me," yelled the giant. "Give me now your answer."

Cornwall swung back to face him. "We are simple pilgrims," he shouted. "We came to carry out a sacred trust. We have no wish to cause any trouble. We only seek the Old Ones."

The messenger guffawed. "The Old Ones," he

134

roared, "if you find them, they will put you to the knife. You must be daft to seek them. And no one goes into the Blasted Plain. It is forbidden country. Thus far you have come; no farther will you go. Give up the prisoner and turn back. If you do, we will not harm you. You have safe passage to the Borderland. On that you have our solemn promise."

"We won't go back," yelled Cornwall. "We haven't come this far to turn tail and run. And we'll not give up the prisoner. He has answered sufficiently to you; now it is us he must answer to."

"So be it," bellowed the giant. "Your own blood is now on your hands and not on ours."

"There need be no blood at all," yelled Cornwall. "No blood on any hands. Simply let us through. Once we find the Old Ones, we'll return to our own lands."

"What about the prisoner? He has many miles to run. Much more screaming he must do. The end of agony is not yet for him. He defiled our sacred soil with a marching army. Once, Sir Scholar, that would have meant war to the very hilt. But these days we grow soft and mellow. Be glad we do, and give us back our plaything."

"If you would kill him quickly. Horribly, perhaps, but quickly."

"Why should we do that? In these boring times there is slight amusement, and we must grasp it when we can. Surely you do not begrudge us that."

"If you do not kill him, then I shall."

"Do that," screamed the giant, "and you will take his place."

"That yet is to be seen," said Cornwall.

"You refuse, then, to give him back?"

"I refuse," said Cornwall.

The giant turned about in a lumbering fashion and went clumping up the hill. The row of Hellhounds on the ridgetop did not move.

Up the hill behind Cornwall another commotion erupted. Cornwall spun about. The trolls and goblins and other little people were fleeing in all directions, and a living horror was emerging from the ground beside the boulders.

The witch was screaming, thumping her broomstick on the ground. "I told you there'd be hell to pay," she shrieked. "He went down the ogre's hole. There isn't anyone can play footsie with the ogre."

The ogre by now had backed entirely from the hole and was tugging at something, pulling it from the hole. Galloping up the hill, Cornwall saw that the thing the ogre was hauling from the hole was Beckett, who was mewling faintly, clawing at the earth, resisting being drawn forth.

The ogre gave a mighty tug, and Beckett popped out of the hole like a cork from a bottle. Hal's bow, somewhat the worse for wear, was still looped around his throat. The ogre flung him contemptuously aside.

"Have you no respect?" the ogre shouted, not at Beckett alone, but at all of them. "Is not one secure in his own habitation? Must the world come pouring in on him? Why are all of you standing there? Tell me what is going on."

"Sir Ogre," said Cornwall, "we regret this exceedingly. It was a happening furthest from our thoughts. Under no circumstances would we willingly have disturbed your rest."

The ogre was a squat beast, almost toadlike. His eyes were saucers, and his mouth was rimmed wtih pointed teeth. His body seemed neither fur nor flesh but an earthy filthiness that fell from him in little patches as he moved.

"Such a thing," the ogre said, "has never happened. The people here know better. It would take an outlander to do what this creature did. Although once, long ago, there was a little minx who delighted in dribbling bark and clods of earth and other sundry items down into my burrow. What pleasure she might have gotten out of it I do not understand."

His saucer eyes swiveled around to fasten on Mary. "And if I am not mistaken," he said, "there is the little minx, quite grown now, I see, but the self-same one."

The witch raised her broom. "Back off," she shrilled. "Do not even think of laying your filthy hands on her. She was just a little tyke and she meant no harm. She was only playful and full of brimming spirits, and there is little enough of good-natured playfulness in this land of ours."

Mary said, "I am truly sorry. I had no idea it would disturb you so. You see, we pretended we were afraid of you, and we'd drop in the sticks and stones—as I remember it, very little sticks and stones—then we'd turn and run."

"You," said the ogre, "and that fiddle-footed brownie and Bromeley, the crazy troll—but, then, all trolls are crazy. You thought I did not know, but I did know and chuckled often over it. I suppose you find it hard to believe that I could ever chuckle."

"I did not know," said Mary. "If I had known that you could chuckle, I'd have come visiting and introduced myself."

"Well, now," the ogre said, seating himself on the ground, "you do know now, and this is as good a time as any. Let's do that visiting."

He patted the ground beside him. "Come over here and sit and we'll do some visiting."

The witch made a little shriek of happiness. "You do just that," she said to Mary. "I'll go and get the pot and we'll have some tea."

She turned and scurried off.

Cornwall saw that Hal and Gib had tight hold of Beckett, who lay quite passively on the ground.

"What are we going to do with him?" asked Hal.

"By rights," said Cornwall, "we should chop off his head. Either that or return him to the Hellhounds, an action I find most repulsive."

"I plead mercy," Beckett whined. "As one Christian to another, I most sincerely plead for mercy. You cannot abandon a fellow Christian to this heathen horde."

"You are at best," said Cornwall, "a very sorry Christian. I would choose ten heathens over a Christian such as you. As a man who tried his best to

137

have me killed, I have slight compunction over whatever happens to you."

"But I never," cried Beckett, struggling to sit up, "I never tried to kill you. How could I? I have never set eyes on you. For the love of God, messire . . ."

"My name is Mark Cornwall, and you did hire men to kill me."

Oliver, popping up beside Cornwall, yelled at him. "You tried to kill him because of a certain manuscript found in the library at Wyalusing. And you would have killed me, too, if you could have managed. There was a certain monk named Oswald, who ran bearing tales to you. He was found, come morning, with his throat slit in an alley."

"But that was long ago!" howled Beckett. "Since I have repented . . ."

"Repentance is no good," said Cornwall. "Make your choice now. The Hellhounds or the sword. A bastard such as you has no right to live."

"Allow me," said Gib. "It is not right that you should stain the good steel of your blade with the blood of such as this. One stroke of my ax . . ."

A pair of claws grabbed Cornwall by the arm. "Hold this talk of killing," screeched the witch. "I put my claim on him. It would be a waste of good man-flesh to kill such a lusty specimen. And I have need of him. Many cold nights have gone by since I've had a man to warm my bed."

She thrust herself past Cornwall and bent to examine Beckett. She reached out a claw and chucked him beneath the chin. Beckett's eyes went glassy at the sight of her.

"He isn't worth the trouble," Oliver said to her. "He will be running off as soon as he has a chance. And there are the Hellhounds . . ."

"Hah!" said the witch, disgusted. "Those little puppy dogs know better than to get gay with me. I'll take my broomstick to them. And as for running off, I'll put a spell on him, and I guarantee there'll be no running off. *Aiee*, the darling," she keened, "I'll make good use of him. Once I get him under covers, I'll break his lovely back. I'll give him loving such as he's never had before. . . ."

"It seems to me," Cornwall said to Beckett, "that your choices now are three. The Hellhounds or the sword or this. . . ."

"That is utter nonsense," screamed the witch. "He has no choice. You heard me say I lay a claim on him." She made a gesture with her hands, and gibberish flowed from out her mouth. She did a little dance and clicked her heels together. "Now turn him loose," she said.

Hal and Gib let loose of him, and Cornwall backed away. Beckett turned over and got on hands and knees, crawling forward to fawn against the witch.

"Like a goddamn dog," said Cornwall, flabbergasted. "If it had been me . . ."

"Look at the darling," the witch exclaimed, delighted. "He likes me already." She reached out and patted him on the head. Beckett wriggled in ecstasy. "Come along, my dear," she said.

She turned about and headed for the house, with Beckett gamboling at her heels, still on hands and knees.

While all this had been going on, the others, excited at the tea party, had paid slight attention to it. The witch, assisted by many willing hands, had brought tea and cakes, which had been placed on a table set before the boulders, underneath which the ogre had his burrow.

Cornwall looked about. There was no sign of the sloppy giant or of the Hellhounds. Quite suddenly the place assumed a happy look. The gentle sun of an autumn afternoon shone down on the knoll, and from far below came the murmuring of the stream as it flowed beneath the bridge.

"Where are the horses?" Cornwall asked.

Hal said, "Down beside the stream, in a little meadow, knee-deep in grass and doing justice to it. Sniveley is there, keeping close watch on them."

Coon came scampering three-legged, one front paw clutching a tea cake. Hal reached down and picked

139

him up. Coon settled contentedly in his arms and munched blissfully at the cake.

"I guess it's all over now," said Cornwall. "Let us join the party."

"I keep wondering," said Gib, "how the Hell-hounds will react when they find Beckett is beyond their reach."

Cornwall shrugged. "We'll handle that," he said, "when we come to it."

●●●●●●●●●●●●●●●●●●●●●●●●●●●●●●●●●●●●

23

THE ogre stuffed a cake into his mouth and leered at Cornwall.

"And who," he asked of Mary, "is this down-at-heels milksop who is acting as your escort?"

"He is no milksop," said Mary, "and if you continue in your pleasantries, you'll feel the full weight of his arm." She said to Cornwall, "He doesn't really mean it. He's only trying to be pleasant. It is a way he has."

"If this is being pleasant," said Cornwall, "I should hate to see him being nasty."

"Well, don't just stay standing there," the ogre boomed at Cornwall. "Here, sit down on the other side of me and have a cup of tea. I would say have a cake as well, but I fear all the cakes are gone. I never in my life have seen such a ravenous assembly. They descended on the cakes as if they were half-starved."

"They couldn't have been," said Mary. "Not after the big feast of last night."

"They are gluttonous," said the ogre. "It is the nature of them. Despite their pretty faces and the winsomeness of them, they are nothing but maws attached to enormous guts."

Cornwall sat down beside the ogre, and a fairy handed him a cup of tea. The cup was tiny, and his large hands had trouble handling it. The cup was only half full; the tea was now in short supply as well.

"The ogre," said Mary, "has been telling me of my parents. It seems he knew them quite well."

"Especially your father," said the ogre. "We found in one another much of common interest. Many an evening we sat here, as the three of us sit now, and talked many hours away. He was an intelligent and perceptive human, and it was a delight to talk with him. He was at once a scholar and a gentleman. He held a vast respect for this land of ours and the people in it, and he held no fear of them—which is an unlikely quality to be found in humans. Although I saw less of his lovely lady than I did of him, I grew quite fond of both, and this sweet child of theirs I loved almost as if she were my daughter—although it is ridiculous to think I might have had such a daughter. I'd lie in my burrow while she threw down stones and dirt and, envisioning in my mind how she then would scamper off in simulated childish terror, I would shake with laughter."

"Somehow," said Cornwall, "it is hard to imagine you shaking with laughter."

"That, my dear sir, is only because you do not know me. I have many excellent, I might say endearing, qualities which are not immediately apparent."

"One thing," said Mary, "that has been sticking in my mind ever since yesterday is whether my parents might have come from the same world Mr. Jones said that he is from."

"I do believe," the ogre said, "that they may have. Not from anything they ever said or did, but since the advent of your Mr. Jones, it has seemed to me I could detect certain similarities—little quirks of temperament, the way in which they looked at things, a certain gentle self-assurance that could, at times, verge on arrogance. Not that they came with all the magic machines that Jones packed along with him; as a matter of fact they came as humble pilgrims, with packs on their backs. I happened to be out sunning myself when the three of you came down the hill together and crossed the bridge, and it was the sweetest sight these old owl-eyes of mine have ever seen. They carried in their packs only those things

142

that might be possessed by a human who lived beyond the Wasteland, and I have wondered since if this were done by deliberate design, so that they would seem what they actually were not."

"And you liked them," Mary said.

"Indeed, I did. I liked them very much. It was a sad day for me when they went into the west, headed for the Blasted Plain. They had intended to take you, my dear, but I talked them out of it. I knew there was no point in trying to persuade them not to go themselves, for they were set on it. As I say, they had no fear in them. They believed that if they went in peace, they'd be allowed to go in peace. They had an almost childish faith in goodness. I think the only reason they left you behind was that never for a moment did they think they would not be coming back. They consoled themselves in leaving you behind in thinking they'd spare you the rigors of the trip. Not the dangers of it, for they never once admitted there would be dangers."

"They went west, then," said Cornwall. "What did they seek there?"

"I'm not sure I ever knew," the ogre said. "Certainly they never told me. There was a time when I thought I knew, but now I'm not so sure. There was something they were looking for. I got the impression they had a good idea where it was."

"And you think they now are dead," said Mary.

"No, actually I don't. I've sat here at the burrow's mouth year after year and stared out across the land. There's never been a time, to say it honestly, when I expected to see them coming back. But if I had ever seen them, I would not have been surprised. There was a sense of the indestructible about them, despite all their gentleness, as if they were unkillable, as if death were not for them. I know this may sound strange, and undoubtedly I'm wrong, but there are times you have a feeling that is beyond all logic. I saw them leave. I watched them until they were out of sight. And now I suppose I'll see you going, too, for I understand that you are about to follow in

143

their path; she is going with you, and I suppose there is no stopping her."

"I wish there were a way to stop her," Cornwall said.

"But there's not," said Mary. "So long as there's a chance of finding them."

"And what can I say to that?" asked Cornwall.

"There is nothing you can say," the ogre told him. "I hope you are more proficient with that sword than I take it you are. You have no look of fighting man to me. You smell of books and inkpot."

"You are right," said Cornwall, "but I go in goodly company. I have stout companions, and the sword I wear is made of magic metal. I only wish I had more training in the handling of it."

"I could suggest," the ogre said, "one other you might add who would make your company the stronger."

"You mean Jones," said Cornwall.

The ogre nodded. "He proclaims himself a coward. But there is great virtue in a coward. Bravery is a disease, too often fatal. It's the kind of thing that gets you killed. Jones would take no chances; he would commit himself to no action unless he were fairly certain the advantage weighed favorably. I would suggest he might carry powerful weapons, although I would have no idea what kind of weapons they might be. He has magic, but a different kind of magic than we have—a more subtle and more brutal magic, and he would be a good man to have along."

"I don't know," said Cornwall, hesitantly. "There is something about the man that makes me uncomfortable."

"The power of his magic," said the ogre. "The power and scope of it. And its unfamiliarity."

"Perhaps you're right. Although I think, uncomfortable or not, I'll make mention of it to him."

"I think," said Mary, "that he may be only waiting for you to do so. He wants to go deeper into the Wasteland and is afraid to go alone."

144

"And how about you?" Cornwall asked the ogre. "Would you join forces with us?"

"No, I would not," the ogre said. "I have long since done with foolishness. Come to think of it, I was never foolish. I have arrived at that time of life when sleeping in my burrow and sitting at its entrance to watch the world go by is all I need and want."

"But you'll tell us what to expect."

"Only hearsay," said the ogre, "and you have enough of that. Anyone can give you that, and you are a fool if you pay attention to it." He looked closely at Cornwall. "I think you are no fool," he said.

24

JONES' camp seemed deserted. The three striped tents still stood, but there was no one to be seen, not even any of the little people. The crude table still stood, and scattered about it and the now dead fire hearths, on which the feast had been cooked, were gnawed bones and here and there a beer mug. Two beer barrels still lay on the wooden horses, where they had been placed for tapping. A vagrant wind came down between the trees and stirred a tiny puff of dust in the road that ran to the battlefield.

Mary shivered. "It's lonely," she said. "After last night it is lonely. Where is everyone?"

The two horses they had ridden to the camp pawed listlessly at the ground, impatient to be back in the knee-deep pasture grass. They tossed their heads, jangling the bridle bits.

"Jones," said Cornwall. He'd meant to make it a shout, but in the moment of shouting some sense of caution toned down his lung power, and it came out as a simple word, almost conversational.

"Let's have a look," he said. He strode toward the larger tent, with Mary at his heels.

The tent was empty. The military cot still stood in its corner and the desk and chair. The corner opposite the desk was still hung with dark drapes, and beside it stood the large metallic cabinet. What Jones had called his cameras were gone. So was the box in which he had kept the little colored miniatures. So were all the other many mysterious objects that had been on the desk.

"He's gone," said Cornwall. "He has left this world. He has gone back to his own."

He sat down on the cot and clasped his hands. "There was so much he could have told us," he said, half talking to himself. "The things he started to tell me last night before the Hellhounds came along."

He glanced about the tent and for the first time felt the alien quality of it—the other-worldness of it—not so much the tent itself or the articles remaining in it, for they were, after all, not so greatly different— but some mysterious sense, some strangeness, a smell of different origins and of different time. And for the first time since he'd started on the journey he felt the prick of fear and an overwhelming loneliness.

He looked up at Mary, standing there beside him, and in a strangely magic moment her face was all the world—her face and eyes that looked back in his own.

"Mary," he said, scarcely knowing that he said it, reaching up for her, and as he reached, she was in his arms. Her arms went around him hard, and he held her close against himself, feeling the soft, yielding contours of her body against the hardness of his own. There was comfort and exultation in the warmth of her, in the smell and shape of her.

She whispered in his ear, "Mark, Mark, Mark," as if it were a prayer, as if it were a pledge.

Tightening his arms, he swung her to the cot and turned so that he was above her. She raised her head to kiss him and the kiss kept on and on. He slid a hand into her robe and felt the nakedness—the soft fullness of the breast, the taut smoothness of the belly, the tender lushness of the pubic hair.

The entire world hammered at him, trying to get in, but he was proof against it. He shut it out in a small tight world that contained only Mary and himself. There was no one else but the two of them. There was nothing that mattered but the two of them.

The tent flap rustled and a tense voice called, "Mark, where are you?"

He surged up out of the private world of him and

Mary and sat blinking at the figure that stood within the parted flap.

Hal said, "I'm sorry—terribly sorry to disturb you at your dalliance."

Cornwall came swiftly to his feet. "Goddamn you to hell," he yelled, "it was not dalliance."

He took a swift step forward, but Mary, rising swiftly, caught him by the arm. "It's all right," she said. "Mark, it is all right."

"I do apologize," said Hal, "to the both of you. It was most unseemly of me. But I had to warn you. Hellhounds are nosing close about."

Gib popped through the flap. "What possessed you," he asked in an angry tone of voice, "to go off by yourselves? Without the rest of us?"

"It was quiet," said Cornwall. "There seemed to be no danger."

"There is always danger. Until we leave these benighted lands, there always will be danger."

"I wanted to find Jones. To ask him if he would join us. But he has left, it seems. It doesn't look as if he's coming back."

"We need no Jones," said Hal. "The four of us, with Oliver and Sniveley, will be quite enough. No two of us alone, perhaps, but all of us together."

25

THE little ones had deserted them. Now they traveled quite alone, the six of them together.

It was nearing evening, and the land had changed but little. Five miles from the knoll where the Witch House stood they had come upon the Blasted Plain. Lying to the far horizon, it was a place of desolation. Drifting sand dunes lay here and there, and in between the dunes the land was parched and empty. Dead grass, dried to the consistency of hay, could be found in the lower areas where water once had lain but now there was no water. Occasional dead trees lifted their bonelike skeletons above the land, clutching at the sky with twisted, broken fingers.

Three of the horses were loaded with water, with the members of the party taking turns at riding the other two. Early in the day, Mary had rebelled at an unspoken conspiracy that would have delegated one of the remaining mounts to her and had done her share of walking. Except in the sand dune areas the walking was not difficult, but it held down the miles they could have made if all had been mounted.

Hal and Cornwall now led the march. Hal squinted at the sun. "We should be stopping soon," he said. "All of us are tired, and we want to be well settled in before darkness comes. How about that ridge over to the left? It's high ground, so we can keep a watch. There are dead trees for fire."

"Our fire up there," protested Cornwall, "could be spotted from a long way off."

Hal shrugged. "We can't hide. You know that.
149

Maybe there is no one watching now, but they knew we started out. They know where we can be found."

"The Hellhounds, you think?"

"Who knows?" said Hal. "Maybe the Hellhounds. Maybe something else."

"You don't sound worried."

"Of course I'm worried. You'd be stupid not to be worried. Even not to be a bit afraid. The best advice we got back there was from the ogre. He said don't go. But we had to go. There was no point in coming that far if we weren't going on."

"I quite agree with you," said Cornwall.

"In any case," said Hal, "you and Gib would have gone on alone. It would have ill behooved the rest of us to do any hanging back."

"I saw no hanging back," said Cornwall.

They trudged along in silence, sand and pebbles grating underneath their feet. They neared the ridge Hal had pointed out.

"Do you agree?" said Hal. "The ridge?"

Cornwall nodded. "You're the woodsman."

"There are no woods here."

"Nevertheless, the ridge," said Cornwall. "You are the one to know. I still remain a city man and know little of these things."

As they climbed the ridge, Hal pointed out a deep valley that gashed its side. "There is dry grass in there," he said. "The horses can do some grazing before dark. Then we'll have to bring them up to the camp for night."

Once they had gathered atop the ridge, Hal took charge. "Mark," he said, "you water the horses. Half a bucket to each horse, no more. After that, take them down to grass. Have them back before dark, and keep a sharp lookout. Mary, you'll be on watch. Watch in all directions. Scream if you see anything at all. The rest of you gather wood from that clump of trees. We'll need a lot of it."

When Cornwall got back to the ridgetop with the horses, the campfire was burning brightly, with a bed of coals raked over to one side, with Mary cooking over them. Sniveley and Oliver were on watch. Hal picketed the horses.

"You go over and have some food," he said to Cornwall. "The rest of us have eaten."

"Where is Gib?" asked Cornwall.

"He's out scouting around."

The sun had gone down, but a faint light hung over the landscape, which had turned to purple. Gazing out over it, there was nothing to be seen. It was a land of shadows.

"The moon will be coming up in an hour or so," said Hal.

At the fire Cornwall sat down on the ground.

"Hungry?" Mary asked.

"Starved," he said. "And tired. How about you?"

"I'm all right," she said. She filled a plate for him.

"Cornbread," she said, "and some bacon, but a lot of gravy. Awfully greasy gravy, but maybe you won't mind. No fresh meat. There was nothing for Hal to shoot. Nothing but those jackrabbits, and with them he had no chance."

She sat down beside him, moved over close against him, lifted her face to be kissed.

"I have to talk with you," she said, "before the others come back. Oliver talked with me, and he was going to talk with you, but I told him no, let me talk with you. I told him it would be better."

He asked, amused, "What did Oliver have to say to you?"

"You remember back at the tent?"

"I'll never forget it. And you? How about you, Mary?"

"I can't forget it, either. But it can't go on. Oliver says it can't. That's what he talked about."

"What the hell has Oliver got to do with it—with you and me? That is, if you feel the same as I do."

She grasped his arm, lay her head against it. "But I do. There were all those days you never even noticed me, and then suddenly you did. When you did,

I could have cried. You are the first one—you must understand that—you are the first. I was a tavern wench, but never . . ."

"I never thought," he said, "I never thought back there at the tent, I never thought of you as an easy tavern wench."

"But Oliver . . ."

"I don't see what Oliver . . ."

She let go of his arm and turned to face him. "He explained," she said. "He was most embarrassed, but he did manage to explain. He said I had to stay a virgin. He said he'd talk to you, but I said—"

Cornwall started to spring to his feet, sending the plate of food flying to the ground, but she caught him by the belt and pulled him back.

"Now see what you've done!" she cried.

"That goddamn Oliver," he said. "I'll wring his neck, just like a chicken. What right has he—"

"The horn," she said. "The unicorn horn. Don't you understand? The magic of the horn."

"Oh, my God," he said.

"I took it from the tree," she said. "The only one who could and only because I'd never known a man. The horn carries powerful magic, but only in my hands. Oliver said we have so little going for us that we may need that magic badly, and it can't be spoiled. I told him I'd try to tell you, and now I have. It's not been easy, but I have. I knew what would happen if he talked to you about it. And we couldn't let that happen. We have to stick together. We can't be fighting one another."

"I'm sorry," he said. "Sorry that you had to tell me. I should have known myself. I should have thought of it."

"Neither of us thought of it," she said. "It happened all so fast there was no time to think. Does it, my darling, always happen to everyone so quickly?"

She leaned against him, and he put his arms around her. "No," he said, "I don't suppose it does. But I couldn't help myself."

152

"Nor could I," she said. "I wanted you so badly. I didn't know it until then, but then I did. There is a buried slut in every woman. It takes the touch of the right man's hand to bring it out."

"It won't last forever," he said. "There'll be a time when the unicorn magic will not be needed. We can wait till then."

She nestled close. "If the time should come when we can't," she said, "when either one or the other of us can't, we'll forget about the magic."

The fire flared as a stick of wood burned through and slumped into the coals. In the east the sky brightened as a signal to the rising moon. Stars pricked out in the heavens.

Feet scuffed behind them, and then she rose. She said, "I'll get you another plate of food. There is plenty left."

•••••••••••••••••••••••••••••••••••••••

26

ON the afternoon of the fourth day they came in sight of the Castle of the Chaos Beast. They first saw it after climbing a steep, high ridge, which broke sharply down into a deeply eroded valley—eroded at a time when there had been water in the land, the naked soil exposed and crumbling, the sun highlighting the many-colored strata, red and pink and yellow.

The castle had a mangy look about it. At one time it must have been an imposing pile, but now it was half in ruins. Turrets had fallen, with heaps of broken masonry piled against the walls. Great cracks zigzagged down the walls themselves. Small trees grew here and there along the battlements.

They stopped atop the ridge and looked at it across the deep and scarred ravine.

"So fearsome a name," said Sniveley, "and what a wreck it is."

"But still a threat," said Oliver. "It still could pose great danger."

"There is no sign of life about," said Gib. "It well could be deserted. I'm coming to believe that nothing lives in this land. Four days and we haven't seen a thing except a jackrabbit now and then and, less often, a gopher."

"Maybe we should try to go around it," suggested Mary. "Double back and . . ."

"If there is anyone around," said Hal, "they would know we're here."

Mary appealed to Cornwall, "What do you think, Mark?"

"Hal is right," he said, "and there seems to be some sort of path across the ravine. Perhaps the only place it can be crossed for miles. Gib may be right, as well. The place may be deserted."

"But everyone back where we came from talked about the Chaos Beast," she said. "As if he still were here."

"Legend dies hard," Sniveley told her. "Once told, a story lingers on. And I would think few cross this land. There would be no recent word."

Hal started down the path into the ravine, leading one of the horses. The others followed, going slowly; the path was steep and treacherous.

Cornwall, following behind Hal, looked up at Coon, who maintained a precarious perch atop the waterbags carried by the horse being led by Hal. Coon grimaced at him and dug his claws in deeper as the horse lurched on uncertain ground, then recovered and went on.

Coon looked somewhat bedraggled, no longer the perky animal he once had been. *But so do all the rest of us*, thought Cornwall. The days and miles had taken their toll. It had been a hard march, and no one knew when the end would be in sight, for the geography of the Wasteland was guesswork at the best. It was told in landmarks, and the landmarks were often ill-defined and at times not even there. *First the Witch House*, he thought, counting off the major landmarks, *then the Blasted Plain, and now, finally, the Castle of the Chaos Beast and after this, the Misty Mountains, whatever they might be*. He remembered he had been told there would be He Who Broods Upon the Mountain, wondering rather idly if one of the Misty Mountains could be the one he brooded on.

But once the Misty Mountains had been reached, the Old Ones could not be far—or so they had been told by Jones, and, once again, what Jones had told would be no more than hearsay gained from his little people. There were no hard facts here, thought Cornwall, no real information. You pointed yourself in a certain direction and you stumbled on, hoping that in time you might find what you were looking for.

They had reached the bottom of the ravine and now started on the upward slope, the horses lunging upward, fearful of the crumbling and uncertain path, scrambling to maintain their footing.

Cornwall did not look up the slope to measure their progress. He kept his eyes on the path, alert to keeping out of the way of the lunging horse behind him. So that the end of it came suddenly and more quickly than he had expected. The path came to an end, and there was level ground beneath his feet.

He straightened from his stooped position and looked across the plain. And the plain, he saw, was no longer empty, as they first had seen it. It was black with Hellhounds.

They were still some distance off, but they were advancing at a steady lope, and in front of the pack ran the sloppy giant he had bellowed back and forth with at the Witch House.

The giant ran slab-sidedly, with his pancake feet plopping on the ground, raising little spurts of dust, but he still was making time, keeping well ahead of the beasts that ran behind him.

Hal stood to one side, with an arrow nocked against the bowstring. There was no excitement in him. He stood straight and steady, waiting, as if what was happening were no more than a target match.

And he knows, thought Cornwall, with a flare of panic, *he knows as well as I do that we can't withstand this charge, that it is the end for us, that the shock of the charging Hellhounds will knock us back into the ravine where, separately, we'll be hunted down.*

Where had the Hellhounds come from? he wondered. There had been no sign of them before. Was it possible they were the denizens of the castle and had hidden there?

His hand went back to the hilt of the sword, and with a jerk he wrenched the blade free of the scabbard. He was somewhat surprised that he should notice, with a thrill of pride, how brilliantly the naked blade flashed and glittered in the sunlight. And, somehow, the flash of it triggered in him an action, a heroic posturing of which he would have believed himself quite incapable. Stepping quickly forward, having no idea whatsoever that he had intended to step forward, he lifted the sword and swung it vigorously above his head so that it seemed a wheel of fire. And as he swung it, there came forth from his throat a battle bellow, a strident challenge—no words at all, but simply a roaring sound such as an angry bull might make to warn an intruder in a pasture.

He swung the sword in a glittering arc, then swung it once again, still roaring out the battle song, and on the second swing the hilt slipped from his hand and he stood there, suddenly weak-kneed and foolish, defenseless and unarmed.

Sweet Jesus, he thought, *I have done it now. I should never have left Wyalusing. I should not be here. What will the others think of me, an oaf who can't even hang onto a sword.*

He gathered himself for a mighty leap to retrieve the blade, praying that it would not fall so far away he could not get it back.

But the sword, he saw, was not falling. It was still spinning out, a wheel of light that refused to fall, and heading straight for the sloppy giant. The running giant tried awkwardly to get away from it, but he was too late and slow. The sword edge caught him neatly in the throat and the giant began to fall, as if he might have stumbled in his running and could not stop himself from falling. A great fountain of blood came gushing from his throat, spraying the ground, covering his head and chest. He hit the ground and bounced, slowly folding in on himself, while the sword came wheeling back toward Cornwall, who put up a hand and caught the hilt.

"I told you," Sniveley said, at his elbow, "that the blade had magic. But I did not dream this much. Perhaps it is the swordsman. You handle it expertly, indeed."

157

Cornwall did not answer him. He could not answer him; he stood, sword in hand, quite speechless.

The loping pack of Hellhounds had suddenly veered off.

"Stand steady," said Hal. "They'll be back again."

Gib said, "I'm not so sure of that. They do not like the sword. They are frightened of it. I wish my ax were as magic as the sword. We would have them then."

"There's something happening," said Mary quietly. "Look, toward the castle."

A ribbon of fog had emerged from one of the castle gates and was rolling swiftly toward them.

"Now what?" asked Hal. "As if we haven't got enough trouble as it is."

"Quick!" said Sniveley. "Get into the fog. Follow it to the castle. Stay in it. The Hellhounds will not dare to enter it. We'll be safe from them."

"But the castle!" Cornwall said.

"We know it's sure death out here," said Sniveley. "For my part, I'll take my chances with the Chaos Beast."

"I agree with Sniveley," said Oliver.

"All right," said Cornwall. "Let's go."

The fog had almost reached them.

"The rest of you go ahead," yelled Cornwall. "I'll take up the rear."

"And I, Sir Scholar," said Gib, "claim a place with you."

They fled down the corridor of fog.

From outside came the frantic, slobbering baying of the cheated Hellhounds.

Running, they reached the castle gate and stumbled through it. Behind them they heard the heavy portcullis slam home.

The castle yard was filled with fog, but now it began to disperse and lift.

Facing them was a row of monstrosities.

Neither group moved. They stood where they were, surveying one another.

No two of the creatures were alike; all were unspeakable. Some were squat, with drooping wings that dragged the ground. Some were semi-human toads with wide mouths that drooled a loathsome slaver. Some were scaled, with the scales falling off in leprous patches. There was one with an enormous belly and a face on the belly. There were many others. All were horrible.

Mary turned and hid her face against Cornwall's chest. Gib was gagging.

Big Belly moved out of line, waddled toward them. The small mouth in the belly spoke. It said, "We seek your help. The Chaos Beast is dead."

THEY had been offered castle room, but had declined it, setting up a camp in the castle yard. There had been plenty of wood to build a fire, and now half a dozen scrawny chickens were stewing in a kettle held on a crane above the blaze.

"It is the only way to cook them," Mary said. "They are probably so tough we couldn't eat them otherwise."

Their hosts had brought them, as well, three large loaves of new-baked bread and a basket of vegetables—carrots, beans, and squash.

And having done that, their hosts had disappeared.

From a far corner of the yard came a startled cackling.

"It's that Coon again," said Hal. "He's after the chickens. I told him there'd be chicken for him, but he likes to catch his own."

The sun had set, and the dusk of evening was beginning to creep in. They lounged about the fire waiting for supper to be done. The castle loomed above them, an ancient heap with mosses growing on the stone. Scrawny chickens wandered about the yard, scratching listlessly. Equally scrawny hogs rooted in piles of rubble. Half the yard was taken up with a fenced-in garden that was nearly at an end. A few cabbages still stood and a row of turnips waited to be dug.

"What I want to know," Cornwall said to Sniveley, "is how you knew we'd be safe inside the fog."

"Instinct, I suppose," said Sniveley. "Nothing I really knew. A body of knowledge that one may scarcely know he has, but which in reality works out to principles. Let us call it hunch. You couldn't have that hunch. No human could have. I did. Something clicked inside me and I knew."

"And now what?" asked Hal.

"I don't know," said Sniveley. "So far we've been safe. I confess I do not understand. The Chaos Beast is dead, they said, and they need our help. But I can't imagine what kind of help they need or why specifically from us. I am troubled, too, by the kind of things they are. They look like off-scourings of this world of ours—no little people, no honest monsters, but something else entirely. We hear stories now and then of creatures such as this. Almost never seen. Not really stories, perhaps. More like legends. And you'll be asking me about the Chaos Beast, perhaps, and I'll tell you now I know no more of it than you do."

"Well, anyhow," said Gib, "they're leaving us alone. They brought us food, then went off. Maybe they're giving us time to get used to the idea of them, and if that's the case, I'm glad. I'm sorry about it, of course, but I gag at the sight of them."

"You'll have to get used to them," said Cornwall. "They'll be back again. There is something that they want from us. . . ."

"I hope," said Hal, "they give us time to eat first."

They did. Supper was finished and full night had come. Hal had built up the fire so that it lighted a good part of the yard.

There were only three of them—Big Belly, Toad Face, and a third that looked as if it had been a fox that had started to turn human and had gotten stuck halfway in the transformation.

They came up to the fire and sat down. Foxy grinned at them with a long jaw full of teeth. The others did not grin.

"You are comfortable," asked Toad Face, "and well fed?"

"Yes," said Cornwall. "Thank you very much."

"There are rooms made ready for you."

161

"We would not feel comfortable without a fire and the open sky above us."

"Humans are seldom seen here," said Foxy, grinning again to show that he was friendly. "Two of you are human."

"You are prejudiced against humans?" asked Hal.

"Not at all," said Foxy. "We need someone who isn't scared."

"We can be just as scared as you," said Cornwall.

"Maybe," Foxy agreed, "but not scared of the same things. Not as scared of the Chaos Beast as we are."

"But the Chaos Beast is dead."

"You still can be scared of a thing when it is dead. If you were scared enough of it while it was alive."

"If you are this scared, why don't you leave?"

"Because," said Toad Face, "there is something that we have to do. The Chaos Beast told us we had to do it once he was dead. He put a charge on us. And we know we have to do it, but that doesn't stop us from being scared to do it."

"And you want us to do it for you?"

"Don't you see," said Big Belly, "it won't be hard for you. You never knew the Chaos Beast. You never knew what he could do."

"Dead he can't do anything," said Gib.

"We tell ourselves that," said Foxy, "but we don't believe it. We tell ourselves and it does no good."

"Tell us about this Beast of yours," said Cornwall. They looked at one another, hesitant.

"Tell us," Cornwall said. "If you don't, there is no deal. And there has to be a deal. We do this chore for you, what do you do for us?"

"Well, we thought . . ."

"You think because you helped us this afternoon . . ."

"Well, yes," said Big Belly, "we sort of did think that."

"I wouldn't be too sure of how much help you were," said Hal. "We were doing rather well. Mark's magic sword and a quiver full of arrows, plus Gib and his ax . . ."

"It was a help," said Mary.

"Don't let these jokers fool you," Sniveley warned. "They have some dirty work . . ."

"I admit," said Cornwall, "that you made some points this afternoon, but it seems to me this calls for more than points."

"You bargain with us?" Foxy asked.

"Well, let us say we should discuss the matter further."

"A sackful of chickens, perhaps," said Foxy. "Maybe a pig or two."

Cornwall did not answer.

"We could shoe your horses," said Toad Face. "We have a forge."

"We're going at this wrong," said Gib. "First we should find out what kind of chore they want done. It may be something we don't want to do."

"Very easy," Big Belly said. "No sweat at all. Provided you have no real fear of the Beast. Fear, of course, but not the kind of fear we have. Even to speak the name, we shudder."

All three shuddered.

"You talk about this Beast of yours and shiver," Sniveley said, tartly. "Tell us what made him so fearsome. Tell us the horror of him. Do not try to spare us. We have stout stomachs."

"He came not of this Earth," said Foxy. "He fell out of the sky."

"Hell," said Cornwall, disgusted, "half the heathen gods descended from the sky. Now, tell us something new."

"Legend says in all seriousness that he came out of the sky," said Big Belly. "Legend says he fell on this spot and lay here in all his fearsomeness. The people of that time fled for their lives, for there were many things about him that they did not like. Those were good days then, or so it is said. There was rain, and the soil was rich, and many people dwelt here in contentment and happiness. But a sickness came

163

upon the land, a rottenness. There were no rains, and the soil lost richness, and there was famine, and the people said it was the Beast who brought the sickness of the land. So they met in council and decided that the Beast must be hedged against the land. With many years of labor they brought here great stones and fenced him in with stones, not around him only, but on top of him as well, leaving only at the very top an opening so that if it were necessary he might be reached. Although why anyone should want to reach him is not well explained. They built a vault to contain him, with deep footings of stone to support the walls, and in the opening at the top they placed a fitted stone to shut him from the land and sky.

"And having done so, they waited for the rain, and there was no rain. The sickness still lay upon the land, the grasses died and the sand began to blow and drift. But the people clung to the land, for once it had been good land and might be good again, and they were loath to give it up. There were certain of these people who claimed they had learned to talk with the vaulted Beast, and these told the others that he wished them to worship him. 'If we worship him, perhaps he'll take the sickness from the land.' So they worshiped him, but the worship did no good, and they said among themselves, 'Let us build a house for him, a very pleasing house. Perhaps if we do that, he will be pleased and take the sickness from the land.' Once again they labored mightily to build this castle that you see, and the people who had learned to talk with him moved into the castle to listen to what he had to say and to do those things he wanted done, and I shudder when I think of some of those acts he wanted done. . . ."

"But it did no good," said Cornwall.

"How did you know that?" asked Foxy.

"For one thing, the land continues sick."

"You are right," said Foxy. "It did no good."

"And yet you stayed here all the time," said Mary.

164

"Since they built the castle. For you are the ones, aren't you, who talked with the Beast?"

"What there are left of us," said Toad Face. "Some of us have died, although all of us lived many times longer than the folk we once were. We lived longer and we changed. It almost seemed that we lived longer to give us the chance to change. Century after century the changes came on us. You can see the changes."

"I am not so certain," said Oliver, "that I believe all this. It seems impossible common folk would become the kind of things these are."

"It was the Beast that did it," said Big Belly. "We could feel him changing us. We don't know why he changed us, but he did."

"You should have left," said Cornwall.

"You do not understand," said Foxy. "We took a pledge to stay. To stay with the Beast. After a time the people left, but we stayed on. We were afraid that if the Beast were left alone, he'd tear down the vault and be loosed upon the Wasteland. We couldn't let that happen. We had to stand between the Wasteland and the Beast."

"And after a time," said Toad Face, "there was no place for us to go. We were so changed there was no place would take us."

"I'm not inclined," said Sniveley, "to believe a word of this. They have told us the story of the forming of a priesthood—a group of selfish, scheming leeches who fastened on the people. They used the Beast to gain an easy living and now, perhaps, the living is not so easy, since the people left, but it was at one time, and that was their purpose in saying they could converse with this Beast. Even now they would have us believe they have a noble purpose, standing, they say, between the Beast and the Wasteland. But they are no more than a gang of slickers, especially that one with the foxy face."

"Perhaps they are," said Cornwall. "Perhaps what you say is right, but let us hear the rest of it."

165

"That's all of it," said Big Belly. "And every word is truth."

"But the Beast is dead," said Hal. "You have no worries anymore. Sure, he told you to do something when he died, but you don't have to do it. You're now beyond his reach."

"Perhaps he can't reach you," said Foxy. "Perhaps not the others of your party. But he can reach us. We have been with him for so long, perhaps becoming so much a part of him, that in many ways he can still live in us, and even in death he can reach out—yes, even in death he can reach out. . . ."

"God, yes," said Cornwall, "it could happen that way."

"We know he's dead," said Big Belly. "His body lies rotting in the vault. He was a long time dying, and we seemed to die a little with him. We could feel the dying and the death. But in the reaches of the night, in the time of silences, he is still there. Perhaps not to others; probably only to ourselves."

"Okay, then," said Hal. "Say we accept your word for all of this. You've taken a lot of time and trouble to build up your story, and you have some purpose in your mind. I submit it is now time to tell us of that purpose. You said there was a chore that you wanted done and that we could do it because we were not as fearful of the Chaos Beast as you are."

"The task requires entering the vault," said Foxy.

"You mean into the vault with that dead monstrosity!" cried Mary.

"But why?" asked Cornwall, horrified. "Why into the vault?"

"Because," said Foxy, "there is something there that must be taken out. Something the Beast said should be taken out."

"You know what this thing is?"

"No, we don't know what it is. We asked and the Beast would not tell us. But we know that it is there. We took the cover from the vault and looked down into it. It took all the courage we had, but we managed it. Not for very long. We just had a glimpse, but we saw the object that must be taken out. We took one look and fled. . . ."

"And you want us to get it out?"

"If you would, please," said Foxy.

"Could you tell us what it is?" asked Mary.

"We saw only a part of it, or I *suppose* we saw only a part of it. We cannot imagine what it is. It appears to be a cage, a round cage. There are strips of metal formed into a cage. It is about so big." Foxy held his hands about a foot apart.

"Embedded in the body of the beast?"

"That is right," said Foxy.

"It will be a nasty job," said Gib.

"I do not like it," said Sniveley. "There is something here that's evil. There is more than they have told us."

"Perhaps," said Cornwall, "but they have a problem, and I suppose there is a price. Not," he said to Foxy, "a few chickens and a pig."

"The goodness of the deed," suggested Foxy. "For the sake of chivalry."

"Don't talk to us of chivalry," snapped Oliver. "Chivalry is dead. It didn't last too long. It was a rotten idea while it did. So come up with something solid. If you don't, come morning we will leave."

"You dare not leave," said Foxy smugly. "The Hellhounds are lurking out there on the plain. They'll snap you up before you've gone a league. The Hellhounds never loved you, and now they love you less since you killed the giant."

"You suggest we're trapped in here," said Hal.

"Perhaps not," said Big Belly. "It's possible we could help you."

"They're working together," Sniveley charged. "These jokers and the Hellhounds. They're putting the squeeze on us."

"If you mean," said Toad Face, "that we are friendly with the Hellhounds and with their aid have devised a devious scheme to get you to do this small service for us, you couldn't be more wrong."

"Come to think of it," said Gib, "we never saw

167

a Hellhound until we saw the castle. We watched and waited for them and they never did show up until we reached the castle. They waited for us here. They could have jumped us anyplace along the way, but they waited for us here."

"For years," said Foxy, "the Hounds have nosed around this castle, thinking they might catch us unaware. It has been war between us almost from the start. In recent years they have grown more cautious, for we have made them smart, and they have sorely learned what we can do to them. Time after time we've whomped them with various kinds of magic, but they still hang around. They've never given up. Now, however, at the very sight of us, they tuck in their tails and scamper. We have them hexed."

"It's the castle they want?" asked Gib. "Not really you they're after, but the castle?"

"That is right," said Foxy. "It's a thing of pride with them, to be possessors of the Castle of the Chaos Beast. They never, you understand, have really amounted to anything at all. They have been the rowdies and the brawlers of the Wasteland. They've been feared, of course, but they've never been respected. But to hold the castle—that might give them status and respect."

"And you say you have them hexed?"

"They dare not lay a hand on us. They won't even come too close. But they hope that through some trick someday they will overcome us. . . ."

"Is it your thought," asked Cornwall, "that you can give us safe escort when we leave the castle?"

"That is our thought," said Foxy.

"We enter the vault and bring out the object, and once that is done, you furnish us escort until there is no longer any danger from the Hellhounds."

"They're lying to us," Oliver said. "They're scared striped of the Hounds. Just like they are scared of the Chaos Beast."

"What difference does it make?" asked Mary. "You all have made up your minds to pull this thing

168

from the vault. You wonder what it is, and you won't rest easy until you find out what it is. . . ."

"Still," said Cornwall to Foxy, "you do promise us escort?"

"That we do," said Foxy.

"And it better be good," said Hal, "or we'll come back and clean out this nest of you."

• •

THE stench was green. It struck the pit of the stomach, it clogged the nostrils, burned the throat, watered the eyes; it made the mind reel. It was an alien foulness that seemed to come from somewhere other than the Earth, a violent corruption deep from the guts of Hell.

They had labored in it for hours, setting up the poles to form the tripod above the opening of the vault (although Cornwall realized he could no longer think of it as a vault, but rather as a pit), rigging the pulley, threading the rope to run in the pulley.

And, now that all was ready, Cornwall leaned over the edge of the opening to glance down into the mass of putrescence that filled the area, a gelatinous matter not quite liquid, not quite solid—a sight he had avoided until now. For the mass itself seemed to have some of the same obscene, stomach-wrenching quality that characterized the stench that came boiling out of it. The stench was bad enough; the stench combined with the sight of the vault's contents was almost unbearable. He doubled over, wracked by the dry wretching that brought up nothing, for the contents of his stomach had been emptied long ago.

"Why don't you let me, Mark?" said Gib, standing at his elbow. "I don't seem to mind it as much—"

"You don't mind it so much," said Cornwall harshly, "that you vomited up your goddamn guts."

"But I am lighter," argued Gib. "I don't weigh more than a third of what you do; I'll be easier to handle on the rope."

"Stop it, Gib," Sniveley said angrily. "We talked

this out hours ago. Sure, you weigh a third less than Mark, you also have only a third the strength."

"Maybe we won't need any strength."

"That thing down there," said Hal, "could be hard to yank out. If it grew out of the body of the Beast, it still could be rooted there."

"The body is a mass of soup," said Gib. "It is nothing but a puddle."

"If it were," said Cornwall, "the cage or globe or whatever it is would have sunk. It wouldn't still be there."

"We can't be sure of that," said Gib. "It could be floating."

"Let's stop this talk," said Cornwall. "As Sniveley said, we decided it. We talked it over and decided it on logic. I have more strength than any of you, and strength may be needed. I grab hold of it, and you guys pull me out along with it; it might take even more strength than I have to hang onto it. The rest of you together can handle the rope—that is, if Mary's here to help. Where the hell is Mary?"

"She went down to start the fire under the kettle," said Sniveley. "We'll need hot water to take baths once we get out of here. . . ."

"If hot water will take it off," said Oliver.

"Big Belly gave us some soap," said Sniveley.

"What would they need of soap?" asked Oliver. "From the smell of them, they never use it."

Cornwall yelled at them. "Cut out the goddamn jabber! What's soap got to do with it? What's hot water got to do with it? If a fire had to be started, any one of you could have started it. We need Mary here to help handle the rope, and what is more . . ."

He let his voice run down, ashamed of himself. What was he doing, shouting at them? It was the stench, he knew—it nibbled the mind, it frazzled the nerves, it squeezed the guts; in time it could turn a man into a shrieking maniac.

"Let's get on with it," he said.

"I'll get Mary," said Oliver. "I'll stay and watch the fire."

171

"Forget the fire," said Hal. "Come back with her. We could need your help."

"If we had a hook," said Hal, "we might be able to hook it out."

"But we haven't got a hook," said Hal, "and no metal to make one. They have a forge down there and no metal. . . ."

"They hid the metal," said Sniveley, "just like they're hiding themselves. There's no hide nor hair of them."

"We could get metal from one of our pots," said Gib.

"It's easier this way," said Cornwall. "Simple and direct. Tie that rope around me and let's get started."

"You'll suffocate," said Sniveley.

"Not if I tie a scarf around my mouth and nose."

"Make sure that knot is tied securely," Sniveley said to Hal. "We can't take a chance. If Mark falls into the mess, we'll never get him out."

"I know about knots," said Hal. "A good slip noose. It will tighten up." He said to Cornwall, "How does it feel?"

"It feels fine. Now give me that scarf."

He wrapped the scarf around his face, covering nose and mouth.

"Hold still," said Gib. "I'll tie it."

Oliver came scampering up the stairs, followed by Mary.

"Everyone's here," said Hal. "Grab hold of that rope, all of you. Hang on for your life. Let him down easy."

Cornwall leaned over the opening and gagged. It was not the smell so much, for the scarf did offer some protection, but the sight—the sea of crawling corruption, a creature dead and rotting, with nowhere for the rot to go, a puddle of putrescence, held within the vault. It was green and yellow, with streaks of red and black, and there seemed to be within it some kind of feeble current that kept it swirling slowly, so slowly that no real motion could be detected, although there was a sense of motion, almost of aliveness.

He gagged, gritting his teeth. His eyes began to smart and water.

He couldn't live down there for long, he knew. It had to be down quickly and out again as fast as possible. He flexed his right hand, as if he wanted to be sure it was in working order when he reached out to grab the cage or whatever it might be that was down there in the pit.

The rope tightened around his chest. "All ready, Mark," said Hal.

He swung over the edge. The rope tightened and held him, lifting him a little. He let loose of the edge of the vault and felt his body swinging to the center of the opening. His body dropped jerkily and was brought swiftly to a halt.

Up above him Hal was yelling, "Watch it! Take it slow! Let him down easy! Not too fast!"

The stench rose up and hit him, engulfing him, smothering him. The scarf was not enough. The stench seeped through the fabric, and he was drowning in it. His belly slammed up and hit him in the face, then dropped into a place that had no bottom. His mouth filled with a vomit he would have sworn he didn't have and was held there by the scarf wrapped about his face. He was blinded and disoriented. He clawed feebly with his hands. He tried to cry out, but no words came in his throat.

Below him he could make out the noisome surface of corruption, and it seemed to be in violent motion. A wave of it rose and reached for him, fell short and dropped back again. It had an oily and repulsive look, and the stench poured out of it. Another wave ran across its surface, struck the opposite wall of the vault and curled on itself, not as water would curl, but slowly, deliberately, ponderously, with a terrible look of power. Then it was flowing back and reaching up again, and this time it hit him. It climbed over his body, covering him, drenching him in its

173

substance. He lifted his hands and clawed in terror to free his eyes of the clinging putridness. His stomach heaved and churned. He vomited weakly, but it was dry vomiting; there was nothing left to vomit.

He could see only blearily, and he had the horrible feeling that he was lost in an otherness that was beyond the ken of all living things. He did not sense the pressure of the rope as the others hauled him up. It was not until he felt hands upon him, hauling him free of the opening of the vault, that he realized he had been lifted free.

His feet hit hardness and his knees buckled under him. He sprawled weakly, still retching. Someone was wiping off his face. Someone was saying, "You're all right now, Mark. We have you out of it."

And someone else, off a ways, was saying, "It's not dead, I tell you. It is still alive. No wonder those slimy little bastards were afraid to go down there. We been took, I tell you. We been took."

He struggled to his knees. Someone threw a pail of water over him. He tried to speak, but the vomit-soaked, stench-drenched scarf still covered his mouth. Hands ripped it off him and his face was free.

He saw Gib's face in front of him. Gib's mouth worked. "What a mess," he said. "Off with those clothes. Down the stairs and in the tub. The water's hot and we have soap."

•••••••••••••••••••••••••••••••••••••

29

Coon and Oliver perched on the edge of the tub. "I say give it up," said Oliver. "The castle people knew what would happen if they went into the vault. They know the thing's not dead. . . ."

"It's dead, all right," said Sniveley. "It's rotting there before your eyes. It's magic. That is what it is. The vault's bewitched. . . ."

"You can't bewitch the vault," protested Oliver. "You can't bewitch a thing. A person, sure, a living thing, but not a thing of stone."

"We have to figure out another way," said Gib. "I've been looking at that iron frying pan we have. We could use the handle of it, heat it, bend it in a hook . . ."

"Go probing down with a hook," said Hal, "and the same thing will happen. The Beast, dead or not, is not about to let us hook that object out of there."

"Any sign of Big Belly or Foxy or any of the rest of them?" asked Cornwall.

"Not a sign," said Hal. "We searched the castle. They're in some hidey-hole."

"If we have to," said Cornwall, "we'll take the place down stone by stone to find them. No one can pull a trick like this on us."

"But we have to get that thing out of there," said Mary. "We made a deal with the castle folk. The plain out there is swarming with Hellhounds. We'll never get out by ourselves."

"What makes you think," asked Sniveley, "they ever meant to keep the deal? They tried to use us.

For some reason they want that thing out of the vault, and they'd have done anything . . ."

"We could tear down the vault," said Gib. "It would take a little time. . . ."

"I think I'm fairly clean," said Cornwall. "I'd better be getting out of here. Hand me my trousers, will you?"

Mary gestured at the makeshift clothesline that had been strung up. "They aren't dry," she said.

"I'll wear them wet," said Cornwall. "We'll have to start doing something. Maybe Gib is right. Tear down the vault."

"Why bother with it anymore?" asked Hal. "We can fight our way through the Hellhounds. With the giant dead, the heart's gone out of them. They won't be all that tough."

"You have only a couple of dozen arrows," said Gib. "Once they're gone, there aren't any more. Then there'll be only Mark's sword and my ax."

"Both the sword and ax are good," said Sniveley. "You'll never find better."

Coon fell in the tub. Cornwall picked him out by the scruff of his neck, reached over the edge of the tub, and dropped him on the ground. Coon shook himself, spattering everyone with soapy, smelly water.

"Here are your pants," said Mary, handing them to Cornwall. "I told you they aren't dry. You'll catch your death of cold."

"Thanks," said Cornwall. "They'll be dry in a little while."

"Good honest wool," said Hal. "No one ever suffers from wearing wet wool."

Cornwall got out of the tub, tugged on his trousers.

"I think we should talk this over," he said. "There's something in that vault the castle folk want out. If it's all that important to them, it might be as important to us. Anyhow, I think we should get it out, find out what it is. And once we get it out, we'll dig out Big Belly and the rest of them from wherever they may be and talk to them by hand. But until we

176

get out whatever's in the vault we can't talk to them too well. All of it may do us no good, and it'll be a messy job, of course . . ."

"There might be another way," said Oliver. "The unicorn horn. The one that Mary has. Magic against magic."

Sniveley shook his head. "I'm not sure it would work. Magic comes in specific packages. . . ."

"I hesitated to mention it," Oliver apologized. "It's no place to send a lovely lady and . . ."

"Lady, hell," Cornwall snorted. "If you think it has a chance, give me the horn and I'll go in again."

"But it wouldn't work with you," said Oliver. "It would only work with Mary. She has to be the one."

"Then we tear down the vault," said Cornwall. "Unless someone can think of something else. Mary, I tell you, is not going down into that vault."

"Now, you listen here," said Mary. "You have no right to say that. You can't tell me what to do. I'm a part of this band, and I claim the right to do whatever I can do. I've packed that horn for miles and it's an awkward thing to carry. If any good can come of it—"

"How do you know it will do any good at all?" yelled Cornwall. "What if it didn't work? What if you went down in there and . . ."

"I'll take the chance," said Mary. "If Oliver thinks it will work, I'll go along with it."

"Let me try it first," said Cornwall.

"Mark," said Hal, "you're being unreasonable. Mary could try at least. We could let her down, and if there were any motion there, if there were anything at all, we could pull her out immediately."

"It's pretty bad down there," said Cornwall. "It is downright awful. The smell is overpowering."

"If it worked," said Oliver, "it would only take a minute. We could have her in and out . . ."

"She could never pull it out," said Cornwall. "It might be heavy. Maybe she couldn't get a grip on it, couldn't hang onto it even if she did get a grip."

"We could fix up that hook," said Hal. "Tie it to

177

a rope. She hooks onto it and then we pull out both her and it."

Cornwall looked at Mary. "Do you really want to?"

"No, of course, I don't want to," she said. "You didn't want to, either, but you did. But I am ready to do it. Please, Mark, let me try."

"I only hope it works," said Sniveley. "I hate to tell you the kind of odds I'd give you that it won't."

••••••••••••••••••••••••••••••••

30

THEY did it differently from the way they had for
Cornwall. For Mary they rigged a seat, like the seat
for a child's swing, and fashioned a hitch so she
could be tied securely into it. They tied a cord about
the horn so it could be looped about her shoulder
and she need not hold it, for it was an awkward thing
to hold. Thus, she had both hands free to handle the
hook, which, tied to another rope, was run through
a second pulley.

Finally it was time to go.

"My robe," said Mary. "It is the only one I have.
It will be fouled."

"Shuck it up," said Hal. "We can tie it into place."

"It might not wash clean," she wailed.

"Take it off," said Sniveley. "Go down in your
skin. None of us will mind."

"No!" said Cornwall. "No, by God, I'll not have
it!"

"Sniveley," Hal said sharply, "you have gone too
far. Modesty is not something you know about, of
course . . ."

Gib said to Mary, "You must excuse him. He had
no way to know."

"I wouldn't mind so much," said Mary. "The robe
is all I have. If none of you ever spoke of it or—"

"No!" said Cornwall.

Mary said to him in a soft, low voice, "You have
felt my nakedness. . . ."

"No," said Cornwall in a strangled voice.

"I'll wash out the robe while you're in the tub,"

Oliver offered. "I'll do a good job on it, use a lot of soap."

"I think," said Sniveley, "it's a lot of foolishness. She'll get splashed. That foul corruption will be all over her. The horn won't work—you wait and see, it won't."

They tucked up the robe and tied it into place. They put a piece of cloth around her face, Oliver having raided the castle kitchen for a jug of vinegar in which the cloth was soaked in hope that it would help to counteract the stench.

Then they swung her over the opening. The putrescent puddle boiled momentarily, then settled down again. They lowered her swiftly. The loathsome pit stirred restlessly, as if it were a stricken animal quivering in its death throes, but stayed calm.

"It's working," said Gib between his teeth. "The horn is working."

Cornwall called to Mary, "Easy does it now. Lean over with the hook. Be ready. We'll let you down another foot or so."

She leaned over with the hook poised above the cage.

"Let her down," said Hal. "She's directly over it."

Then it was done. The hook slipped over two of the metal strips and settled into place. Gib, who was handling the hook-rope, pulled it taut. "We have it," he shouted.

Cornwall heaved on the rope tied to Mary's sling and brought her up swiftly. Hands reached out and hauled her to safety.

She staggered as her feet touched solid rock, and Cornwall reached out to steady her. He ripped the cloth off her face. She looked up at him with tearful eyes. He wiped the tears away.

"It was bad," she said. "But you know. You were down there. Not as bad for me as it must have been for you."

"But you are all right?"

"I'll get over it." she said. "The smell . . ."

"We'll be out of here for good in a little while. Once we get that thing out of there." He turned to Gib. "What have we got?"

"I don't know," said Gib. "I've never seen its like."

"Let's get it out before something happens."

"Almost to the top," said Hal. "Here it comes. The Beast is getting restless."

"There it is!" yelled Oliver.

It hung at the end of the rope, dripping slime. It was no cage or globe. The globe was only the upper part of it.

"Quick!" warned Hal. "Reach over and pull it in. The Beast is working up a storm."

A wave of the vault's contents rose above the opening, curled over, breaking, sending a fine spray of filth over the edge of the opening.

Cornwall reached out, fighting to get a grip on the thing that dangled from the hook. It had a manlike look about it. The cage formed the head, its tanklike body was cylindrical, perhaps two feet through and four feet long. From the body dangled three metallic structures that could be legs. There were no arms.

Hal had a grip on one of the legs and was pulling it over the edge of the opening. Cornwall grasped another leg and together they heaved it free of the vault. A wave broke over the lip of the opening. The noisome mass sloshed out over the platform that ringed the top of the vault.

They fled down the stairs and out into the court-yard, Gib and Hal dragging the thing from the vault between them. Once in the courtyard, they stood it on its feet and stepped away. For a moment it stood where they had set it, then took a step. It paused for a short heartbeat, then took another step. It turned about slowly and swiveled its head, as if to look at them, although it had no eyes, or at least none that were visible.

"It's alive," said Mary.

They watched it, fascinated, while it stood unmoving.

181

"Do you have any idea," Hal asked Sniveley, "what in the world it is?"

Sniveley shook his head.

"It seems to be all right," said Gib. "It isn't angry at us."

"Let's wait awhile," cautioned Hal, "before we get too sure of that."

Its head was the cage, and inside the cage was a floating sphere of brightness that had a tendency to sparkle. The cage sat atop the tanklike body, and the body was networked with many tiny holes, as if someone had taken a nail and punched holes in it. The legs were so arranged that there was no front or back to the creature; at its option it could walk in any direction. It seemed to be metal, but there was no surety it was.

"Son of the Chaos Beast," said Cornwall speculatively.

"Maybe," said Hal. "The son? The ghost? Who knows?"

"The castle folk might know," suggested Mary. "They were the ones who knew about it."

But there was still no sign of the castle folk.

31

BATHS had been taken, clothing washed, supper cooked and eaten. A faint stench still, at times, wafted from the direction of the vault, but other than that, everything was peaceful. The horses munched methodically at a pile of ancient hay stacked in one corner of the courtyard. The pigs continued to root here and there, but the chickens had ceased their scratching and had gone to roost.

None of the castle folk had made an appearance.

"I'm getting worried about them," said Cornwall. "Something must have happened to them."

"They're just hiding out," said Sniveley. "They made a deal they know they can't deliver on, and now they're hiding out and waiting for us to leave. They're trying to outwait us."

"You don't think," said Mary, "they can help us with the Hellhounds?"

"I never did think so," said Sniveley.

"The place still is stiff with Hounds," said Gib. "I went up on the battlements just before sunset and they were all around. Out there and waiting."

"What are we going to do?" asked Oliver. "We can't stay here forever."

"Wait and see," said Cornwall. "Something may turn up. At least we'll sleep on it."

The moon came tumbling over the eastern horizon as night settled in. Hal piled more wood on the fire and the flames leaped high. The thing they had taken from the pit prowled restlessly about the courtyard; the rest of them lounged about the fire.

"I wonder what is wrong with Tin Bucket over

183

there," said Hal. "He seems to have something on his mind. He is jittery."

"He's getting oriented," said Gib. "He's been jerked into a new world and he's not sure he likes it."

"It's more than that," said Hal. "He acts worried to me. Do you suppose he knows something we don't?"

"If he does," said Sniveley, "I hope he keeps it to himself. We've got enough to worry about without him adding to it. Here we are, locked up in a moldering old stone heap, with the owners of it hiding in deep dungeons and Hounds knee-deep outside. They know we'll have to come out sometime, and when we do, they'll be there, with their teeth all sharpened up."

Cornwall heaved himself to his feet. "I'm going up on the wall," he said, "and see if anything is going on."

"There are stairs over to the left," Gib told him. "Watch your step. The stones are worn and slippery."

The climb was long and steep, but he finally reached the battlement. The parapet stood three feet high or so, and the stones were crumbling. When he reached out a hand to place it on the wall, a small block of stone came loose and went crashing down into the moat.

The ground that stretched outward from the walls was splotched with moonlight and shadow, and if there were Hounds out there, he realized they would be hard to spot. Several times it seemed he detected motion, but he could not be certain.

A chill breeze was blowing from the north and he shivered in it. And there was more than the wind, he told himself, that might cause a man to shiver. Down at the fire he could not admit his concern, but here, atop the wall, he could be honest with himself. They were caught in a trap, he knew, and at the moment there was no way to get out. It would be foolishness, he knew, to try to cut their way through. A sword, an ax, a bow (with two dozen arrows at best) were the only weapons they had. A magic sword, of course, but a very inept swordsman. An expert at the bow, but what could one bow do? A stout man with an ax, but a small man, who would go under in the first determined Hellhound rush.

Somewhere out on the darkened plain a night bird was startled into flight. It went peeping its way across the land, its wings beating desperately in the night. Something was out there to have startled it, Cornwall told himself. More than likely the entire plain was alive with watching Hounds.

The peeping went away, growing fainter and fainter as the bird blundered through the darkness; but as the peeping faded, there was a cricket chirping, a sound so small and soft that Cornwall found himself straining to hear it. As he listened, he felt a strange panic stirring in him, for it seemed to him he had heard the same sound once before. Now the cricket-chirping sound changed into another sound, not as if there were a new sound, but as if the chirping had been modified to a sort of piping. And suddenly he remembered when he had heard the sound before—on that night before they had stumbled on the battlefield.

The quavery piping swelled into a wailing, as if some frightened thing in the outer dark were crying out its heart. The wailing rose and fell and there was in it something that hinted at a certain madness—a wild and terrible music that stopped one's blood to hear.

The Dark Piper, Cornwall told himself, *the Dark Piper once again.*

Behind him came a tinkling sound as a small bit of stone was dislodged and went bouncing down the inside wall. He swung about and saw a little sphere of softly glowing light rising above the inner wall. He stepped back in sudden fright, his fist going to the sword hilt, and then relaxed as he realized what it was—Tin Bucket making his slow and cautious way up the slippery flight of stairs.

The creature finally gained the battlement. In the light of the risen moon his metallic body glinted, and the luminous sphere inside his head-cage sparkled in a friendly manner. Cornwall saw that Tin Bucket had sprouted arms, although arms was not quite the word.

185

Several ropelike tentacles had grown, or had been extruded, from the holes that pierced his body.

Tin Bucket moved slowly toward him, and he backed away until he came up against the parapet and could go no farther. One of the ropelike arms reached out and draped itself across one of his shoulders with a surprisingly gentle touch. Another swept out in an arc to indicate the plain beyond the wall, then doubled back on itself, the last quarter of it forming into the shape of the letter "Z." The "Z" jerked emphatically and with impatience toward the darkness beyond the castle.

The piping had stopped. It had been replaced by what seemed a terrible silence. The "Z" jerked back and forth, pointed to the plain.

"You're insane," protested Cornwall. "That's the one place we aren't going."

The letter "Z" insisted.

Cornwall shook his head. "Maybe I'm reading you wrong," he said. "You may mean something else."

Another tentacle stiffened with a snap, sternly pointing backward to the stairs that led down from the wall.

"All right, all right," Cornwall told him. "Let's go down and see if we can get this straightened out."

He moved away from the parapet and went carefully down the stairs, Tin Bucket close behind him. Below him the group around the fire, seeing the two of them descending, came swiftly to their feet. Hal strode out from the fire and was waiting when they reached the courtyard.

"What is going on?" he asked. "You having trouble with our friend?"

"I don't think trouble," said Cornwall. "He tried to tell me something. I think he tried to warn us to leave the castle. And the Dark Piper was out there."

"The Dark Piper?"

"Yes, you remember him. The night before we came on the battlefield."

Hal made a shivering motion. "Let's not tell the others. Let's say nothing of the Piper. You are sure you heard him? We didn't hear him here."

186

"I am sure," said Cornwall. "The sound may not have carried far. But this fellow is insistent that we do something. I gather that he wants us to get going."

"We can't do that," said Hal. "We don't know what is out there. Maybe in the morning . . ."

Tin Bucket strode heavily forward to plant himself before the gate. A dozen tentacles snapped out of his body and straightened, standing stiffly, pointing at the gate.

"You know," said Hal, "I think he does want us to leave."

"But why?" asked Gib, coming forward and catching what Hal had said.

"Maybe he knows something we don't know," said Hal. "Seems to me, if I remember, I said that just a while ago."

"But there are Hounds out there!" gasped Mary.

"I doubt," said Oliver, "that he would want to do us harm. We hauled him from the pit and he should be grateful."

"How do you know he wanted to be taken from the pit?" asked Sniveley. "We may have done him no favor. He may be sore at us."

"I think, in any case," said Cornwall, "we should get the horses loaded and be set to raise the gate. Be ready to get out of here if anything happens."

"What do you expect to happen?" Sniveley asked.

"How should any of us know?" snapped Hal. "There may nothing happen, but we play this one by ear."

Gib and Oliver already were catching up the horses and bridling them. The others moved rapidly, getting saddles on the animals, hoisting and cinching on the packs.

Nothing happened. The horses, impatient at being hauled from the hay on which they had been feeding, stamped and tossed their heads. Tin Bucket stood quietly by the fire.

"Look at him," said Sniveley, disgusted. "He started all this ruckus and now he disregards us. He stands off by himself. He contemplates the fire. Don't tell me he expects anything to happen. He is a mischief maker, that is all he is."

"It may not be time as yet for anything to happen," Gib said, quietly. "It may not be time to go."

Then, quite suddenly, it was time to go.

The wheel of fire came rushing up from the eastern horizon. It hissed and roared, and when it reached the zenith, its roar changed to a shriek as it sideslipped and turned back, heading for the castle. The brilliance of it blotted out the moon and lighted the courtyard in a fierce glow. The stone walls of the castle reared up with every crack and cranny outlined in deep shadow by the blinding light, as if the castle were a drawing done by a heavy pencil, outlined in stark black and white.

Cornwall and Gib sprang for the wheel that raised the castle gate, Hal running swiftly to help them. The gate ratcheted slowly upward as they strained at the wheel. The circle of fire came plunging down, and the screaming and the brilliance of it seemed to fill the world to bursting. Ahead of it came a rush of blasting heat. It skimmed above the castle, barely missing the topmost turrets, then looped in the sky and started back again. The horses, loose now, were charging back and forth across the courtyard, neighing in terror. One of them stumbled and, thrown off balance, plunged through the fire, scattering smoking brands.

"The gate is high enough," said Cornwall. "Let us catch those horses."

But the horses were not about to be caught. Bunched together, screaming in panic, they were heading for the gate. Cornwall leaped for one of them, grabbing for a bridle strap. He touched it and tried to close his fingers on it, but it slipped through his grasp. The plunging forefoot of a horse caught him in the ribs and sent him spinning and falling. Bellowing in fury and disappointment, he scrambled to his feet. The horses, he saw, were hammering across the drawbridge and out onto the plain. The

188

lashings that bound the packs on one of the saddles loosened, and the packs went flying as the horse bucked and reared to rid himself of them.

Hal was tugging at Cornwall's arm and yelling, "Let's get going. Let's get out of here."

The others were halfway across the drawbridge. Coon led them all, scampering wildly in a side-wheeling fashion, his tail held low against the ground.

"Look at him go," said Hal, disgusted. "That coon always was a coward."

The plain was lighted as brilliantly as if the sun had been in the sky, but the intensity of the glow from the screaming wheel of fire played funny tricks with shadows, turning the landscape into a mad dream-place.

Cornwall found that he was running without ever consciously having decided that he would run, running because the others were running, because there was nothing else to do, because running was the only thing that made any sense at all. Just ahead of him, Tin Bucket was stumping along in a heavy-footed way, and Cornwall was somewhat amused to find himself wondering, in a time like this, how the metal creature managed the running with three legs. Three, he told himself, was a terribly awkward number.

There was no sign of the horses, or of the Hell-hounds, either. There would, of course, he told himself, be no Hellhounds here. They had started clearing out, undoubtedly, at the first appearance of the wheel of fire—they probably wouldn't stop running, he thought with a chuckle, for the next three days.

Suddenly, just ahead of him, the others were stumbling and falling, disappearing from his view. They ran into something, he told himself, they ran into a trap. He tried to stop his running, but even as he did, the ground disappeared from beneath his feet and he went plunging into nothingness. But only a few feet of nothingness, landing on his back with a thump that left him gasping for breath.

Sniveley off a ways, was yelping, "That clumsy Bucket—he fell on top of me!"

"Mark," said Mary, "are you all right?" Her face came into view, bending over him.

He struggled to a sitting position. "I'm all right," he said. "What happened?"

"We fell into a ditch," said Mary.

Hal came along, crawling on his hands and knees. "We'd better hunker down and stay," he said. "We're well hidden here."

"There are a half a dozen wheels up there," said Mary.

"I don't believe," said Hal, "they are after us. They seem to be concentrating on the castle."

"The horses are gone," said Gib from somewhere in the shadow of the ditch, "and our supplies went with them. We're left here naked in the middle of the wilderness."

"They bucked off some of the packs," said Oliver. "We can salvage some supplies."

Sniveley's agonized voice rose in petulance. "Get off me, you hunk of iron. Let me up."

"I guess I better go," said Hal, "and see what's wrong with him."

Cornwall looked around. The walls of the ditch or hole, or whatever it might be, rose five feet or so above the level of its floor, helping to shelter them from the intense light of the spinning wheels of fire.

He crawled to the wall facing the castle and cautiously raised himself so he could peer out. There was, as Mary had said, more wheels now. They were spinning above the castle, which stood out against the landscape in a blaze of light. Their roaring had changed to a deep hum that seemed to shake his body and burrow deep into his head. As he watched, one of the castle's turrets toppled and fell down. The grinding crunch of falling stone could be heard distinctly over the humming of the wheels.

"There are five of them," said Mary. "Have you the least idea what they are?"

He didn't answer her, for how was one to know? Magic, he thought, then forced the answer back, remembering how Jones had scoffed at him for saying magic whenever he faced a situation he could not comprehend. Certainly something not in the memory of man, for in all the ancient writings he had read, there had been no mention of anything like this— although wait a minute, he told himself, wait just a goddamn minute—there had been something written and in a most unlikely place. In the Book of Ezekiel, chapter one. He tried to remember what had been written there and was unable to, although he realized that there was a lot more to it than simply wheels of fire. He should have, he told himself, spent less time with ancient manuscripts and more time with the Bible.

The wheels had spaced themselves in a circle just above the castle and were spinning rapidly, one following the other, closing in and moving down until it seemed there was just one great fiery, spinning circle suspended above the ancient structure. The deep hum rose to an eerie howling as the ring of fire picked up speed, contracting its diameter and steadily settling down to encompass the castle.

Towers and turrets were crumbling, and underneath the howling could be heard the grinding rumble of falling blocks of masonry. Blue lightning lanced out of the wheel of fire, and the sharp crackling of thunder hammered so hard against the ground that the landscape seemed to buck and weave.

Instinctively Cornwall threw up his arms to shield his head but, fascinated by the sight, did not duck his head. Mary was huddling close against him and off somewhere to his right, someone—Sniveley more than likely, he thought—was squealing in terror.

The air was laced with lightning bolts, etched with the brilliance of the flaming wheel, the very earth was bouncing and the noise was so intense it seemed in itself a force that held one in its grasp.

From the center of the circle of fire, a great cloud was rising, and as Cornwall watched, he realized that what he saw was the dust of shattered stone rising through the circle as smoke from a fire rises through a chimney.

191

Suddenly it was over. The wheel of fire rose swiftly in the air and separated into five smaller wheels of fire that shot quickly upward, swinging about to race to the east. In seconds they disappeared.

As quickly, the world resumed its silence, and all that could be heard were the clicking and crunching sounds of settling masonry, coming from the mound of shattered stone that marked the spot where the Castle of the Chaos Beast had stood.

•••••••••••••••••••••••••••••••••

32

LATE in the afternoon of the third day they came on water. The character of the land had changed. The bleak desert of the Blasted Plain had gradually given way to a still dry, but less forbidding, upland. On the evening of the first day they had seen far in the distance the great blue uplift of the Misty Mountains and now, as they went down to the little stream, the mountains stood, perhaps no more than a day away, a great range that climbed into the sky, leaping from the plain without the benefit of foothills.

They had run out of water before noon of the second day, having been able to salvage only a small skin bag of it from the packs the fleeing horses had bucked off. They had spent some futile hours trying to reach the well in the courtyard of the castle, but the way had been blocked by a mass of fallen stone and still-shifting rubble.

The campfire had been lit, and supper was cooking.

"There'll be enough left for breakfast and that is all," said Mary. "We're down to the last of the cornmeal."

"There'll be game up ahead," said Hal. "Rough going, maybe, but we won't starve."

Sniveley came down the hill and hunkered by the fire. "Nothing stirring," he said. "I scouted all about. Not a thing in sight. No tracks, not even old tracks. No tracks of any kind. We're the only living beings that have ever come here. And we shouldn't be here. We should have gone back."

"It was as far back as it was forward," said Gib.

"Maybe farther. And there is still the ax we're carrying for the Old Ones."

"The Old Ones," said Sniveley, "if we ever find them, whatever they may be, will take that precious ax of yours and smash our skulls with it."

"Quit your complaining, Sniveley," said Hal. "Sure, we've had tough luck. We lost our horses and most of our supplies, but we came out of all that ruckus at the castle without a scratch, and this is more than we could have reasonably expected."

"Yeah," said Sniveley, "and I suppose that when He Who Broods Upon the Mountain comes down and takes the last stitch off our backs and boots us so hard he leaves the mark of footprints on our rumps, you'll be saying we are lucky that he didn't—"

"Oh, stop it," Mary cried. "Stop this squabbling. We are here, aren't we? We all are still alive. We found water before we suffered from the lack of it and—"

"I got thirsty," Sniveley said. "I don't know about the rest of you, but I got so thirsty I was spitting dust."

Bucket came ambling over to the fire and stopped. He stood there, doing nothing at all.

"I wish," said Gib, "I could figure that one out. He doesn't do a thing. He can't talk, and I'm not too sure he hears."

"Don't forget," said Cornwall, "that he was the one who warned us back there at the castle. If it hadn't been for him, we might have been caught flat-footed. . . ."

"Don't forget, as well," said Hal, "that he carried more than his fair share of the supplies we salvaged. He ran out those ropes he uses for arms and latched onto the packs . . ."

"If it hadn't been for him," protested Sniveley, "we never would have got into this mess. Them wheels were after him, I tell you. Whatever they might have been, they never would have bothered with us or with that bunch of creeps who were living

194

in the castle. None of us were that important to them. It was either the Chaos Beast or Tin Bucket that was important to them. They were the ones they were out to get."

"If it hadn't been for the wheels," Gib pointed out, "we still would be penned back there in the castle. The wheels scared the Hellhounds off, and we took some roughing up, but it all worked out for the best."

"It's funny," said Oliver, "how we now can talk so easily of the wheels. At the time we were scared out of our wits of them, but now we can talk quite easily of them. Here is something that we didn't understand, something frightening, something entirely outside any previous experience, and yet now we brush off all the mystery of it and talk about the wheels as if they were common things you might come upon at any corner you turned."

"Thing is," said Hal, "there's been too much happening. There has been so much strangeness that we have become numbed to it. You finally get to a point where you suspend all wonder and begin accepting the unusual as if it were everyday. Back there in the world we came from all of us lived quite ordinary lives. Day followed day without anything unusual happening at all, and we were satisfied that nothing ever happened. We were accustomed to nothing ever happening. On this trip we have become so accustomed to strangenesses that we no longer find them too remarkable. We do not question them. Maybe because we haven't the time to question."

"I have been doing a lot of wondering about the wheels," said Cornwall, "and I'm inclined to agree with Sniveley that their target was either the Chaos Beast or Bucket. More likely the Chaos Beast, it seems to me, for they probably did not know, or those who sent them did not know, the Chaos Beast was dead. It would seem unlikely they would have known of Bucket."

"They could have," Sniveley objected. "Somehow

they could have been able to calculate the time, if they knew about the Beast, when Bucket was about to hatch."

"Which brings us to the question," said Cornwall, "not only of what the wheels were, but what was the Chaos Beast, and what is Bucket? Is Bucket another Chaos Beast?"

"We don't know what the Chaos Beast looked like," said Gib. "Maybe Bucket is a young Chaos Beast and will change when he gets older."

"Perhaps," said Cornwall. "There is a man at Oxford, a very famous savant, who just recently announced that he had worked out the method by which, through some strange metamorphosis, a worm turns into a butterfly. It is unlikely, of course, that he is right. Most of his fellow savants do not agree with him. He has been the butt of much ridicule because of his announcement. But I suppose he could be right. There are many strange occurrences we do not understand. Maybe his principle is right, and it may be that Bucket is the worm that in time will metamorphose into a Chaos Beast."

"I wish," said Mary, "that you wouldn't talk that way in front of Bucket. As if he were just a thing and not a creature like the rest of us. Just a thing to talk about. He might be able to hear, he might understand what you are saying. If that is so, you must embarrass him."

"Look at Coon," said Oliver. "He is stalking Bucket."

Hal half rose from his sitting position, but Cornwall reached out and grabbed him by the arm. "Watch," he said.

"But Coon . . ."

"It's all right," said Cornwall. "It's a game they're playing."

The end of one of Bucket's arms had dropped onto the ground, was lying there, the tip of it quivering just a little. It was the quivering tip of the tentacle that Coon was stalking, not Bucket himself. Coon made a sudden rush; the arm tip, at the last moment, flicked out of his reach. Coon checked his rush and pivoted, reaching out with one forepaw, grasping at the tentacle. His paw closed about it and he went over on his back, grabbing with the second forepaw, wrestling the tentacle. Another tentacle extruded and tickled Coon's rump. Coon released his hold on the first tentacle, somersaulted to grab at the second one.

"Why, Bucket's playing with him," Mary gasped. "Just like you'd use a string to play with a kitten. He even let him catch the tentacle."

Hal sat down heavily. "Well, I'll be damned," he said.

"Bucket's human, after all," said Mary.

"Not human," said Cornwall. "A thing like that never could be human. But he has a response to the play instinct, and that does make him seem just a little human."

"Supper's ready," Mary said. "Eat up. We have breakfast left and that is all."

Coon and Bucket went on playing.

197

33

TOMORROW, Cornwall thought, they'd go on toward the mountains, where they'd seek out, or try to seek out, the Old Ones. And after they had found the Old Ones, or had failed to find them, what would they do then? Surely they would not want to turn about and come back across the Blasted Plain, without horses and more than likely with Hellhounds in wait for their return. One could not be sure, he knew, that the Hellhounds would be waiting, but the possibility that they might be was not something that could be ignored.

He sat on a sandy slope of ground that ran down to the stream, leaning back against a boulder. Off to his left the campfire gleamed through the dark, and he could see the silhouettes of the rest of the party sitting around it. He hoped that for a while they would not miss him and come looking for him. For some reason that he could not completely understand, he'd wanted to be off by himself. To think, perhaps, although he realized that the time for thinking was past. The thinking should have been done much earlier, before they had gone plunging off on this incredible adventure. If there had been some thought put to it, he knew, they might not have set out on it. It had all been done on the impulse of the moment. He had fled the university once he learned that his filching the page of manuscript was known. Although, come to think of it, there had been no real need to flee. There were a hundred places on the campus or in the town where he could have holed up and hidden out. The imagined need to flee had been no more than an excuse to go off on a hunt to find the Old Ones. And from that point onward the expedition had grown by a chain of unlikely circumstances and by the same emotional response to them as he, himself, had experienced—responses that were illogical on the face of them. An unknowing fleeing perhaps, from the sameness of the ordinary life that Oliver and Hal had talked about just a few hours before.

At the sound of a soft rustling behind him, he leaped to his feet. It was Mary.

"I wondered where you were," she said. "I came looking for you. I hope you don't mind."

"I've been saving a place for you," he said. He reached out a hand to guide her to a seat against the boulder, then sat down beside her.

"What are you doing out here?" she asked.

"Thinking," he said. "Wondering. I wonder if we were right to come, what we should do now. Go on, of course, and try to find the Old Ones. But after that, what? And what if we don't find the Old Ones? Will we still go on, stumbling from adventure to adventure, simply going on for the sake of going, for the sake of new things found? A course like that could get us killed. We've been lucky so far."

"We'll be all right," she said. "You've never felt this way before. We will find the Old Ones, and Gib will give them the ax, and everything will work out the way it should."

"We're a long way from home," he said, "and maybe no way back. Or at least no easy way. For myself I don't mind so much. I never had a home except the university, and that wasn't really home. A university is never more than a stopping place. Although for Oliver, I suppose it might be. He lived up in the rafters of the library and had been there for years. But Gib had his marsh, and Hal and Coon had their hollow tree. Even Sniveley had his mine and metal-working shop. And you . . ."

"I had no home," she said, "after my foster parents died. It makes no difference to me now where I am."

199

"It was a thing of impulse," he said, "a sort of harebrained plan that rose out of nothing. I had been interested in the Old Ones—perhaps no more than an academic interest, but somehow it seemed very real. I can't tell you why. I don't know where their attraction lies. I had studied their language, or what purported to be their language. No one, in fact, seemed sure there were such things as Old Ones. Then I ran across the manuscript in which an ancient traveler . . ."

"And you had to go and see," said Mary. "I can't see there's so much wrong with that."

"Nothing wrong with it if only myself were involved. If only the Hermit hadn't died and left the ax in Gib's keeping, if Gib had not saved me from the wolves, if Hal hadn't been a woodsman and a friend of Gib's, if Sniveley had not forged the magic sword—if these things hadn't happened, none of this would be happening now. . . ."

"But it did happen," said Mary, "and no matter about the rest of it, it brought the two of us together. You have no right to shoulder guilt because there is no guilt, and when you try to conjure it up and carry it, you're doing nothing more than belittle the rest of us. There are none of us here against our will. There are none of us who have regrets."

"Sniveley."

"You mean his complaining. That is just his way. That's the way he lives." She laid her head against his shoulder. "Forget it, Mark," she said. "We'll go on and find the Old Ones, and it will be all right in the end. We may even find my parents or some trace of them."

"There's been no trace of them so far," he said. "We should have asked at the castle, but there were so many other things that we never even asked. I blame myself for that. I should have thought to ask."

"I did ask," said Mary. "I asked that dirty little creature with the foxy face."

"And?"

"They stopped at the castle. They stayed for several days to rest. There were Hellhounds all about, there always were Hellhounds hanging around the castle, but they didn't bother them. Think of it, Mark, they walked in peace through the Blasted Plain, they walked in peace through packs of Hellhounds. They're somewhere up ahead, and that is another reason for us to go on."

"You hadn't mentioned that you asked."

"As you said, there were so many other things."

"They walked in peace," said Cornwall. "They must be wonderful. What is there about them—Mary, how well do you remember them?"

"Hardly at all," she said. "Just beauty—beauty for my mother, beauty and comfort. Her face I can remember just a little. A glow with a face imprinted on it. My father, I can't remember him. I love them, of course, but I can't remember why I do. Just the beauty and the comfort, that is all."

"And now you're here," said Cornwall. "A long march behind you, a long march ahead. Food almost gone and one garment to your name."

"I'm where I want to be," she said. She lifted her head, and he cupped her face in his two hands and kissed her tenderly.

"The horn of the unicorn worked," he said. "Oliver, damn his hide, was right."

"You thought of that?" she asked.

"Yes, I did think of that. You still have the horn. How about mislaying it or losing it or something?"

She settled down against him. "We'll see," she said in a happy voice.

THEY stumbled on the Old Ones when they were deep into the mountains. Climbing a sharp ridge that lay between two valleys, they came face to face with them as they reached the crest. Both parties stopped in astonishment and stood facing one another, not more than three hundred feet apart. The little band of Old Ones appeared to be a hunting party. They were short, squat men clothed in furs and carrying stone-tipped spears. Most of them wore grizzled beards, although there were a couple of striplings still innocent of whiskers. There were, altogether, not more than a dozen of them.

In the rear of the band two men shouldered a pole, on which was slung a carcass that appeared disturbingly human.

For a moment no one spoke, then Cornwall said, "Well, we have finally found them. I was beginning to doubt in the last few days that there were any Old Ones."

"You are sure?" asked Hal. "How can you be sure? No one knows what the Old Ones are. That has worried me all along—what are we looking for?"

"There were hints in the accounts written by ancient travelers," said Cornwall. "Never anything specific. No eyewitness accounts, you understand, just hearsay. Very secondhand. No solid evidence. Just horrific little hints that the Old Ones were, in some horrible way, humanoid. Humanoid, but overlaid with abundant myth content. Even the man, whoever he might have been, who wrote the Old

Ones' vocabulary and grammar had nothing to say of the Old Ones themselves. He may have, and that part of his manuscript may have been lost or stolen or for some reason suppressed by some fuddy-duddy churchman centuries ago. I suspected they might be human, but I couldn't be sure. That ax Gib carries smells of human fashioning. Who other than a human could work stone so beautifully?"

"Now that we've found them," said Sniveley, "what do we do about them? Does Gib just go rushing down and give the ax to them? If I were you, Gib, I would hesitate to do that. I don't like the looks of the game they carry."

"I'll go down and talk to them," said Cornwall. "Everyone stand fast. No sudden motions, please. We don't want to frighten them away."

"Somehow," said Sniveley, "they don't look nearly as frightened as I would like them to."

"I'll cover you," said Hal. "If they act hostile, don't try to be a hero."

Cornwall unbuckled his sword belt and handed it and the sword to Mary.

"We're dead right now," wailed Sniveley. "They'll gnaw our bones by nightfall."

Cornwall lifted his hands, with the palms extended outward, and began pacing slowly down the slope.

"We come in peace," he shouted in the language of the Old Ones, hoping as he spoke the words that his pronunciation was acceptable. "No fighting. No killing."

They waited, watching closely as he moved toward them. The two who were carrying the carcass dropped it and moved up with the others.

They made no response to the words he spoke to them. They stood solid, not stirring. Any facial expressions were hidden behind the grizzled beards. They had as yet made no menacing gesture with the spears, but that, he knew, could come at any minute and there'd be nothing to forewarn him.

Six feet away from them he stopped and let his arms fall to his side.

203

"We look for you," he said. "We bring a gift for you."

They said nothing. There was no flicker of expression in their eyes. He wondered fleetingly if they understood a word he said.

"We are friends," he said, and waited.

Finally one of them said, "How we know you friends? You may be demons. Demons take many shapes. We know demons. We are demon hunters."

He gestured at the thing slung upon the pole. A couple of them stepped aside so Cornwall could see it better. It was of human form, but the skin was dark, almost blue. It had a long slender tail and stubby horns sprouted from its forehead. The feet were hoofed.

"We trapped him," said the spokesman for the band. "We trap many. This one is small. Small and young and probably very foolish. But we trap the old as well." He smacked his lips. "Good eating."

"Eating?"

"Cook in fire. Eat." He made a pantomime of putting something in his mouth and chewing. "You eat?"

"We eat," said Cornwall. "But not demons. Not men, either."

"Long ago eat men," said the Old One. "Not now. Only demons. Men all gone. No more men to eat. Plenty demons. Old campfire tales tell of eating men. Not miss men as long as plenty demons. This one"—he gestured at the carcass tied to the pole— "be very tender eating. Not much to go around. Only one small piece for each. But very tender eating." He grinned a gap-toothed grin at the thought of how tender it would be.

Cornwall sensed an easing of the tension. The Old One was talkative, and he took that to be a good sign. You don't gossip with a man you are about to kill. He swiftly examined the other faces. There was no friendliness, but neither was there animosity.

"You sure you are not demons?" asked the Old One.

"We are sure," said Cornwall. "I am a man like you. The others all are friends."

"Demons tricky," said the Old One. "Hate us. We trap so many of them. They do anything to hurt us. You say you have gift for us."

"We have a gift."

The Old One shrugged. "No gift to us. Gift to Old Man. That is the law."

He shook his head. "You still could be demons. How are we to know? You would kill a demon?"

"Yes," said Cornwall, "we would be glad to kill a demon."

"Then you go with us."

"Glad to go with you."

"One more trap to see. You kill demon we find in it. Then we know you not demon. Demon not kill demon."

"What if there is no demon in the trap?"

"There will be demon. We use good bait. No demon can pass by without being caught. This time very special bait. Sure to be a demon. We go. You kill the demon. Then we go home. Good eating. Eat and dance. Give gift to Old Man. Sit and talk. You tell us, we tell you. Good time had by all."

"That sounds good to me," said Cornwall.

All the other Old Ones were grinning at him, lifting their spears across their shoulders. The two who had been carrying the demon picked up the pole. The demon dangled, its tail dragging on the ground.

Cornwall turned and beckoned to those waiting on the hilltop. "It's all right," he shouted. "We are going with them."

They came rapidly down the hill. The talkative spokesman for the Old Ones stayed with Cornwall, but the rest of the hunting party went angling up the slope, heading toward the north.

"What's going on?" asked Hal.

"They've invited us to go along with them. They are trapping demons."

"You mean that thing they're carrying?" asked Oliver.

205

Cornwall nodded. "There's one more trap to visit. They want us to kill the demon to prove we aren't demons."

"That wouldn't prove a thing," Sniveley pointed out. "Men kill men. Look at all the men who are killed by other men. Why shouldn't demons kill demons?"

"Maybe," said Oliver, "the Old Ones just aren't thinking straight. Lots of people have strange ideas."

"They think we are demons?" Mary asked. "How can that be—we have no tails or horns."

"They say demons can change their shapes." He said to the Old One, "My friends cannot speak your tongue. They are telling me they are happy we have met."

"You tell them," said the Old One, "we have big demon feast tonight."

"I'll tell them," Cornwall promised.

Mary handed Cornwall his sword, but before he could strap it on, the Old One said, "We must hurry on. The others are ahead of us. If we aren't there, they may be driven by excitement to kill the demon in the trap, and you must kill that demon. . . ."

"I know we must," said Cornwall. He said to the others, "Let us get going. We can't afford to linger."

"When do I give them the ax?" asked Gib, trotting along beside Cornwall.

"Later on," said Cornwall. "You have to give it to the Old Man of the tribe. Tribal law, I guess. There'll be big doings. A big feast and a dance."

"A feast of what?" asked Sniveley, eyeing the demon dangling from the pole. "If it's the kind of feast I think it will be, I will not eat a bite. I'll starve before I do it."

The Old One was hurrying them along. "I hope there is a big, fat one," he said. "The one we have is small and skinny. We need a big, fat one."

They had crossed the ridge and were running down a steep ravine, with the hunting band a short distance ahead of them. The ravine made a sharp turn, and as the hunters went around the bend, a mighty shouting went up. They came around the bend and there, ahead of them, the hunters were leaping up and down, waving their spears and yelling.

"Wait!" screamed the Old One. "Wait! Don't kill him. Wait for us."

The hunters swung around at the shout and stopped their yelling. But someone else was shouting.

"Let me out of here, goddamnit! What do you think you're doing? A gang of filthy savages!"

Cornwall broke through the milling hunters and skidded to a halt.

"That is no demon," Gib said. "That is our old friend, Jones."

"Jones," yelled Cornwall, "what are you doing here? Whatever happened to you? How did you get in there?"

Jones stood in the center of a small clearing from which rose a great oak tree. Broad bands of shimmering light ran in a brilliant triangle between three metallic poles set in the ground in such a fashion as to enclose the clearing and the oak. Jones was standing near one of the shimmering bands, carrying in one hand a singular contraption made of wood and metal. A naked girl crouched against the oak tree. She didn't seem too frightened.

"Thank God it's you," said Jones. "Where did you pop out from? You made it all the way, it seems, across the Blasted Plain. I never thought you would. I was on my way to hunt for you, but my bike broke down. Now, get me out of here." He waved the strange contraption. "It would be a pity to be forced to mow all the beggars down."

The Old One was jigging up and down. "You can talk with it," he squealed. "You can talk with demons."

"He is no demon," Cornwall said. "He is the same as me. You must turn him loose."

The Old One backed swiftly away. "Demons!" he shouted. "All of you are demons."

Cornwall's hand went to his sword hilt. "Stay where you are," he shouted, drawing the sword with

207

an awkward flourish. He flicked a glance toward the other Old Ones. Spears leveled, they were moving in, but very cautiously.

"Hold it!" Jones shouted and even as he shouted, there was a vicious chattering. Little puffs of dust and flying gouts of earth stitched a line in front of the advancing spearmen. The end of the sticklike contraption in his hands twinkled with an angry redness, and there was the bitter scent of something burning.

The line of spearmen came to a halt. They stood half-frozen, but with the spears still leveled.

"Next time," Jones said calmly, "I'll hold it a little higher. I'll blast out your guts."

The Old One who had backed away had stopped in his tracks. Staring in fascination at the sword held in Cornwall's hand, he sank slowly to his knees.

"Throw down the spears," yelled Cornwall. The line of spearmen dropped their weapons.

"Watch them, Hal," said Cornwall. "If they make a move . . ."

"The rest of you get over to one side," said Hal. "Jones has some sort of weapon, and he needs a clear field for it."

The Old One who had fallen to his knees now was groveling on the ground and moaning. Cornwall, sword still in hand, walked forward and jerked him to his feet. The man shrank back and Cornwall hauled him closer.

"What is your name?" asked Cornwall.

The Old One tried to speak, but his teeth were chattering and no words would come.

"Come on, speak up," said Cornwall. "Tell me your name."

The Old One broke into speech. "The shining blade," he wailed. "The shining blade. There are tales of the shining blade."

He stared in fearful fascination at the glittering sword.

"All right," said Cornwall. "So it is a shining

blade. Now tell me your name. I think the two of us should know one another's names."

"Broken Bear," the Old One said.

"Broken Bear," said Cornwall. "I am Cornwall. It is a strange name, Cornwall. It is a magic name. Now say it."

"Cornwall," said Broken Bear.

"Let me out of here," bawled Jones. "Won't someone let me out?"

Bucket walked toward the shining fence. He snapped out a tentacle and seized one of the poles. Sparks flared all about him, and the shining bands wavered, crackling and popping. With a heave Bucket uprooted the pole and flung it to one side. The shining bands were no longer there.

"And so," said Sniveley, "there is the end to all this foolishness. Why don't you, Mark, give that old friend of yours a swift kick in the pants?"

"There is nothing I'd like better," Cornwall said, "but it would be wiser not to do it. We want them to be friends."

"Some friends they turned out to be," said Sniveley.

Jones came striding toward Cornwall, the weapon held carelessly in the crook of one arm. He held out his hand, and Cornwall grasped it.

"What was that all about?" asked Jones, gesturing toward Broken Bear. "I couldn't understand a word of it."

"I spoke the language of the Old Ones."

"So these are the Old Ones that you talked about. Hell, they're nothing but a bunch of Neanderthals. Although I must admit they are very skillful trappers. They use the proper kind of bait. There was this girl, not so bad to look at, although not ravishing, but naked as a jaybird, tied to the tree and doing a moderate amount of screeching because there were wolves about—"

"Neander-whats?"

"Neanderthals. A very primitive kind of men. In

209

my world there aren't any of them. Died about thirty thousand years ago or more. . . ."

"But you said that our two worlds split much more recently than that, or at least you implied it."

"Christ, I don't know," said Jones. "I don't know anything anymore. Once I thought I did, but now it seems I know less and less and can't be certain of anything at all."

"You said you were coming to meet us. How did you know where to look for us and what happened to you? We went up to your camp and it was apparent you had left."

"Well, you talked about the Old Ones, and I got the impression you were hell-bent to find them, and I knew you'd have to cross the Blasted Plain to reach them. You see, I tried to steal a march on you. You said something about a university, something, I gather, that that funny little gnome of yours had told you."

"So you went hunting for the university?"

"Yes, I did. And found it. Wait until I tell you—"

"But if you found it—"

"Cornwall, be reasonable. It's all there, all the records, all the books. But in several funny kinds of script. I couldn't read a line of it."

"And you thought perhaps we could."

"Look, Cornwall, let's play ball. What difference does it make? Our two worlds are separated. We belong to different places. But we can still be reasonable. You do something for me, I do something for you. That's what makes the world go round."

"I think," said Hal, "we'd better get this expedition moving. The natives are getting jittery."

"They still aren't convinced we aren't demons," Cornwall said. "We'll have to gag down some demon meat to prove it to them. Once they get a fool idea planted in their minds . . ."

He turned to Broken Bear. "Now we go home," he said. "We all are friends. We eat and dance. We will talk the sun up. We will be like brothers."

210

Broken Bear whimpered, "The shining blade! The shining blade!"

"Oh, Christ," said Cornwall, "he has the shining blade on the brain. Some old ancient myth told and retold for centuries around the campfire. So all right, I'll put it away."

He sheathed the sword.

He said to Broken Bear, "Let us get started. Pick up the bait you used. All of us are hungry."

"It is lucky," said Broken Bear, "we have something else than demon or it would be a starving feast. But we have at home a bear, a deer, a moose. There will be plenty. We can wallow in it."

Cornwall flung an arm about his shoulder. "Fine for you," he said. "We shall grease our faces. We shall eat until we can eat no more. We shall do it all with you."

Broken Bear grinned his snaggle-toothed grin. "You no demons," he said. "You are gods of shining blade. The fires burn high tonight and everyone is happy. For the gods come visiting."

"Did you say something about a feast?" asked Jones. "Look, coming down the hill. The son of a bitch can smell out good eating a million miles away."

It was the Gossiper, his rags fluttering in the wind, his staff stumping sturdily as he strode along. The raven perched on his shoulder, squalling obscenities and looking even more moth-eaten, Cornwall thought, than he had seen it.

Behind the Gossiper, the little white dog with spectacles limped along.

35

THE Old Man was not in good shape. He had only one eye and a scar ran down from where the missing eye had been, slantwise across the cheek to the base of the neck.

He touched the empty socket with his forefinger and with it traced the scar. The hand had three fingers missing; there was only the forefinger and the thumb.

He fixed Cornwall with his one remaining, glittering eye.

"Hand to hand," he said. "Me and him. An old boar bear almost as mean as I was. And I was the one who walked away. Not the bear. He tore me up, but I was the one who walked away. We ate him. We dragged him home and cooked him, and he was the toughest meat I ever knew. Tough to eat, hard to chew. But his was the sweetest flesh I have ever eaten."

He cackled at his joke. Most of his teeth were gone.

"I couldn't eat him now," he said. He pointed at his still open mouth. "The teeth fell out. Do you know why teeth fall out?"

"No, I don't," said Cornwall.

"I'm no good no more," said the Old Man. "I'm stiff in the legs. I have only one good hand. One eye is gone. But these fellows here," he said, gesturing at the group of Old Ones who squatted behind and to either side of him, "these fellows, they don't dare to tackle me. They know I am mean and tricky. I was always mean and tricky. Wouldn't have lived this long if I hadn't been mean and tricky. I hear you are a god and carry a shining blade."

"I carry a shining blade," said Cornwall, "but I never claimed to be a god. It was Broken Bear—"

The Old Man made a disrespectful noise. "Broken Bear is full of wind," he said. He jerked out his elbow and caught Broken Bear squarely in the ribs. "Aren't you, Broken Bear?" he asked.

"No more than you, broken man," said Broken Bear. "You have more wind than any of us. It all comes through your mouth."

"He would like to take my place," said the Old Man. "But he won't. One hand on that big neck of his and I would strangle him. The good hand, not the bad hand. I'd take care to grab him with the good hand." He guffawed toothlessly.

"You talk a good fight," said Broken Bear, "but someone has to help you up. You can't get to your feet alone."

"I wouldn't have to get to my feet to strangle you," said the Old Man. "I could do it sitting down."

"What's all this jabbering about?" asked Jones.

"He's bragging about how beat up he is," said Cornwall.

Out beyond the corner where they sat, three great fires had been built on the ledge that extended out from the rock shelter. Grills of green wood had been set up over the fires, and on them meat was cooking. There was a great scurrying about, women bustling with the importance of the moment, racing children romping about and getting underfoot, packs of dogs circulating haphazardly, with a wary eye kept out for a flailing foot, but at the same time maintaining a close watch on the carcasses on the grills.

Coon, crouched between Hal and Mary, peeked out to have a quick look at the dogs. Mary hauled him back. "You stay put," she said. "I know you licked a half dozen of them, but now you are outmatched."

213

Hal grinned. "Did you ever see the like of it? They never even laid a tooth on him. Let him get backed into a corner and he can hold his own."

"Nevertheless," said Mary, "he stays here. He hasn't anything to prove. He handled those that jumped him and that's enough for one day."

Gib nodded at the Old Man. "When do I give him the ax?" he asked.

"Give him time," said Jones. "He's probably building up to it. Broken Bear would have told him there was a gift, so he must know. But there's tribal protocol in a thing like this—very solemn protocol. He can't appear too anxious. He must be very urbane. He must uphold his dignity."

The Old Man was saying, "You have traveled far. You come from unknown lands. You crossed the Blasted Plain. You outran the Hellhounds. But how did you get past the Castle of the Chaos Beast?"

"We did not outrun the Hellhounds," Cornwall told him. "The Hellhounds ran from us. We stopped at the castle and the castle now is a heap of ruins. The Chaos Beast is dead."

The Old Man raised his hand to his mouth to express amazement. "Truly," he said, "you indeed are gods. And this one who travels with you who is not honest flesh and that travels on three legs, as would no honest man . . ."

"He is magic," Cornwall said, "as is my shining blade."

"And the horn the female carries? It is magic, too? It comes from a unicorn."

"You know of unicorns? There are still unicorns about?"

"In the Place of Knowing. There are unicorns in the Place of Knowing." He made a gesture out into the darkness. "Beyond the gorge," he said. "No man travels there. It is guarded by Those Who Brood Upon the Mountain."

Cornwall turned to Jones. "He is telling me about the Place of Knowing. He must mean the university. He talks about a gorge and says that it is guarded by

214

Those Who Brood Upon the Mountain. Not, you will note, He Who Broods Upon the Mountain."

Jones nodded. "Undoubtedly he has it right. He should know. A bit of bad translation on the part of someone. That is all it is. And there is a gorge. It is the very gorge we traveled to reach this place. I know. I traveled it."

"Seeing none of Those Who Brood Upon the Mountain?"

"Not a one," said Jones. "But I traveled on a bike and, as you may recall, it makes hell's own amount of noise. Maybe I scared them off. Maybe they like to know what they are guarding against. Too, I was traveling the wrong way. I was traveling from the university, not toward it. There's something I want to talk with you about. This robot of yours . . ."

"What is a robot?"

"The metal man who's traveling with you."

"Later," Cornwall said. "I will tell you later." He turned back to the Old Man. "About this Place of Knowing. Could we travel there?"

"It would be death to try it."

"But there must have been others who traveled there. Just a few seasons ago. A man and woman . . ."

"But they were different," said the Old Man.

"How different?"

"They went in peace. They traveled hand in hand. They had no weapons, and there was only goodness in them."

"They stopped here. You saw them?"

"They stayed with us for a time. They could not talk with us. They did not need to talk. We knew the goodness in them."

"You tried to warn them?"

"We did not need to warn them. There was no need of warning. They could walk in safety anywhere they wished. There is nothing that could touch them."

Cornwall spoke softly to Mary, "He says your parents were here. Then went on to the university. He

215

says it was safe for them. He says there was nothing that could hurt them."

"Anywhere anyone else can go, we can go," said Jones.

"No," said Cornwall. "Mary's folks had something special. It is past all understanding. . . ."

"Broken Bear tells me," said the Old Man, "that you carry something for us."

"That is right," said Cornwall. "Not a gift. Not from us. It is something that belongs to you."

He motioned to Gib. "Give him the ax," he said.

Gib held out the package, and the Old Man grasped it in his one good hand. He put it on the ground in front of him and unwrapped it. Once it was unwrapped, he sat there staring at it, unspeaking. Finally, he lifted his head and stared intently at Cornwall with his one good, glittering eye.

"You mock us," he said.

"Mock you!" Cornwall exclaimed. "All we are doing—"

"Listen," said the Old Man. "Listen very closely. . . ."

"What is going on?" asked Gib. "Did I do something wrong?"

"Something's wrong," said Cornwall. "I don't know what it is."

"The old stories say," the Old One said, "that this ax was given long ago, in friendship, to a man of another place who passed our way. Now you bring it back and the friendship ends."

"I don't know," said Cornwall. "I know none of this."

The Old Man bellowed at him, "Our head is in the dust. Our gift has been thrown back into our face. There is now no friendship."

He surged to his feet and kicked the ax to one side. Behind him the other Old Ones were rising, gripping their spears.

Cornwall came to his feet, jerking out the sword.

Behind him came a snicking sound. "I'll mow 'em down," said Jones. "You stack 'em to one side."

"Not right yet," said Cornwall. "Maybe we can reason with them."

"Reason, hell," said Jones in a disgusted tone.

"We fear no gods," the Old Man said. "We will not be mocked by gods. We die before we're mocked."

"We did not mock you," Cornwall said, "but if you want to do some dying, now's the time to start."

The Old Man staggered forward a step or so, lifting his arms as if to ward off an unseen enemy. Something protruded from his chest and blood ran down his belly. Slowly he collapsed, fighting to stay erect. Cornwall, startled, stepped back to give him room to fall. When he fell, it could be seen that a spear shaft protruded from his back.

Broken Bear stood, with empty hands, behind him.

"And now," he said, "the old bag of wind is dead. You and I can talk."

A deathly silence had fallen. The children no longer ran and screamed. The women stopped their chatter. The dogs swiftly slunk away. The men who stood with Broken Bear said nothing. They stood unmoving, spears grasped in their hands, faces hard.

Broken Bear motioned toward the fallen leader. "He would have got us killed," he said. "Some of us, all of you. We didn't want that, did we?"

"No," said Cornwall. "No, I guess we didn't."

"I still do not know," said Broken Bear, "if you be gods or demons. I think one thing one time, then I think the other. The one thing I do know is we do not want you here."

"We will gladly go," said Cornwall.

"But first," said Broken Bear, "you barter for your lives."

"I am not sure," said Cornwall, "that we will barter with you. All of us, you say, and you may be right. Some of you, you say, but let us change that to say an awful lot of you. And I promise you, my friend, you will be the first."

"We will not be greedy," said Broken Bear. "All we want is the stick that smokes."

217

"What is going on?" asked Jones.

"He wants the stick that smokes. Your weapon."

"It would do the damn old fool no good. He'd probably shoot himself. You have to know how to use the thing. And I'll not give it up."

"He says it is dangerous to one who does not know it," Cornwall told Broken Bear. "It can kill the one who has it if you're not friends with it. It is powerful magic and not for everyone. Only a great wizard can learn how to use it."

"We want it," insisted Broken Bear, "and the horn the female carries and the shining blade."

"No," said Cornwall.

"Let us talk deep wisdom," said Broken Bear. "You give us the stick, the horn, the blade. We give you your lives." He made a thumb at the fallen Old Man. "Better than he offer. He have many dead."

"Don't bicker with the bastard," said Jones.

Cornwall put out a hand and shoved Jones' weapon to one side.

"They have us surrounded," said Hal. "We're in the middle of them. The women and the kids have grabbed up clubs and stones—"

Someone from behind shoved Cornwall roughly to one side.

"Hey, what's going on?" yelled Jones.

A ropelike tentacle reached down and wrenched the sword from Cornwall's grip.

"You can't do that!" yelled Cornwall.

Another tentacle slammed against his chest and thrust him off his feet. As he scrambled up, he saw that there were many tentacles—as if the air were full of writhing, darting ropes. They extended up and out into the press of Old Ones who were shrinking back against the shelter wall. The tentacles among them were snapping in and out, snatching spears out of their hands. One tentacle had a dozen bundled spears and, as Cornwall watched, snapped up another.

"What the hell is going on?" yelped Jones. "He took away the rifle—"

218

"Bucket," Cornwall bellowed, "what the hell are you doing?"

The Old Ones who had been with Broken Bear were huddled against the wall, but out around the cooking fires there was a screeching and a running as the women and children rushed wildly about. Dogs went yelping, tails tucked between their legs.

Bucket was hurling the spears he had collected out beyond the shelter's edge, out into the darkness of the gorge. Other tentacles, sweeping across the area out around the fires, scooped up clubs and rocks that had been dropped by the women and the children, heaving them after the spears.

"He's gone mad," yelled Mary. "He even grabbed the horn."

"I'll cave him in," screamed Jones, "if he damages that rifle."

Bucket bristled with tentacles. He seemed to be a metal body suspended from many tentacles, bearing some resemblance to a spider dangling in a sagging, broken web. Tentacles seemed to have issued from each of the holes that perforated his body.

Now the tentacles were pushing them along, herding them across the ledge, to where the path wound up from the gorge.

"He's got the right idea," said Gib. "Let's get out of here."

Down in the gorge there was a howling and screaming. Some of the women and children had either fallen or had scrambled down in the darkness, escaping from the ledge. The group of Old Ones who had been huddled against the wall were moving out, but very cautiously.

As Cornwall and the others came to the path, Bucket pushed them along. He handed the horn back to Mary, the ax to Gib, the bow to Hal, and the sword to Cornwall. Jones' rifle he hurled out into the center of the ledge.

"Why, goddamn you!" frothed Jones. "I'll bust you up for scrap. I'll dent you out of shape—"

219

"Move along," growled Cornwall. "He knows what he's doing."

Bucket snapped out a twirling tentacle, wrapped it around the bear roasting on the grill, holding it well up in the air. Drops of sizzling grease spattered on Cornwall's face.

"Now we get supper," said Oliver, licking his chops.

"And," said Sniveley with relief, "we'll not have to eat any demon meat."

36

●●●●●●●●●●●●●●●●●●●●●●●●●●●●●●●●●●●●●

"WE'RE safe here," said Hal. "They can't try to
follow us. They're no great shakes, I'd judge, at
prowling in the dark. And they're scared purple of
the gorge."

"You're sure this is the gorge they spoke of?"
asked Cornwall.

Jones nodded. "It is the one I followed out of the
university. I must have passed right by the Old Ones'
camp and not even noticed it. And now, suppose you
tell me about this robot of yours? If I had a sledge
at hand, I'd so some hammering on him. Although
I do admit he managed to get us out of a tight spot
in a most efficient manner. I only wish he could have
warned us a bit ahead of time."

"He couldn't warn us," said Hal. "He can't talk."

"That was a good gun," Jones mourned. "It set
me back a heap. What made him do it, do you
think?"

"I wouldn't try to answer that," said Cornwall.
"He's not been with us very long, and I suppose
he'd have to be with us for years before we began
to understand him. Apparently he thought it was not
a good idea for you to retain your weapon. I can't
agree with him, of course, but he must have had a
reason."

"Maybe it was because this thing you call a weapon was too far out of its time," said Sniveley. "Maybe he felt it had no right to be here. There's a name
for something like that. Anachronism, I think, although that doesn't sound quite right."

"Much as I regret losing it," said Jones, "I must admit that I feel no great compulsion to go back to get it. If I never see an Old One again, it will be much too soon. And in any case it is probably out of kilter. This Tin Bucket of yours did not toss it easily. When it hit, it bounced."

After traveling for miles, stumbling down the gorge in the light of a sickly moon, they had finally stopped to build a fire in the shelter of a huge pile of tumbled boulders. They had feasted on the bear and then had settled down to talk.

"I'm dying to know what is going on," said Jones. "Perhaps now you'll tell me."

Lounging against a boulder, Cornwall told the story, with much help from the others, especially Sniveley.

"The rings of fire," said Jones. "Most intriguing. They sound very much like the flying saucers with which my world is both amused and plagued. You say they were destructive."

"Extremely so," said Cornwall. "They pulverized a castle."

"After the Chaos Beast was dead."

"We think it was dead," said Hal. "It seemed to most of us that we experienced abundant evidence it was. We are considerably unsure why the wheels of fire incident should have come about. By and large we are inclined to believe the attack was aimed at Bucket. They probably figured they would hit the castle about the time that he was hatched. As it chanced, we speeded up the hatching by a few hours' time."

"The Chaos Beast must have known the danger," said Jones. "That is why it ordered the people of the castle to haul Bucket out as soon as it was dead."

"Bucket probably knew as well," said Gib. "He was the one who insisted that we leave the castle."

Jones asked, "Have you had any chance to study this stormily born robot? Have you any data on him?"

Cornwall frowned. "If you mean by data, facts and

observations laboriously arrived at, the answer is no. I would suspect your world is much more concerned with data than we are. We know only a few things— that he seems to be made of metal, that he has no eyes and yet can see, that he cannot talk nor does he eat, and still it seems to me . . ."

"He gave us warning to flee the castle," said Gib. "He turned himself into a packhorse for us, carrying more than his share when we crossed the Blasted Plain. He destroyed the magic of the demon trap and this night he extracted us from a situation that could have cost our lives."

"And he plays with Coon," said Mary. "Coon likes him. And I don't think we should be talking like this about him, with him just standing over there. He must know what we are saying, and it may embarrass him."

Bucket didn't look embarrassed. He didn't look like anything at all. He stood on the other side of the fire. All his tentacles were retracted with the exception of one that was half-extruded, the end of it shaped in an intricate, boxlike form, resting on what one might think of as his chest.

"That tentacle is a funny business," said Oliver. "I wonder if it has any meaning. Are we supposed to notice it and get some meaning from it?"

"It's ritual," said Sniveley. "Some silly ritualistic gesture, probably done for some satisfaction that its symbolism may afford him."

Jones squinted at him. "I think," he said, "he is not of this earth. I think the Chaos Beast was not of this earth, either, or the wheels of fire. I think that here we deal with alien beings from deep outer space. They all came from some distant star."

"How could that be?" asked Cornwall. "The stars are no more than celestial lights set by God's mercy in the firmament. From a magic world, perhaps, from some place hidden and forbidden to us, but not from the stars."

"I refuse," Jones said icily, "to conduct a seminar

for you on what the astronomers of my world have discovered. It would waste my time. You are blind to everything but magic. Run up against something that you can't understand and out pops that all-inclusive concept."

"Then," Hal said, soothingly, "let us not discuss it. I agree there can be no meeting of the minds. Nor is it essential that there should be."

"We have told you our story," Mary said. "Now, why don't you tell us yours? We went seeking you, to ask if you would join us in our journey across the Blasted Plain, but we found you gone."

"It was Cornwall's doing," said Jones. "He dropped a hint about a university. He did not seem to place too much emphasis on it, but he was wonderfully intrigued. Although he did not say so, I had the impression that the university was in fact his goal. So, in my devious and unmoral way, I decided I'd steal a march on him."

"But how could you know the location of it?" asked Cornwall. "And how could you have gotten there?"

"The location," said Jones, grinning. "Mostly a guess. I studied a map."

"But there are no maps."

"In my world there are. In my world these are not the Misty Mountains, nor the Blasted Plain. They are normal geographies settled by normal people, surveyed and mapped and with roads running into the far reaches of them. So I used the machine that enables me to move between my world and yours and went back to my world. There I studied the maps, made my guess, had my machine trucked—by that I mean I used another machine to move my traveling machine to the point in my world that corresponds with the same terrain I believed the university was located in your world. If this all sounds confusing . . ."

"It does," said Sniveley, "but proceed in any case."

"I then came back to this world, and my guess had been a good one. I landed only a couple of miles from the university. I spent a few days there, enough to know I needed help. As I told you, I found books and documents, but couldn't read a word of them. Then I thought of you. I knew you would try to make it across the Blasted Plain, and I hoped that Cornwall, with his years of study at Wyalusing, might be able to read the books. And I also had a hunch you might need some help. So I started out. You know the rest of it.

"The university? I've never seen anything quite like it. One huge building, although from a distance it has the look of many buildings. A place you might think fairies had built. A place, Sir Mark, such as your magic might have built. It looks like froth and lace, as if the hand of man had no part in it. . . ."

"Perhaps," said Sniveley, "the hand of man had not."

"There were farmlands and garden plots about it, and, while the crops had all been harvested, it was quite apparent that someone had worked to grow the crops and to take in the harvest. There was cattle. There were pigs and chickens and a few rather scrawny horses—peacocks, ducks, geese, pigeons. Enough animals and fowl and farmland to feed a substantial population. But there was no one there. At times, as I prowled about, it seemed there was someone watching, and at times I thought I caught sight of figures scurrying out of sight, but no one came forth to greet me, no one watched me leave. They, whoever they might be, were hiding from me."

"We are glad, of course," said Sniveley, "to have heard this tale from you, for it is a most intriguing one. But the question now is what do we do?"

"We have to go on," said Cornwall. "We can't go back across the Blasted Plain. Without horses we would never make it."

"There are the Hellhounds, too," said Gib.

225

"We can't go back, you say," said Sniveley. "That's because you are dying to see the university. The point of it is that you should not see it, none of us should see it. You have your holy places and we have ours, and many of ours have been desecrated and obliterated. The university is one of the few places we have left, and it is left only because the knowledge of its existence has been closely guarded."

"I don't know about the rest of you," said Mary, "but I am going on. My parents passed this way, and if they are still alive, I mean to find them."

"Your parents," said Jones. "I know but little of them. I searched the Witch House for some evidence of them but found nothing. I would wager that if you strung that witch up by her heels and built a good fire underneath her, there'd be evidence forthcoming. But I had not the stomach for it. Up in my world there is no record of them, of anyone other than myself who has come into this world. But from what little I have heard I would gather they are people from my world. Perhaps people who were born some centuries after me. For witness: I must use a technological contraption to travel here, and there is no evidence they used a machine at all. In the centuries beyond my time investigators from my world may be able to travel here without benefit of machinery."

"There is a great deal in what Sniveley has to say about the university's sacred status," Cornwall said with a judicious air. "We should not intrude where we are not wanted, although the hard fact of the matter is, that we have nowhere else to go. I think everyone is agreed we can't go back. Not only are there the Hellhounds on the Blasted Plain, but now there are the Old Ones as well. By morning they will have retrieved their spears and regained their courage. I doubt very much they'll follow us down the gorge, for their fear of it seems quite genuine; but I would think it might be dangerous for us to attempt to make our way back past them. The best we can

226

say, Sniveley, is that we pledge ourselves to keep our lips forever sealed and that we will commit no desecration."

Sniveley grumbled. "It's nothing I would count on, for most people, given a chance, become blabbermouths. But I suppose it must be accepted, for we are forced to it. I agree we can't go back the way we came."

"It was a wild goose chase all around," said Cornwall, "and I am sincerely sorry that we made it. I feel responsible."

"The fault was mostly mine," said Gib. "I was the one who insisted that I must deliver with my own hands the ax made by the Old Ones."

"It was no one's fault," said Mary. "How could anyone have ever guessed the Old Ones would react as they did?"

"So we go on," said Hal. "I wonder what we'll find."

Somewhere far off a wolf howled, and, listening to the howl in the fallen silence, they waited for another howl to answer, but there was no answer. The fire was burning low, and Hal threw more wood on it.

Up the gorge a twig snapped loudly in the silence and they leaped to their feet, moving away from the fire.

A tattered figure came blundering down the gorge, his staff thumping on the ground as he walked along. The ragged raven clutched his shoulder desperately, and behind him the little white dog limped faithfully along.

"My God," exclaimed Cornwall, "it is the Gossiper. We had forgotten all about him."

"He intended that we should," Sniveley said nastily. "He slips in and out of your consciousness. It is the nature of him. Now you see him, now you don't. And when you don't see him, you never even think of him. You forget him easily because he wants you to forget. He is a slippery character."

227

"Dammit, man," Jones bellowed at the Gossiper, "where have you been? Where did you disappear to?"

"If my nostrils do not deceive me," said the Gossiper, "there is good roast meat about. A very gorgeous roast. I hunger greatly. . . ."

"Hell," said Jones, "you forever hunger greatly."

• •

37

IT was late afternoon and they were almost through the gorge when the first dot appeared in the sky. As they stood and watched, there were other dots.

"Just birds," said Gib. "We are getting jumpy. We are almost there but are convinced from what the Old Ones told us that something is bound to happen. You said we were almost through the gorge, didn't you, Master Jones?"

Jones nodded.

"What bothers me about those dots," said Hal, "is that the Old Ones talked about Those Who Brood Upon the Mountain. And the things that brood are birds, hatching out their eggs."

"You came through the gorge," Cornwall said to Jones, "and nothing happened to you. Nothing even threatened you."

"I'm convinced," said Jones, "that it was only because I was going in the right direction. It would seem logical that whatever's here is here to protect the university. They'd pay no attention to someone who was leaving."

There were more dots now, circling but dropping lower as they circled.

The walls of rock rose up from the gorge's narrow floor, shutting out the sun. Only at high noon would there be sunlight in this place. Here and there trees, mostly cedar and other small evergreens, sprouted from the rock faces of the wall, clinging stubbornly to little pockets of soil lodged in the unevenness of the rock. The wind moaned as it blew along the tortuous course the gorge pursued.

"I don't like this place," said Sniveley. "It puts a chill into my bones."

"And here I stand," lamented Jones, "without a weapon to my hand other than this driftwood cudgel I managed to pick up. If I only had the rifle. If that stupid robot had not thrown away my rifle . . ."

The stupid robot stood unperturbed by what Jones had said—if, indeed, he had heard what had been said. All his tentacles were retracted except for the one on his chest, which lay arranged in a boxlike fashion.

The dots were dropping lower, and now it could be seen that they were enormous birds with a monstrous wingspread.

"If I only had my glasses, I could make out what they are," said Jones. "But, no, of course, I haven't got my glasses. I persuaded myself that I had to travel light. It's a goddamn wonder I brought anything at all. The only two things I had that counted were the rifle and the bike, and now both of them are gone."

"I can tell you what they are," said Hal.

"You have sharp eyes, my friend."

"He has forest eyes," said Gib. "A hunter's eyes."

Hal said, "They are harpies."

"The meanest things in the Enchanted Land," screeched Sniveley. "Meaner than the Hellhounds. And us out in the open."

Steel rasped as Cornwall drew his blade. "You're getting good at that," Hal said nonchalantly. "Almost smooth as silk. If you'd practice just a little."

The harpies were plunging down in a deadly dive, their wings half-folded, their cruel, skull-like human faces equipped with deadly beaks thrust out as they dived.

Hal's bowstring twanged, and one of the harpies broke out of the dive and tumbled, turning end for end, its folded wings coming loose and spreading out limply in the air. The string twanged again, and a second one was tumbling.

The others waited for them and the Gossiper,

backed against a rocky wall, held his staff at ready. The little lame dog crouched between his feet and the raven reared on his shoulder, squalling.

"Let me get just one good crack at them," said the Gossiper, almost as if he were praying or, more likely, talking to himself. "I'll crack their stupid necks. I hate the filthy things. I need not be here, but I cannot go away right yet. I've greased my gut with this company, not once but twice, and my Fido and their Coon get along together."

"Get down," Cornwall told Mary. "Close against the ground. Stay right here beside me."

Sniveley and Oliver had hastily gathered a small pile of rocks and now stood on either side of it, with rocks clutched in their hands.

The harpies were almost on top of them and now shifted the direction of their dive, pivoting in midair so that they presented their massively taloned feet rather than their beaked heads.

Cornwall swung his sword and the singing blade sliced off the feet of a plunging harpy. The heavy body, falling to the ground, bounced and rolled. The vicious beak of the wounded monster stabbed at Hal's leg as it rolled past, but missed the stroke.

Standing close to the Gossiper, Bucket was the center of a network of lashing tentacles, knocking the diving harpies off their mark, catching them and hurling them against the stony walls.

Jones, swinging his club with lusty will, knocked down two of the attackers. The third got through, fastening one claw on his arm, trying to reach his face with the other. The mighty wings beat heavily to lift him. Hal, hearing Jones' startled yell, swung about and sent an arrow into the body of the monster. Both the harpy and Jones fell heavily. Jones jerked free, and with his club beat in the harpy's skull. His left arm, streaming blood, hung limply.

The Gossiper beat off an attack with his staff, the raven screaming in triumph. Oliver and Sniveley sturdily kept on pegging rocks.

Gib cut down two of the attackers with his ax

231

while Cornwall, swinging a deadly, gleaming blade, fought off harpy after harpy. A half a dozen wounded harpies hopped and fluttered about the rocky floor of the gorge. The air was filled with floating feathers.

One of the harpies, missing its plunge at Sniveley, perhaps diverted by the barrage of rocks that Oliver and Sniveley kept up, apparently quite by accident hooked one of its claws in Sniveley's belt and started to beat skyward. Sniveley squalled in terror, and Hal, seeing what had happened, winged an arrow that drove through the creature's neck. It fell heavily, dragging Sniveley with it.

The harpies drew off, laboring mightily to drive their massive bodies skyward.

Cornwall lowered his sword and looked about. Mary crouched at his feet. Sniveley, snarling oaths, was pulling himself free of the dead harpy's grasping talon. Hal lowered his bow and watched the retreating harpies.

"They'll be back," he said, "taking only enough time to regroup. And I have but three arrows left. I could retrieve some from the bodies of the harpies, but that will take some time."

Sniveley, still spitting fury, came limping up the gorge. He raged at Hal, "That arrow you loosed almost hit me. I could feel the wind of it going past my ear."

"Would you rather I had let it haul you off?" asked Hal.

"You should be more careful," Sniveley yelled.

Cornwall asked Jones, "How badly are you hurt?"

"My arm is deeply cut. It will stiffen, and I fear there will be infection." He said to Hal, "I thank you for your shot."

"We'll be hard pressed," said Cornwall, "to fight them off next time. We were lucky this time. I think that our resistance considerably surprised them."

Now heavy shadows lay within the gorge. The sun no longer lighted anything but a thin segment of the soaring walls of rock. Black pools of darkness lay here and there in the sharp angles of the floor.

"There is a way," said the Gossiper, "by which we may be able to evoke some help. I am not too certain, but I think it might work."

Bucket stood stolidly where he had been standing all the time, his tentacles now retracted except for the one, folded in its boxlike conformation, resting on his chest.

The Gossiper reached out his staff and touched the folded tentacle with the tip of it, holding out his other hand.

"Please," he said. "Please give it to me. It may be the one thing that will save us."

Bucket stirred, began deliberately to unwind the tentacle as they watched. Finally, they could see what he had been holding—the fist ax of the Old Ones.

"He cleaned the floor of the shelter of all the stones and clubs," said Gib. "That was when he got it."

Bucket held out the ax to the Gossiper.

"Thank you," said the Gossiper, taking it.

He fit it in his hand and raised it high into the air, beginning a wild, melodious chant. The narrow walls caught the singsong phrases and flung them back and forth so that the little area between them seemed to be filled with many-voiced chanting, as if a choir were chanting. As the chant went on, the shadows deepened even further, and in the shadows there was a stirring and a sound—the sound of many padding feet.

Mary screamed, and Cornwall jerked up his sword, then lowered it slowly. "God save us now," he said.

There seemed to be hundreds of them, little more than shadows in the shadows, but delineated enough even in the gloom so they could be seen for what they were—great brutish gnarly men, naked for large part, although some of them wore pelts about their middles. They slouched on knees that did not want to straighten out, and they walked bent forward from the waist. They carried shafts with crude stone points attached, and their eyes gleamed redly in the gloom.

High in the brightness of the sky, the ranks of harpies ceased to spiral upward and began their dive.

They hurtled down in a mass attack and Cornwall, watching, knew that this time there was no chance to stop them. He reached out his free arm and drew Mary close against him.

Savage yells drowned out the chanting of the Gossiper. The gnarly men were screaming in a frenzy and shaking their spears at the diving harpies. The shadowy men moved in closer, crowding in. The gorge seemed filled with them.

The harpies plunged down between the looming walls. Then, suddenly, the charge was broken. In midair they windmilled their wings to check their plunge, bumping into one another, a flurry of beating wings and flying feathers. They squalled in surprise and outrage, and beneath them the gnarly men howled in exultant triumph.

The Gossiper ceased his chanting and cried out in a loud voice. "Now, run! Run for your lives!"

Cornwall pushed Mary behind him. "Follow me," he said. "Stay close. I'll open up a path."

He lowered his head and charged, expecting resistance from the press of bodies all about him. But there was no resistance. He plowed through the gnarly men as if they had been a storm of autumn-blown leaves. Ahead of him Jones stumbled and fell, screaming as his mangled arm came in contact with the stone beneath him. Cornwall stooped and caught him, lifting him, slinging him across his shoulder. Ahead of him all the others, including Mary, were racing through the drifts of shadowy gnarly men. Glancing upward, he saw that the harpies were breaking free from the constrictions of the rock walls of the gorge, bursting out into sunlit sky.

Just ahead was light where the gorge ended on what appeared to be a level plain. The gnarly men were gone. He passed the Gossiper who was stumping along as rapidly as he could, grunting with his effort. Ahead of the Gossiper, the little white dog skipped along with a weaving, three-legged gait, Coon loping at his side.

Then they were out of the gorge, running more easily now. Ahead of them, a few miles out on the little plain, which was ringed in by towering mountains, loomed a fairy building—as Jones had said, all froth and lace, but even in its insubstantiality, with a breath-taking grandeur in it.

"You can let me down now," said Jones. "Thank you for the lift."

Cornwall slowed to a halt and lowered him to his feet.

Jones jerked his head at the injured arm. "The whole damn thing's on fire," he said, "and it's pounding like a bell."

He fell into step with Cornwall. "My vehicle's just up ahead," he said. "You can see it there, off to the right. I have a hypodermic— Oh, hell, don't ask me to explain. It's a magic needle. You may have to help me with it. I'll show you how."

Coming across the meadow that lay between them and the fairy building was a group of beings, too distant to be seen with any distinctness except that it could be seen that one of them stood taller than the others.

"Well, I be damned," said Jones. "When I was here before, I wandered all about and there was no one here to greet me, and now look at the multitude that is coming out to meet us."

Ahead of all the others ran a tiny figure that yipped and squealed with joy, turning cartwheels to express its exuberance.

"Mary!" it yipped. "Mary! Mary! Mary!"

"Why," Mary said, astounded, "I do believe it is Fiddlefingers. I have wondered all along where the little rascal went to."

"You mean the one who made mud pies with you?" asked Cornwall.

"The very one," said Mary.

She knelt and cried out to him, and he came in with a rush to throw himself into her arms. "They told me you were coming," he shrieked, "but I could not believe them."

He wriggled free and backed off a way to have a

235

look at her. "You've gone and grown up," he said accusingly. "I never grew at all."

"I asked at the Witch House," said Mary, "and they told me you had disappeared."

"I have been here for years and years," the little brownie said. "I have so many things to show you."

By now the rest of those who were coming in to meet them had drawn close enough for them to see that most of them were little people, a dancing, hopping gaggle of brownies, trolls, elves, and fairies. Walking in their midst was a somber manlike figure clothed in a long black gown, with a black cowl pulled about his head and face. Except that it seemed he really had no face—either that or the shadow of the cowl concealed his face from view. And there was about him a sort of mistiness, as if he walked through a fogginess that now revealed and now concealed his shape.

When he was close to them, he stopped and said in a voice that was as somber as his dress, "I am the Caretaker, and I bid you welcome here. I suspect you had some trouble with the harpies. At times they become somewhat overzealous."

"Not in the least," said Hal. "We gently brushed them off."

"We have disregarded them," said the Caretaker, "because we have few visitors. I believe, my dear," he said, speaking to Mary, "that your parents were here several years ago. Since then, there have been no others."

"I was here a few days ago," said Jones, "and you paid no attention to me. I think you made a deliberate effort to make it seem that this place was deserted."

"We looked you over, sir," said the Caretaker. "Before we made ourselves known to you, we wanted to find out what kind of thing you were. But you left rather hurriedly. . . ."

Mary interrupted him. "You say that they were here," she said, "my parents. Are they here no longer, then?"

"They went to another place," said the Caretaker.

236

"I will tell you of that and much more a little later on. All of you will join us at table, will you not?"

"Now that you speak of it," said the Gossiper, I believe that I could do with a small bit of nourishment."

38

THE Caretaker sat at the head of the table, and now it was apparent that he, indeed, did not have a face. Where the face should have been, underneath the cowl, was what seemed an area of fogginess, although now and then, Cornwall thought, watching him, there were at times faint, paired red sparks that might take the place of eyes.

He did not eat but sat there while they did, speaking to them pleasantly enough but of inconsequential things, asking them about their journey, talking about how the crops had been, discussing the vagaries of the weather—simply making conversation.

And there was about him, Cornwall thought, not only a fogginess about his face but about his entire being, as if he might be some sort of wraith so insubstantial that one would not have been amazed if he had disappeared altogether, blown by the wind.

"I do not know what to make of him," Sniveley said to Cornwall, speaking in a confidential whisper. "He fits in with nothing I've ever heard of as dwelling in the Wasteland. A ghost one might think at first, but he is not a ghost, of that I am quite certain. There is a certain misty character to him that I do not like."

The food was in no way fancy, but it was good and solid fare, and there was plenty of it. The Caretaker kept urging them to eat. "There is plenty of it," he kept saying. "There is enough for all."

But finally it became apparent that everyone had eaten all they could, and the Caretaker said, "Now that we are finished, there is much explanation that is due and there may be some questions you want to ask."

Sniveley piped up hurriedly, "We have been wondering . . ." But the Caretaker waved him down.

"You're the one who has been wondering what I am," he said, "and I think it is only fair I tell you, which I would have in any case, but in its proper time. I told you I am the Caretaker and, in a sense, I am. But basically I'm what you might call a philosopher, although that is not the word exactly. There is no word in your world that can precisely describe what I am. 'Philosophical engineer' probably would come as close as any, and you, Mr. Jones, and you, Sir Mark, if you wish to make dispute of this, please to wait a while. . . ."

"We'll hold our questions," Cornwall said, "but there is one thing that I demand to know. You are acquainted with our names, but we have never told you them."

"You will not like me when I tell you," the Caretaker said, "but the honest answer is I can see into your minds. Very deeply, should I wish, but to go deeply would be impolite, so I merely brush the surface. Only the surface information: who you are and where you've been. Although should I go deeply and unearth your inmost secrets, you need feel no embarrassment. For I am not of this planet and my values are not entirely your values, and even should they coincide, I would not presume to judge you, for I I know from many eons the great diversities of minds—"

"Before the rest of you get in with your questions," Mary said, hurrying before anyone else could speak, "I want to know what happened to my folks."

"They went back home," the Caretaker said.

"You mean they went without me. They never even thought of coming back to get me."

"You will hate me for this," said the Caretaker, "as you very rightly should. But I persuaded them, and supplied convincing evidence, that you had died."

"What a hateful thing to do," said Mary scornfully.

239

"What a nasty thing. I hope you had a reason. . . ."

"My dear, I had a reason. And I consoled myself that it would work out in the end. . . ."

"So you're clairvoyant, too," said Jones. "With all your other creepy qualities."

"Well, not exactly," said the Caretaker, a little flustered. "I have, rather, a certain sense of destiny. In the sort of work I do it is necessary, and—"

"Forget about the destiny," said Mary coldly, "and tell us what was so important—"

"If you'd quit shouting at me and give me a chance."

"I wasn't shouting," Mary said.

"We'll give you your chance," said Cornwall, "and I warn you, sir, your reason had better be a good one."

"Perhaps," said the Caretaker, "I had best begin at the beginning, which is what I should have done to start with. My race is an ancient one, and it rose on the planet situated well within the galactic core. Long before there was such a thing as a human being, perhaps before the first life crawled out of the sea, we had built a great civilization. And I know, Sir Mark, that you are confounded and perhaps a bit incensed . . ."

"He'll be all right," said Jones. "He can ask his questions later; he is achieving an open mind in seeing that there is more than magic. So please get on with it."

"All right, then, I will," the Caretaker said. "We could have advanced to a very lofty culture that would have set us aside from the galaxy, perhaps from the universe. For we were among the first intelligence and had a head start on all the others. We could have fashioned for ourselves a way of life that by now would have been beyond anything even we ourselves can imagine, but there were certain wise men among us in very ancient times who saw the loneliness of such a course, if it should be taken. They knew that if we continued as we were going, we would stand alone, cutting ourselves off from all other life. Facing a decision, we made it, and the decision was that we would not live for ourselves alone but for the other intelligences that might evolve throughout the galaxy.''

"Mister," Jones said harshly, "I know your kind. In my world, we are up to our armpits in them. Dogooders who make it their business to interfere with other people, who would be much happier without the interference."

"You mistake me," said the Caretaker. "We are observers only. We try not to interfere. It is only at a crisis point—"

"And you think this is a crisis point?"

"I have a feeling that it might be. Not that any great catastrophe is about to happen, but through the fear that something that could happen may fail to happen. Here, on this little plot of ground, there exists a chance for greatness. If the greatness does not come about, a unique culture will be lost to the galaxy, perhaps to the universe. And if it will make you feel any better, Mr. Jones, it is not you people here with whom I am concerned, but with the citizens of the galaxy.

"I would have you believe that we are not missionaries. We are not welfare workers. We are only observers. We merely watch and hope. We reveal ourselves and take a hand in things only when there seems no alternative."

"This is all well and good," said Cornwall, "and it sounds very pretty in the telling, but it still leaves me confused. And the greatest confusion of all is by what means you see greatness in this place. A repository, of course, for Wasteland lore, and that certainly is worth the saving. . . ."

"Not the Wasteland lore, alone, my friend, but the lore, the hopes, the potentialities of three great civilizations, all springing from a common source, three divergent philosophies, which, if they could be fused together . . ."

"Three," said Jones. "I think I see what you are getting at, but there are only two, not three. The culture of the Wasteland and of Cornwall's world and

241

the culture of my world. Magic and technology, and I agree they might work in tandem."

"There is another world," the Caretaker said. "The world of Mary's people. Your world split not once, but twice. You are three worlds in one."

"I have enough difficulty with two worlds, let alone with three," said Cornwall. "We had thought that Mary's people came from the same world as Jones, perhaps some centuries in his future. . . ."

"And it was this third world that my folks went back to," Mary said. "Why was it so important—"

"I could not take the chance," said the Caretaker, "that they would slip from my grasp. If something happened to them, there was no guarantee—nay, only the slightest possibility—that someone else from the third world would ever show up. I prevailed upon them to go back to their own world to bring back to this one the documentary culture . . ."

"You've got it all worked out," said Jones. "All laid out neat and simple."

The Caretaker nodded. "I would hope so. Make this place the depository of the knowledge of three worlds. From your world, Mr. Jones, the technology; from the world of Mary's people, the great humanistic concept that both this world and yours would seem, somehow, to have missed. Put it all together, meld it all together, build a cultural concept that is not of any of the worlds, but the best of all of them. Bring in scholars from distant reaches of the galaxy, some of them representing disciplines that you have never heard of . . ."

"I take it," said Cornwall, "that you do have here a large body of ancient writings. I can hardly wait to see them. I have some small capability in some of the ancient languages. Although I think quite likely that my goblin friend may, in many instances, have much more than I do. He spent many years in the library at Wyalusing."

"This is fine for you," said Gib, "but what about the others of us? You can settle down with the ancient writings and fill your days with them. But Hal and

Coon and I would have no purpose here. We have accomplished what we set out to do. We delivered the ax to the Old Ones, and we could have saved our time, but we got it done. And we went on to find this place—"

"We can't even read," said Hal. "We were never taught to read. None of the Marsh People or the Hill People—"

"For that matter," said Sniveley, "neither can I, although that has nothing to do with my wanting to go back. I have a mine to run and there are friends I left behind. Both Gib and Hal have business that they must attend to. But if there is any other way to manage it, we do not want to go back the way we came."

"I can take you back," said Jones. "I must go to my own world to get my arm attended to. With the injection that Mark gave me and the bandaging that Mary did, it is quite comfortable, but—"

"I am certain," said Oliver, "that if you'd give me the time to scan some of the old tomes, I could hit upon some magic . . ."

Jones groaned. "I have my belly full of magic. I am going back to where they have antibiotics. I can take the others with me, move my machine to what is equivalent in my world to their old stomping grounds and return them home quite neatly. The only thing is that they would have to remain under cover. I could not take the chance of their being seen."

"Most willingly," said Gib. "We'll be as quiet as mice."

"But you will return?" the Caretaker asked of Jones.

"Christ, yes!" said Jones. "I wouldn't miss this for the world. Not for the sake of your precious galaxy, you understand, not to try to build that magnificent culture you are twittering about, but for the laughs that will be in it. I can see some of them now."

"And you will bring with you the basic documents of your technologies, the philosophies that go with it, what your great men have written . . ."

"You must be kidding," Jones said. "You don't know what you're talking about. I'll bring tons of it, and there still will be tons of it left behind. What do you want—technical handbooks, blueprints, theories, white papers, scientific journals? Oh, hell, I'll try to bring the best I can, and I'll stand around and chuckle while you try to make some sense of it."

"I am pleased," said the Caretaker, "that you think you will get some enjoyment out of it."

"There are three of us I know for certain will be staying," said Cornwall. "And I suppose Bucket, too. You say you can scan our minds. Can you scan his as well? He cannot talk with us, although he seems to understand. Would it be ethical to tell us what you know of him?"

"He is well disposed toward you," said the Caretaker, "if that is your question. He is grateful to you, and he is a friend. You can place all trust in him. But as to what he is, I have no idea, for he does not seem to know himself. Perhaps in time he will, but he still is very young. He carries some instinctive knowledge imparted by his parent, who was, it seems, a refugee from some far point in space. He is not the image of his parent, as you probably are aware. The race from which he springs, it seems, had the capability to alter the genetics of their offspring to any form they wished, and I gather, on a very primal level, with no details at all, that the Bucket's parent fashioned this offspring of his in such a way that it possessed survival values it might find handy as the child of a hunted being, the hunters more than likely extending their hunting from the father to the child. But I gather that as yet the Bucket has no realization of the capabilities that his father imprinted in him. The likelihood is that he'll find them one by one as the need occurs. We must wind up by concluding that he is still an unknown factor."

"Which," said Jones, "is a damn funny way of putting it."

"Perhaps, Mr. Jones. But I think you must agree that in an unknown factor may often lie the greatest hope."

"I hope," said Jones, "that this unknown factor

doesn't rise up and slug us in the chops. After the rifle incident . . ."

"Hush, Mr. Jones," the Caretaker said. "There is one other who has not spoken yet. Master Gossiper, have you anything to say?"

"I am a mere messenger," said the Gossiper, "a runner of the errands, a patcher-up of small difficulties, one who sees that everything's in place and that nothing is forgotten."

"You don't intend to stay?"

"I have too much to do, too many leagues to cover. I must neaten things all up, and I might as well begin."

He reached into the pocket of his robe and hauled forth the Old Ones' ax.

"Since the Old Ones spurned this," he said, "it must be returned to the one who carried it and guarded it all the weary way. It may be poor payment for all the trouble that he went to, but it is at least a token."

He tossed the ax and Gib caught it, grinning.

"It'll be a thing to show when I tell the tale," he said. "I thank you kindly, Gossiper."

The Gossiper reached out a scrawny hand to Mary. "And now," he said, "if you please, the horn of the unicorn. You have no further need of it. Please to give it to me."

"Most willingly," said Mary, "but I don't understand."

"It must be taken back," said the Gossiper, "and securely inserted into the great oak once again so it will be there and ready when the next pilgrims come along. You must understand that the horns of unicorns are in very short supply and that we must make the best possible use of them."

●●●●●●●●●●●●●●●●●●●●●●●●●●●●●●●●●●

39

Now they were gone, the good companions of the pilgrimage. Along with Jones' machine, they had been whisked into nothingness.

Cornwall turned heavily to follow the rest of the party across the nighttime meadow, back toward the fairy structure that glimmered in the moonlight. The little folks skipped blithely along, and in their midst the Caretaker seemed to float along. Off to one side, still by himself, as if he did not quite belong, Bucket jerked ahead with his unsteady gait.

So this was the end of it, Cornwall thought, the end of the long trail that had started at Wyalusing when he'd found the hidden manuscript—and a different ending from the one he had imagined, an ending that, at that time, he could not have imagined. He had set out to find the Old Ones, and now the Old Ones no longer mattered, for they had been something other than he had expected.

He remembered that night when they had reached first water after crossing the Blasted Plain and he had gone off by himself, sunk in guilt for having led the pilgrimage, and wondered what could be done when the end should come, knowing that it would be almost certain death to return by the route they had come. Now it all was finished, and there was no need of going back, for a lifetime's work, more than a lifetime's work, lay here in this little meadow ringed in by the peaks of the Misty Mountains.

Here, if the Caretaker were correct, lay the opportunity to merge three great cultures into one even greater culture, with the aid, perhaps, of strange scholars from strange worlds, equipped with unknown arts and philosophies. And there was, as well, he thought, an unknown factor in the person of the lurching Bucket, which might give to the project a dimension of which there was, as yet, no hint.

Beside him, Mary said, "Don't feel so bad, Mark. They are going home. That's where they want to be."

He shook his head. "There was nothing I could say to them. At the very end there was nothing I could say. I guess, as well, there was nothing they could say to us. All of us, I think, did a little dying back there. They did so much for me . . ."

"You did as much for them," said Mary. "You filled their lives for them. They'll spend many winter nights in the years to come talking of the trip—Sniveley at his mine, Hal and Coon in their hollow tree, Gib in his marsh."

"Thank you, Mary," Cornwall said. "You always know exactly what to say. You take away the hurt."

They walked in silence for a time, then Mary said, "Fiddlefingers told me there'd be new clothes for us, and this is something that we need. You are out at knees and elbows, and this old gown of mine is worth little except as a dusting rag. He said that if I wanted, I could have a gown of cloth of gold. Can you imagine me dressed up in cloth of gold? I'd be like a princess."

He put out a hand to stop her, turning her to face him. "Without cloth of gold," he said, "you are still a princess. I love you best in that very gown you wear, with some of the stink of the Chaos Beast still in it, worn and rent and ragged, spattered with bacon grease from the cooking fire. Promise me you'll never use it as a dusting cloth."

She came to him, put her arms around him, and he held her close.

"It'll be a good life, Mark," she whispered. "Cloth of gold or not, it'll be a good life for us."

About the Author

Clifford D. Simak was born and raised in southwestern Wisconsin, a land of wooded hills and deep ravines which he often uses as the background locale for his stories. Over the years he has written over 25 books, and he has some 200 short stories to his credit. A retired newspaperman, Simak and his wife, Kay, live in Minnesota. They have two children. His most recent novel, also published by Del Rey Books, is *Special Deliverance*.

Dear Reader,

Your opinions are very important to us so please take a few moments to tell us your thoughts. It will help us give you more enjoyable DEL REY Books in the future.

1. Where did you obtain this book?

Bookstore	☐1	Department Store ☐4	Airport	☐7	5
Supermarket	☐2	Drug Store ☐5	From A Friend ☐8		
Variety/Discount Store	☐3	Newsstand ☐6	Other_____		

(Write In)

2. On an overall basis, how would you rate this book?

Excellent ☐1   Very Good ☐2   Good ☐3   Fair ☐4   Poor ☐5   6

3. What is the main reason that you purchased this book?

Author ☐1   It Was Recommended To Me ☐3   7
Like The Cover ☐2   Other_____

(Write In)

4. In the same subject category as this book, who are your two favorite authors?

_____ 8
_____ 9
_____ 10
_____ 11

5. Which of the following categories of paperback books have you purchased in the past 3 months?

Adventure/		Biography ☐4	Horror/		Science	
Suspense	☐12-1	Classics ☐5	Terror	☐8	Fiction	☐x
Bestselling		Fantasy ☐6	Mystery	☐9	Self-Help	☐y
Fiction	☐2	Historical	Romance	☐0	War	☐13
Bestselling		Romance ☐7			Westerns	☐2
Non-Fiction	☐3					

6. What magazines do you subscribe to, or read regularly, that is, 3 out of every 4 issues?

_____ 14
_____ 15
_____ 16
_____ 17

7. Are you: Male ☐1   Female ☐2   18

8. Please indicate your age group.

Under 18 ☐1   25-34 ☐3   50 or older ☐5   19
18-24 ☐2   35-49 ☐4

9. What is the highest level of education that you have completed?

Post Graduate Degree ☐1	College Graduate ☐3	Some High	20
Some Post Graduate	1-3 Years College ☐4	School	
Schooling ☐2	High School	or Less ☐6	
	Graduate ☐5		

(Optional)

If you would like to learn about future publications and participate in future surveys, please fill in your name and address.

NAME_____

ADDRESS_____

CITY _____ STATE_____ ZIP_____ 21

Please mail to: Ballantine Books
DEL REY Research, Dept.
516 Fifth Avenue — Suite 606
New York, N.Y. 10036

F-15